Also by Terry Spear

Heart of the Wolf

Heart of the Jaguar

A HIGHLAND WOLF CHRISTMAS

WITHDRAWN

TERRY SPEAR

sourcebooks
casablanca

Copyright © 2014 by Terry Spear
Cover and internal design © 2014 by Sourcebooks, Inc.
Cover design by Juliana Kolesova
Cover photos © chudakov/dreamstime.com, Dmitrij/dreamstime.com

Published by Sourcebooks Casablanca, an imprint of Sourcebooks, Inc.
P.O. Box 4410, Naperville, Illinois 60567-4410
(630) 961-3900
Fax: (630) 961-2168
www.sourcebooks.com

Printed and bound in Canada.
MBP 10 9 8 7 6 5 4 3 2 1

*To Deborah Hill, who has accompanied me to zoos
and the Saint Francis Wolf Sanctuary in Texas
to make my research even more fun.
We worked together at a local library,
and our lunch and movie dates
always inspire me to write more.
Thanks, Deborah, for being a great friend!*

Chapter 1

IN A RUSH TO PACK BEFORE HER EX-FIANCÉ DISCOVERED her home alone, Calla Stewart felt jittery, on edge. She knew that breaking up with Baird McKinley had been the best thing for her to do—though she wished she'd taken her good friend Cearnach MacNeill's advice *way* before she reached the altar. Wedding and mating Baird was the worst thing she could have done. She should be relieved and happy now, moving forward with her life. Except for one thing. The wolf wasn't giving her up easily.

The Celtic Christmas harp music playing and the Christmas lights sparkling on her tabletop tree did little to lighten her mood as she hurried to pack the rest of her things for her stay at the MacNeills' Argent Castle.

Normally, her home—the carriage house behind her parents' manor house—was a place of joy where she could recharge her batteries, relax, and enjoy some peace and solitude after the often hectic days and nights she spent operating her party-planning business.

But her parents were on their way to Ireland to visit family, so they wouldn't be around to help her out if she had trouble. Their trip was so sudden—unusual, given the way they always planned things far in advance— that she had asked if they were taking it because of the upset over the wedding. But they'd assured her they just needed a vacation. They hadn't taken one in years because they'd been busy managing their own chain of hotels. They *had* looked frazzled and worn out. Calla hated that she'd upset them with the wedding fiasco, but they'd been relieved that she hadn't gone through with it.

She still couldn't believe her dad had gotten his flight times so wrong. She'd thought she was going to have all day to pack. Had she known their flight was so early, she would have already been packed, taken her parents to the airport, and then driven straight from there to Argent Castle. Instead, she'd had to take them to the airport, then come home to finish packing, and finally set out for the castle. Her mother had assured her that next time she was taking charge of the itinerary.

With a snowstorm on the way, Calla tucked an extra pair of winter gloves in the pocket of her field pack and felt something. She pulled out a picture of Baird and her that a photographer had taken for their Save the Date cards. She'd thought she'd gotten rid of any reminder of that photo shoot. She tossed the picture in the trash.

God, she regretted having been such a fool. How could she have allowed herself to be taken in so completely by Baird's charm?

Calla shook her head, glad the MacNeills had extended the invitation to stay with them while she planned their Christmas celebration—it gave her a place to regroup after the disastrous end to her almost-marriage.

She turned off her Christmas-tree lights and was about to haul her bags out to the car when she heard car doors slam out front. Four of them.

Her heart skittered. It could be nothing, she told herself. Maybe the MacNeills had sent someone to take her to the castle, concerned about the weather, or worried about Baird and his kin. She peeked out the curtains and saw Baird stalking toward her front door, two of his brothers and a cousin leaning against his car and waiting for him.

Her skin prickled with goose bumps.

Taking a deep breath, she tried to get her wildly beating heart under control. She desperately wanted to ignore Baird's knock on the door. But her car was sitting near the front door, not hidden in the garage, and he would guess she was here. Besides, their car was blocking her path, and she couldn't leave until they moved it.

She wasn't afraid of Baird, as long as he was simply trying to cajole her into coming back to him, but she wanted his constant harassment to end. She worried that he might take this further if he finally realized he couldn't convince her to return to him.

"Come on, Calla. I know you're home," he said, sounding a little annoyed, though he was trying hard to sound more like someone who was attempting to appeal to her.

He wouldn't want to appear as though he was pleading when his brothers and his cousin were watching him and listening to him. Not when he had been their pack leader, in charge and making the rules, for only the last two years. How would that look to the rest of the pack? If he couldn't sway one stubborn she-wolf to come back to him.

If she ignored him, she was afraid they'd delay her so long that she'd be stuck here until the roads were cleared. Worse, what if he and his kin were stuck here too? She'd be sorely tempted to let them sit out in the freezing weather in their wolf coats.

Resolved to deal with him one last time, she went to the door and unlocked and opened it. "It's over—"

He brushed past her, slamming the door behind him. *Damn him.*

"I didn't want to talk in front of my kin," he said, sounding exasperated.

"Then don't bring them next time. Rather—don't come here again. It's over between us."

He moved toward her as if to give her a hug, but she held her hand out to keep him from drawing closer. "Nay, Baird. We're not there any longer."

Big mistake. He seized her hand and pulled her into his arms, but she quickly jerked away from him.

"Baird, you listen to me. We are done. Through. Finished. We're not getting back together—today, tomorrow, or ever," she said, as pissed off as she could be. Partly because he'd scared her by getting physical, trying to force an intimacy between them that she no longer wanted.

He wore a stupid smile as if he knew better. Which irked her completely. Then he noticed her packed bags and his face darkened. "Where are you going? To join your parents in Ireland?"

How did he know about that? Not that he couldn't have found out somehow, but it wasn't exactly public knowledge. As far as she knew, her parents weren't talking to him, either. Unless he'd been badgering them, trying to get them to change her mind about going back to him. They hadn't said anything to her about it, though.

"You're going to Argent Castle, aren't you? What did the MacNeills tell you about me? What lies?" Baird growled.

"Your actions at the wedding revealed just how you would be toward any of my friends. The MacNeills didn't have to say a thing about you. And if they did say anything adverse about you, I didn't listen." *Unfortunately*. "Your own actions, or inactions, ruined our relationship."

Baird shook his head. "All right. I've tried to be reasonable about this. The truth is that I love you and I want you back. I'll…do whatever it takes for us to work through this." He didn't sound like his words came from the heart. More like he had to say them, although he desperately wanted to tell her that she was coming back to him, or else. Like he would dictate to a pack member who was way out of line.

"I'm not mating you. Can't you get that through your head?"

"Two weeks, love. Two weeks to change your mind." He was smiling, but the look was not sweet or warm, and the implied threat was there. *Do it, or else.*

"Or what?" she asked, glowering at him.

He shrugged and headed for the door. Once he walked outside, she stood in the entryway and watched him join his kin. He talked to them casually, his voice so low she couldn't hear his words, even with her enhanced wolf hearing. They weren't making a move to get into the car. Damn the lot of them.

Already snow was accumulating on the cobblestone drive, which made her feel the urgency of leaving now. While Baird and his kin kept talking, Calla grabbed her bags.

She tried to ignore them, tried not to pay attention to the way her skin felt icy with concern as she packed her luggage in her car. If he wanted to show her how much he cared, he could have packed her car for her. Which she wouldn't have wanted. But he was showing his alpha side—he wanted his way in this and wouldn't help her do anything that wasn't what he wished of her.

She locked her place up, hoping no one would break into it while she was gone—just to prove she shouldn't have run off to stay with the MacNeills. The whole time, the wolves watched her, trying to unnerve her. She was pissed off at them, but worried too. She wasn't any match for four male wolves if they decided to force the issue of her returning to Baird. And she didn't trust them in the least.

When they still didn't move their vehicle, she pulled out her cell phone and said to them, "Please move your car so I can leave." Or she'd call the police, she implied with her tone of voice. Even though she knew that if she did, Baird would leave well before the police arrived, and she'd be stuck staying behind to give a full report. That could make her even later if the weather slowed her down. Besides, in the long run, wolves had to handle wolves. Incarcerating a *lupus garou* wasn't safe for their kind.

"We're getting married," Baird said. "You'll see. And everything will be like it was before."

Over her dead body. Though she didn't want to say it in case that was exactly what he was thinking.

They could *never* go back to the way it was.

To her relief, Baird and his kin all piled into their car and left, yet she couldn't help but be troubled by his veiled threat. What did he plan to do if she didn't go back to him?

She glanced down at her car, the tires nestled in deep snow, and realized that it wasn't that the snow had reached so high on the tires, but that they were no longer inflated. If his kin had cut her tires while she and Baird were inside, she would kill Baird, since he was their pack leader and ultimately responsible for his pack mates' deeds.

She hurried to the garage, located her tire pump, and then began filling the first tire with air. To her guarded relief, it began to expand. She suspected they'd just let the air out of the tires to show her she wasn't going to have an easy time of it if she didn't agree to be Baird's mate.

With the clock ticking, she was getting further behind in trying to beat the brunt of the storm. She stored her tire pump, got into the car, and traveled in the direction of Argent Castle, hoping she hadn't forgotten anything.

Trying to get her mind off Baird, she thought about how thrilled she was that the MacNeill gray-wolf-pack leaders, Ian and Julia, had hired her to help plan their first mated Christmas celebration, which would be a mix of Scottish and American traditions. The only damper on Calla's plans was her concern that Guthrie, one of Ian's younger quadruplet brothers and the financial manager for the pack, would contest any expenditure she suggested. At least, Julia had warned her about that possibility.

Calla should have been more worried about the weather. It had only been lightly snowing when she left, but by the time she was nearing the castle, she could barely see in the blinding blizzard. The snow blew sideways across the narrow road, and she soon lost track of where the road ended and the land dropped off. Snowplows wouldn't be out until later on the more isolated country roads, including this one that led to Argent Castle.

Driving at a wolf's crawl, she squinted to discern where the road was. Snow and ice clung to branches on the fir trees on either side of the pavement. A haze of grayish white cloaked the area, lending a somber cast to the evergreens. Visibility was limited to only a couple of feet ahead of her.

Despite the trouble Baird had caused her, she'd still left home three hours early. It should have taken her only an hour and a half to reach Argent Castle. She thought she had only a little more than five miles to go, as long as she didn't accidentally drive off the road and get stuck. Her tires slipped again. She gripped her steering wheel harder, her skin prickling with tension. The roads were worsening, getting icier with every mile, and she was afraid she would slide right off the asphalt at any moment. As soon as she had that notion, a herd of red deer bolted across the road.

"Damn!" Her heart nearly stopped as she slammed on her brakes.

Her car slid on the ice, her heart jumping into her throat. Steering away or toward the slide had no effect. Braking made it worse.

The car sailed off the road into the deep ditch. Teeth gritted, she braced for impact. The car crashed into a tree with a jolt. The dead stop forced her to jerk forward, her seat belt catching her. Thankfully, she hadn't hit the tree hard enough to do herself any injury.

She gunned the engine in reverse, hoping for a

miracle. With a whirring, grinding noise, the tires spun around and around. Ticked off to the max, she peered out through the fogged-up windows. Her vehicle was buried in a snowdrift, the cold, wet flakes reaching to just below her door handle. *Great.* She tried reversing again. Her tires continued to spin, and the front bumper felt like it was hung up on something because it moved a little, but wouldn't budge any farther.

As early as the sun set in winter, darkness would descend soon. Only another half hour or so, which was the problem with winter in Scotland. As soon as three thirty arrived, the sun would vanish. She shut off her engine. Without the heater running, the temperature in the interior of the car quickly plummeted. She looked around in the backseat to see if she had anything she could use for traction.

A blanket. Not that she wanted to ruin it, but she always kept one in the car during the winter for emergencies, and this constituted an emergency.

She pulled her cell out of her purse and called Julia, but she didn't answer. Calla tried Cearnach's number. He was Ian's second oldest brother and the only other one in the MacNeill pack she had a number for, but no answer there, either. *Fine.* She texted both of them so they'd know approximately where she'd left the car, when, and the direction she'd taken to get to the castle.

If she ran as a wolf, she'd most likely get there before her anticipated arrival and no one would think she'd had car trouble in the meantime. Well, that and she'd told them she wasn't coming until after she dropped her parents off at the airport, which had turned out to be a totally different time than expected.

She tried to open the door, but a wall of snow was wedged against it. She let her breath out in exasperation. She shoved, making a small gap between the door and the snowbank. She'd never make it out of the car that way. *Damn it!* She closed the door.

Climbing over the console, she peered out the passenger window. The snow was not quite as deep here. She shoved the door open, grabbed her blanket, and waded through the snow. The ditch was maybe three feet deep, with as much snow piled up in it, and she didn't think she could get her car out on her own. Not to be deterred without at least trying, she placed the blanket against the back tires and then climbed back into the car. She gunned the engine again, but no matter how much gas she gave it, the car wasn't budging.

She silently fumed, got back out of the car, and retrieved her blanket.

"This really sucks."

Even though it would get dark soon, and the blinding snow would make it difficult to see, she could still find her way to Argent Castle using her enhanced wolf sense of smell. She wasn't sitting here and waiting for a rescue.

Inside the car, she yanked off her wool coat and then realized she'd have to leave her purse, phone, and everything else behind… No, she'd use her wolf teeth to grab the strap of her waterproof field pack. That would slow her down even more, but it couldn't be helped. Tucking her purse into the pack, she tossed everything she could live without into the backseat.

She quickly stripped out of the rest of her clothes, then grabbed her bag. Naked and hoping nobody would find her like this and think she was in some kind of confused, hypothermic state, she squeezed out through the narrow opening. *Cold, cold, cold.* Snow reached her thighs, and the upper part of her body was bare to the freezing wind. She slammed the door, hit the lock button, threw her keys in the bag's side pocket, and zipped it up.

Dropping the bag in the snow, she called on the urge to shift. The chill of the snow against her feet and legs was bad enough, but the wind whipping the snow mixed with ice against her back and arms stung like icy needles. Internally, her body warmed as her muscles and bones reshaped into the wolf. As soon as her wolf's double coat covered her skin, she sighed with relief. For a second, she shivered until her natural fur coat helped to warm her against the biting cold that had already chilled her to the bone.

Grabbing the bag with her teeth, she rethought taking it with her. It was heavier than she'd thought it would be. Carrying it over her shoulder was not the same as dragging it, clenched in her wolf teeth, through chest-deep snow.

She'd gone maybe a mile when she saw movement between a couple of fir trees and stopped dead in her tracks. She thought she saw the gray tail of a wolf. Was it one of the MacNeill clansmen in his wolf coat, coming to greet her? That seemed odd. Unless Cearnach or Julia had gotten her messages and had sent someone to find her. A MacNeill would have made his presence known, though, not lurked in the woods.

Something moved behind her, not just the branches blowing in the wind. She dropped her bag, the instinct to protect herself coming to bear, and swung around.

Baird McKinley stood in the woods in his dark gray wolf form, along with his two brothers and cousin, also in their wolf forms. They had to have been waiting here for her. The deer must have caught wind of the wolves and panicked, fleeing the area and probably causing her accident—which infuriated her even more.

Baird watched her reaction before he made a move. He gave her an expression of appeal, like he still wanted to make up with her, his eyebrows arched, his eyes wide, not narrowed and threatening. Maybe he thought he'd have a better chance at convincing her in his wolf form.

Then again, she could imagine the four of them talking about her on the way here, suggesting ways to get her to capitulate, agreeing that he couldn't let her slip into Argent Castle without one last-ditch effort to appeal to her.

Heart pounding, she knew how nasty Baird could be with others in his pack when he didn't get his way. And with her, he *wasn't* getting his way. Just the fact that he'd been waiting for her to arrive—especially when he had a show of force instead of just trying to see her alone? Not good.

She turned, grabbed her bag, and took off running through the virgin snow. She couldn't make good headway while dragging her field pack. But if she dropped it so she could move faster, they could get all her stuff, including the keys to her car if they wanted to steal it. *Damn, damn, damn.*

That brought the memories flooding back of Baird's kin stealing Cearnach MacNeill's and his mate's cars and other belongings, and stranding them in wolf form—at Baird's direction. That was why she had dumped Baird's butt at the altar in the first place.

Baird bolted in front of her and snarled and snapped, forcing her to lunge around to his right flank. She would have bitten him if her teeth hadn't been clenched around the strap to her bag. His kin quickly surrounded her and she stopped dead. She watched Baird, her heart beating furiously against her ribs. Her gaze met his.

His brown eyes were hopeful that she'd give in. That she'd want to come back to him. So she was certain he wouldn't attack. The other wolves continued to flank her, not allowing her to move in any direction. Their panting breaths appeared as frosty mist, carried away in the blowing wind. They waited for her to give in or bolt.

She wasn't going with Baird, and she wasn't standing here all day in the freezing cold, even though her wolf coat kept her warm. She had a meal and friends waiting for her at Argent Castle. Hating to, she let go of her pack.

All eyes were on her, all ears perked up, as the wolves watched to see what her next move would be. Wolves were good at reading the slightest body movements. So they would know exactly what she was going to do next as soon as she lifted her chin. She didn't have much of a choice.

Guthrie MacNeill was helping his brothers and several other male kin carry the Christmas tree into the great hall when he thought again about Calla. "Have you tried calling her, Cearnach?" Guthrie asked.

Cearnach glanced back at him as they struggled to get the tree into the hall. "We've been kind of busy."

"Snowstorm's worsening," Guthrie reminded him.

"I assumed she'd stay put," Cearnach said, "until the roads are clear."

Guthrie didn't say anything, still worried about her, as he would be about anyone coming to the castle in bad weather conditions. Given all the trouble he and his clan had had with the McKinleys both before and after Calla left Baird at the altar, he was certain she'd have more trouble with Baird before long.

Guthrie took a deep breath. He shouldn't be worrying needlessly. Cearnach had her number, and Guthrie would call to ensure she was still at home. Well, once he wasn't helping to carry this monstrous tree inside.

As they got the tree situated, Julia hurried to inspect its location. She smiled and said, "Perfect!"

Guthrie was glad for that. Wolves *could* get hernias!

"Julia," Heather, Guthrie's cousin, said, nearly out of breath. "You got a message." She handed her the phone.

Julia checked her text messages. "Oh my God. Calla's stranded and on her way here in her wolf coat about five miles out. From the time of the text, she is probably about here, but somebody should go and make sure she's all right."

Guthrie was already stripping, not waiting for their pack leader, Ian, to decide who would go. His brother smiled a little at him, and then told their brothers Cearnach and Duncan to come with Guthrie and him, along with a few other men.

Just as Julia opened the door for them so that the men in their wolf forms could race across the inner bailey and out the open gates, they heard the howl of a she-wolf in distress. Guthrie and the others ran full out. His heart thundered as his blood heated with a fresh surge of adrenaline.

Chapter 2

CALLA GOT OUT ONE GOOD HOWL BEFORE VARDON, one of Baird's older brothers, lunged at her. Her heart skipped a bit as she tried to jump out of his path. The snow and his sudden movement precluded that. He slammed into her and forced her onto her side.

Growling fiercely, she snapped at him with wickedly sharp canines meant to tear. Her heart was beating triple time. She wasn't putting up with this.

He jumped back, avoiding her biting teeth and snarling at her. She rolled off her side to lie on her belly.

Baird was studying her, not making a move and not growling at Vardon, which would have told her he didn't approve of what his brother had done. As usual, Baird was using his kin to fight his battles.

She lifted her head to howl again. She suspected one of the wolves would try to stop her. Nobody tackled her this time. Instead, Baird came up close to greet her nose to nose. She snarled, angry that he would keep her from going where she wished. He persisted. She snapped. He growled back, his true personality coming through in an instant.

She didn't care if she ticked him off. He was irritating the hell out of her with his constant pestering.

Howls from the distance called to her. Relief flooded through her.

Ian and some of his kin were on their way. Thank

God. She didn't really want to bite Baird or his kin. But she would, if they kept this up.

Baird glanced at her bag.

Barks and woofs from the direction of the castle grew closer, letting her know just how far away they were now. Telling her to hold on until they could reach her. They couldn't know why she was distressed, or why she didn't respond. Then Baird barked at her, still trying to make up to her. The MacNeills would know now. Baird was here, blocking her from reaching them.

She stood, wary of him and the others.

Baird turned and made a low, rumbling moan at the MacNeill wolves before they were even in sight. Calla grabbed her bag, but Vardon seized it and began a tug-of-war with her, pulling her away from Argent Castle. *Damn him!*

She growled low and he did the same. She wasn't letting go! But Vardon was heavier than she was, and stronger. He was dragging her, despite how fiercely she tugged and viciously she snarled, trying to make some headway. Her feet dug into the snow-covered ground as she attempted to keep him from budging her. Nothing was working. She kept sliding through the snow as he yanked the bag with him—and her along with it.

Hating to give up her bag, she let go and Vardon fell on his butt, dropping the field pack.

Baird, who was still watching in the direction of the castle, yipped a retreat. But not before Vardon seized her bag again.

Calla snarled and chased after him, meaning to bite him in the butt or the tail, whichever she could sink her teeth into. She suspected he didn't want the bag as much as he was trying to draw her away from the MacNeill wolves. Ian's brother Cearnach howled. She was too busy trying to reach Vardon to respond, his longer legs propelling him forward and keeping him just out of reach of her teeth.

The deep, powdery snow and the wind whipping the flakes into her eyes didn't help matters. She was squinting, nearly blinded by the snow.

Vardon stumbled in a drift and she ran into him, not meaning to. He snarled at her, and she growled right back at him. One of the other wolves, Baird's cousin Robert Kilpatrick, grabbed her bag and took off running. *Damn!*

She sprinted after him, feeling like this was a wolf relay game, and then Baird barked, and she heard the wolves behind her growling. *Closer.*

Thank God.

Robert dropped her bag and ran full out to avoid a clash with Ian and his men. Ten MacNeill clan wolves greeted her quickly, checking her over, and then raced off after Baird and his men. All except for one wolf. She was grateful that he'd stayed with her.

The third oldest of the quadruplets, Guthrie MacNeill, a gray wolf with a beautiful white mask, greeted her. He licked her face and made sure she was unharmed. He barked at her, seized her bag, and motioned with his head for her to follow.

Gladly.

Before the castle towers came into view, she heard the sound of wolves running to catch up to them. She and Guthrie turned, making sure the approaching wolves were Ian and his family, and not Baird and his pack.

Relieved to see Ian and the rest of his clansmen, she ran with them as a pack, her breath frosty in the blizzard wind, the heat of their bodies stretching out to her. She wasn't used to being with a pack like this, and she loved feeling the protectiveness and the strength in numbers. As soon as they were inside the walls, the gate guards lowered the portcullis, and then closed the gates.

Ian's wife, Julia, hurried out to greet her in the inner bailey. Calla hadn't wanted her to come out into the cold, dressed the way she was in just a sweater, slacks, and boots, with snowflakes collecting on her red hair. Julia's worried green eyes took in Calla and the rest of the wolves. Several more of their clansmen hurried out to greet them, moving aside to let them into the keep. Julia took Calla's bag from Guthrie.

"Come, Calla," Julia said to her. "I have prepared the blue bedchamber for you."

Before long, Calla was dressed and warming herself in front of a great fire in the cozy den.

Guthrie and his brothers stood nearby, now dressed and with their arms folded across their broad chests, waiting to hear what had happened.

"All my bags are in the car," Calla said, as if Ian and his kin wouldn't already know that.

"We're headed out to find your car, and if we can't move it, we'll haul all your things here, lass," Ian assured her. "We won't leave them in the car overnight."

"Aye. I wasn't sure when the snow would melt enough to budge it," Calla said.

"In a couple of days, most likely. We'll get your things for you in the meantime so you don't have to worry," Ian said.

"After the McKinleys stole my and Elaine's cars, we don't trust them not to steal yours," Cearnach said, repeating Calla's own concerns. He was Ian's second-in-command of the pack and had been a friend of hers when they were young.

Calla sipped her hot tea, the sweet and spicy cinnamon flavor sliding down her throat and warming her, while Ian made arrangements for more of the men to go back to her car.

"Thanks for coming to my rescue." Calla still couldn't believe Baird would do something as stupid as this. She was trying to move on and wished he would too. It was one thing to come to her house and try to convince her to renew their friendship, but quite another to confront her in the MacNeill wolves' territory.

"Aye, lass, which is all the more reason we need to have a bodyguard detail watch over you," Ian said.

She'd objected earlier, not thinking bodyguards were necessary and assuming Baird would realize sooner or later that things were over between them. He was proving to be much too stubborn for that. Still, she had hoped they could remain—well, maybe not friends, but not enemies, either.

Most of all, she loved how she felt so secure among the MacNeill wolves, though hating Baird for making her feel unsafe without them.

"Thanks for carrying my bag, Guthrie. Sorry it weighed so much." Calla realized as soon as she spoke the words that she might have offended his masculinity.

Especially when his brothers chuckled. Men.

"It was no trouble." The sparkle in Guthrie's green eyes dispelled the idea that anything would be too heavy for him.

When the men left to get her personal items out of the car, Julia sat down on one of the chairs by the fireplace. "I'm so sorry that Cearnach and I didn't get your messages right away. I was in your room getting it ready and had left my phone charging in the kitchen. And then I came down to supervise where the men would set up the Christmas tree. Cearnach was helping bring it into the castle. With the bad weather, we thought you would have changed your mind and waited."

"Nay, I'd promised. I really did think I would arrive long before it got that bad, though."

"Well, I'm glad you're here now. You will help us to decorate the tree, won't you?"

"I'd love to." Calla loved how Julia had taken her in like she was part of their family. Calla had already helped decorate her own family's tree, as well as hers, even though she hadn't planned to be home to enjoy it. Still, before she left, she had wanted to feel the Christmas spirit.

"We'll have dinner tonight and decorate it tomorrow. I have to show it to you first."

Julia led Calla into the great hall where she stared at the tree in awe. Not a cut tree, but a beautiful Nordmann fir—a deep, rich green, bristling with full, rounded needles, and redolent with the luscious scent of citrus. Divine. Best of all, it was living.

"You're going to plant it after Christmas?" Calla asked, excited. She would love to return and see the pack members plant it. Help, even, if she could.

"Yes. Isn't it beautiful? You know that Duncan's mate, Shelley, is a botanist. She had the brilliant idea of buying a tree that we could plant after the holidays. Just think, over the years, we could have a whole new forest."

Calla took in a breath of the Christmas scent. "It's the most beautiful Christmas tree I've ever seen." She reached out and touched the soft needles. She'd never known anyone personally who had a living Christmas tree in their home for the holidays.

Julia smiled, but then her expression turned serious. "Calla, I have to ask you. Is there anything more to Baird's wanting you to return to him so badly? Something more than what we assume it's all about?"

"Other than him being a jerk and an alpha who doesn't like to lose? Nay."

Julia glanced at the doorway, but she and Calla were the only two people in the great hall at the moment. A lot of chatter and laughter were coming from the kitchen, however, while the dinner was being prepared.

"One other thing, are you…going to be able to manage Guthrie?" Julia asked.

Calla wasn't sure what Julia was asking. About the Christmas party expenditures? That was Julia's job. But yeah, Calla assumed he'd be all negative about the cost of the party.

"Concerning what?" Calla asked.

"A courtship." Julia smiled broadly.

Chapter 3

GUTHRIE WASN'T SURE HOW TO TAKE CALLA STEWART, party planner entrepreneur. He still couldn't get over how she'd stolen his shorts and hung them on the pirate's flagpole the ladies had put up during the hen party a couple of weeks ago. Many in the pack had teased him mercilessly about how Calla had the hots for him. And they wanted to know what he was going to do about it.

What he'd like to do was one thing. Her real intentions were another.

He and nearly everyone else in the pack had thought Calla and Cearnach would be mated wolves someday, especially when she'd moved back into the area a year ago. But both his brother and Calla had insisted they were just friends. Cearnach mating Elaine had finally assured the pack of that.

Guthrie had just come off a roller-coaster ride with a she-wolf he'd seriously intended to mate—if not for her previous boyfriend and her subsequent change in attitude. At first, Tenell had adored Guthrie. What alpha male wolf could resist a woman who worshipped him?

But a month into their relationship, Tenell began to compare Guthrie to her former beau, and not in a good way. That got old quickly. Then Guthrie learned her old boyfriend had cheated on her—which was the reason for their breakup. When she saw her ex-boyfriend while out shopping alone one day, she went back to him and told Guthrie it was over between them.

Maybe Calla would be over Baird for good in another six months to a year. No chance of rebound by then, hopefully. Then Guthrie would consider dating the lass. If she was ready. If she was still available. And *if* they were both interested.

He sighed and helped carry her bags up to her guest chamber, then headed downstairs with the rest of the men to eat dinner.

"Told you so," Cearnach said as he and Guthrie descended the stairs behind the other men.

"*About…?*" Guthrie said, elongating the word, not sure what sage advice his brother had given him this time.

"That I wasn't interested in mating Calla. That we were just good friends."

"Aye, so you were."

"And?"

"And what?" Guthrie asked, annoyed. He *wasn't* a mind reader.

"Come on, Brother. She's free, but she won't be forever. Court her."

Guthrie said, "You know what happened the last time I dated a woman who was just getting over a breakup."

"Aye. But Calla's different."

"Right. She needs protection from the bastard. But what if she changes her mind? Women are known to do that. You had a devil of a time getting her to see his true face. She was completely hung up on the guy. What if we started to court each other, and lo and behold, she decides Baird wasn't so bad after all."

"She's over him. It's over between them. Finished. Through," Cearnach assured him.

"That's what Tenell told me. You know how well that ended."

Cearnach shook his head as they made their way to the great hall where the conversation was already a dull roar. Chairs scraped across the stone floor while people took their seats. "Tenell was extremely needy. She wanted both the emotional and physical support you offered her at the time. And I believe she was using you, to an extent."

Guthrie had realized that also, but too late.

"She wanted to prove to her old boyfriend that she had what it took to get another wolf interested in her. So you were convenient."

Okay, so Cearnach wasn't mincing words now. Guthrie hated to admit his brother was right.

"She was biding her time. Once she learned that her boyfriend had dumped the woman he'd been seeing on the side when he and Tenell had been courting, Tenell went back to him. *Good riddance*. Calla isn't like that."

So Cearnach said.

The other stumbling block was Guthrie's proclivity for making money and saving it. Rather than spending money frivolously, he'd always been concerned about saving for a wintry day. In 1779, when he was a lad, Elaine's pirate uncles had stolen a ship full of merchandise belonging to the MacNeills. The clan had to scrimp to make it through the harsh winter with very little to eat, an experience Guthrie had not forgotten.

Calla was in the business of making money off people's wasteful spending habits. Guthrie had a hard time seeing that what she did for a living was good for anyone's pocketbook. That was all well and good for other people—it wasn't *his* concern if they wanted to throw away their hard-earned money. But now that she was here to put on a lavish Christmas celebration for the MacNeills, it was more personal—since he handled the clan finances and she intended to spend them.

"Give it a chance, Guthrie," Cearnach said, smiling at him. "You never know where it might lead. Don't wait. I doubt the lass will be free for very long before another wolf snatches her up."

If she was suffering from a case of rebound, that wouldn't be a good scenario for either her or the new guy she hooked up with.

They both surveyed the great hall and spied Calla sitting at the end of a table. Their redheaded cousin, Oran, was sitting next to her, smiling and talking with his hands, looking like he was already putting the moves on her.

Cearnach shook his head. "Got to move on this one, Brother. She's worth it." Then he headed for the main table and his wife, Elaine, who was already seated.

Guthrie had no intention of observing the lassie as he took his new seat next to his younger brother, Duncan, and his mate, Shelley.

"Oran's already going after her," Duncan teased him.

Guthrie drank his mug of beer and fully intended to change the subject. He was opening his mouth to speak about the weather, or about anything that had nothing to do with Calla, when Duncan said, "You know Oran's only pulling your leg, don't you?"

"What?" Guthrie said frowning.

"He likes the lass, aye. But he knows she's interested in you."

"*Duncan…*" Guthrie said, so exasperated that his brother smiled at him.

"Julia moved her into the guest chamber close to yours so if our ghostly cousin Flynn hassles her, you can rescue her. The scenario worked wonders for Cearnach and Elaine. You know how Flynn is. I am still hopeful that he will outgrow the rakish ways that led to his death centuries ago."

"I doubt Flynn will ever change. Though he doesn't bother her. At least he hasn't in the past. I have no idea why he disturbs some of the lassies and not others. He's left her well enough alone whenever she's visited."

"Aye, well, for any other reason, then." Duncan buttered a slice of bread. "Ian asked me to go on her guard detail tomorrow night."

"Where is she going?"

"A clan reunion she's set up. But I had already promised Shelley I'd help her with some Christmas shopping. Would you mind going in my place?"

"Christmas shopping?" Guthrie couldn't believe it. Duncan was the warrior of the bunch, always ready for a battle. Shopping was *not* one of Duncan's favorite pastimes. To give up guarding Calla to go Christmas shopping with his mate? Guthrie suspected it had more to do with Duncan giving Guthrie a chance to protect Calla instead. What better way to prove a wolf's interest than in offering his protection? He shook his head. "I've…"

"Good. I already talked to Ian about the schedule changes, and you're in charge of the detail. Shelley's uncles Ethan and Jasper will accompany you. Their brother, Teague, is busy with the cattle."

Guthrie frowned at Duncan. He was going to say he would have to check his schedule. Wolf packs typically homeschooled kids of their kind, and a large pack like the MacNeills' was no different. Their method of homeschooling was having the individuals with the most knowledge of a subject provide training for the kids in that area of expertise. The *lupus garou* children didn't usually attend a human-run public or private school—too much of a risk if a child became angry, lost his head, and showed off his fully wolfish side.

Guthrie was responsible for the math curriculum, and sometimes he tutored students at night. He was giving a couple of final classes this week before they took Christmas break, but he didn't think he had any night sessions scheduled.

But why did Duncan know about this outing before Guthrie? A pecking order existed among the brothers. He was older than Duncan by five minutes. He should have been told first.

He glanced over at Calla, who was laughing at something Oran said. She was so animated, always cheerful. Although, when they'd found her in the woods trying to hold her own against Baird and his kin, he'd smelled a mixture of anxiousness and anger rolling off her in waves for the first time since he'd known her. She probably had smelled the same on him. He couldn't help but admire how she'd stood her ground.

Yet, wasn't that the way Tenell had acted? Like she wanted nothing further to do with her old boyfriend—and then the next thing Guthrie knew, he was no longer courting a she-wolf.

When Tenell had broken up with her ex-boyfriend a second time, Guthrie had stayed clear of her, despite her calling to make it up to him. She was still trying to reach him through his kin, which amused them. No one had any intention of encouraging him to go back to her.

Calla's pretty strawberry blond hair curled about her shoulders, looking as soft as her blue sweater. Her green eyes suddenly glanced in his direction as if her wolf half had realized someone was watching her. He would not look away. It was an alpha *lupus garou*'s way of showing interest. Because he *was* interested. She smiled at him, and then Oran glanced his way.

Guthrie bowed his head a little to her, and only then did he look away. Was she like Tenell? Emotionally and physically feeling a void that she needed filled with another man—and any wolf would do?

He let out his breath. There wasn't any way he wanted to go through that again. Especially not if she went back to Baird.

Calla was so glad the MacNeills had come to help her out with Baird and his pack mates. She did not really want to be "guarded" anytime she left Argent Castle, but otherwise she was looking forward to seeing what pack life was like here. She loved how everyone was a wolf. That meant she didn't have to guard against saying anything pertaining to wolves that only her own kind could understand.

She glanced again at Guthrie as he talked to Duncan.

Even though he was the financial advisor for the pack, he was in as good shape for fighting as the rest of his brothers. His green eyes were lighter than hers, his reddish hair more brown. His coloration appealed to her. Being a redhead herself, redheads often caught her eye. To her chagrin, Duncan turned to see her observing Guthrie. Duncan winked, the devil, and that had Guthrie turning to see who he'd winked at.

She quickly cut up another slice of pork. That would teach her to ogle Guthrie while others were watching. She sighed. After what she'd done at the hen party—when she'd been perfectly innocent—she supposed everyone would watch the two of them while she was staying here. It was like olden times when courtiers gossiped about trysts between other members of the court. Especially since she was someone new to gossip about.

Oran was regaling her with all his fishing mishaps with Guthrie and Duncan when they were lads. He finished his pork and said to her, "Once, Guthrie got so excited about catching his first trout that he tipped the boat and we all ended up in the icy river. Duncan was ready to punch him. But in a good-hearted way. We had a devil of a time catching up with the boat. That was the end of that fishing trip."

She hadn't asked Oran to share everything about his life, although she did find it entertaining. But if Oran was interested in her, why did he say so much about Guthrie in all the humorous incidents he brought up? Surely, Oran could have shared stories that didn't include him.

"So then there was this time that we decided to reach the tree in the center of the pastureland, where one of our bulls was penned."

"Nay," she said, tilting her chin down, not believing the lads could have been that reckless.

"Aye. You know, lass, if we didn't have a clan battle to win, we had to do something with our time."

"Cearnach didn't go with you, did he?"

"Aye, he did. Ian didn't. He was always running things at the castle, even when he was sixteen. Guthrie said it would be a good way to keep up our physical training. And we were all for it."

"Guthrie did?" She thought that if Cearnach had gone with them, it had been his idea, since he was always in charge when Ian wasn't around.

"Aye, lass. Don't believe for a minute that all Guthrie does is calculate profits and expenses. He's a wild wolf, that one."

She smiled at that. He always seemed the quietest of the brothers. Maybe he'd had his wild fun in his youth, learned a thing or two from his experiences, and changed his ways. She wondered what he'd think if he knew Oran was telling all about him. She was glad she had no one here to tell on her.

⁓⁓

Early the next morning, Ian and his kin still weren't able to move Calla's car because of the snowdrift. Calla just hoped that Baird and his men couldn't move her car, either.

The fir trees were still covered in the soft, wet flakes, and the rising sun peered through the white clouds, coloring everything soft shades of yellow and pink. Calla was invited to join the fun of a snowman-building contest before the snow melted too much.

Bundled in coats, scarves, hats, and gloves, pack kids and adults alike were busy building snowmen in the parklike setting beyond the castle walls. Some of their Irish wolfhounds were playing in the snow too, biting at it, rolling in it, and acting as though they'd never seen the stuff before.

Ian and Duncan were constructing a snowman with their mates, when Cearnach stole their head for his, Elaine's, and Guthrie's creation. Getting the biggest kick out of it, Calla watched along with everyone else as Cearnach raced back to Guthrie and Elaine with the snowman's head in his gloved hands.

"Hurry, Cearnach!" Elaine and Guthrie cheered.

"Stop him, Ian!" Julia threw the first snowball at Cearnach in lighthearted retaliation, smacking him in the back. Everyone was laughing.

Ian pelted Cearnach with the next snowball, shouting, "That was only practice. The next head will be even better."

Calla had been helping Logan, the teen who took care of the dogs, and some of the other teens, to make a snowman, but with snowy missiles coming from all directions, the snowmen were forgotten. From the youngest to the oldest clan member, the battle was on.

As good-natured as both Ian and Cearnach were as the male leaders of the pack, they were bombarded the most. Julia was the female leader of the pack, but Calla noticed that nobody targeted her, probably not wanting to earn Ian's wrath if anyone accidentally hurt her.

Barking, the dogs chased after the flying balls of snow.

Calla hadn't ever participated in anything like this

with a wolf pack, and she couldn't stop laughing. Her stomach hurt as she gathered up more snow.

She formed a nice-sized ball and threw it at Cearnach. When he moved out of her path, her snowball smacked Guthrie in the forehead. He had been standing nearby, ready to pelt his brother with one. Guthrie turned to see who his attacker was. And smiled when he caught her eye.

He had the most devilishly wolfish look about him—a mixture of impending payback with a snowball and something a wee bit more intimate, like a tackle in the snow. But he wouldn't. Not in front of his clansmen. Not when they weren't courting. At least, she hoped not.

Cearnach was about to pelt him, but then turned to see what had stolen Guthrie's attention. She felt like her suddenly heated body would melt all the snow surrounding her, and she quickly bent to serve up another snowball. As soon as she threw it at Cearnach again, Julia got in the way and the ball of snow splatted against her back.

She turned to see who had targeted her and found Calla grinning. "I was aiming at Cearnach," Calla shouted over the laughs and squeals and threats of retaliation all around her.

"I'm not buying it!" Julia called back, and quickly readied her own ammunition.

Calla had never had so much fun in her life.

Guthrie was getting strong wolf vibes that Calla was interested in him. He felt the same way about her. His wolfish urges encouraged him to chase after her and tackle her—to get her back for socking him with the snowball, just for fun. If they'd been alone, he would have. He could tell from the way she was watching him that she knew just what he had in mind. Her mouth had curved up a hair, her cheeks turning rosy.

Guthrie's gaze had strayed to her a few times. He told himself it was because she was a guest, and he was ensuring that she was having a good time and not feeling left out. He'd never seen her this way—letting her hair down, so to speak—playing with other pack members and acting as though she were just one of the family.

She'd lived away from packs most of her life, so he'd been curious how she'd fit in. He and his brothers and Julia had been concerned that she might fold under Baird's persistence in attempting to get her back. They'd all shared the consensus that she needed to be with a pack that showed her a more supportive and loving family of *lupus garous*, unlike what the McKinley pack could offer her.

Even so, Guthrie was dying to get her back for that snowball. But not in front of everyone here. Sure, they were all busy playing in the snow, but still, everyone was watching out for her. Seeing to her needs. Ensuring she felt as though she belonged. He was certain that if he targeted her, and she got him back, everyone would think there was more to it than just playing.

He smiled at her as Julia threw a snowball at Calla that missed her by a mile. Grinning, Calla quickly armed herself and threw one at Julia; only it missed her too and hit Guthrie in the crotch. Good thing it was soft snow. He grinned and wiped off the snow, slowly, deliberately, wolfishly.

Calla looked like she could burst into flames, she was so red faced. He started laughing.

A half hour later, Ian called a truce so they could

finish the snowmen and head inside. A few knit caps were placed on top of the snowmen, and some sticks added for arms. A couple wore plaid scarves, and one of the girls brought out a couple handfuls of carrots from the kitchen to use as noses for several of them. Buttons and stones were added to create all kinds of faces—surprised, smiling, downturned—and then it was time to eat the noon meal.

Guthrie loved this time of year. Everyone was excited—the kids, the adults, even the wolfhounds. The pack gathering to do fun activities in the snow, the decorating and preparing special meals, made it truly an extraordinary time.

Everyone quickly put away their damp cold-weather gear and gathered in the great hall.

Guthrie started walking toward his usual seat when this many pack members ate together. Ian and Cearnach and their mates sat at the head table with Aunt Agnes, Lady Mae, and Shelley's uncle Ethan. Guthrie had begun sitting at one of the lower tables. Duncan and his mate, Shelley, were likewise sitting at a lower table now, so that they could be together. One big, happy family.

Guthrie glanced around to see where Calla was and found that Logan was sitting next to her. He was chatting away to her—Guthrie figured about the dogs—but he also noticed that the seat on her other side was suspiciously vacant.

He talked to several others as they made their way to their tables. He headed to the spot where he normally sat, next to Duncan, but he realized the seat to his brother's left had been taken. Oran, who normally sat nearer the door, was filling it now.

Guthrie shouldn't have cared, but it was unsettling to be bumped from his seat once again. He hated to admit how at home he felt in a particular place, and then how uncomfortable when he had to move. He glanced around and noticed that nearly all the seats were taken on this side of the great hall. He didn't want to be the last person seated, as Cook and her assistants were already bringing the trout served on toasted bread to the high table. He spied a spot but discounted it, realizing that one of the family's pairs of twin girls was short a twin, and sure enough, she dashed by him to get to her saved seat.

Two seats were available by the drafty window. He glanced again at the one by Calla, expecting it to be filled. It wasn't. Julia was watching him but quickly looked away, a wicked smile gracing her lips.

He'd been trying to let Calla have some space, but he'd been thwarted this time. He shook his head and strode toward the vacant chair before he ended up having to sit in one of the chilly window seats.

When he approached Calla, she looked grateful. He smiled. He supposed he'd saved her from Logan's dog talk. Logan said to her, "Will you ride with me on the hayride tonight?"

"Um, I have an engagement tonight. A Highland reunion I'm in charge of," Calla hastily said, sounding relieved that she had work to do.

"Ahh. Well, maybe another time." Logan brushed his brown hair out of his eyes. "Why are you sitting over here?" he asked Guthrie, as if he'd just noticed that Guthrie had joined them.

"Oran stole my seat." Guthrie thanked the lady who brought them their lunches.

"What did he do that for?" Logan asked and began eating his fish.

"Maybe he needed to talk to Duncan about something. I don't know." Guthrie suspected it was a conspiracy, yet he wondered why Oran hadn't been trying to make more headway in getting to know the lass. Maybe he was concerned about the same thing—that her relationship with Baird had ended too recently to consider dating her.

Logan glanced around the room, then grinned. "You didn't want the drafty chairs." He pointed at the two nearest the window.

"Good guess." Nobody wanted to sit there in wintertime.

Calla smiled and then began to eat her lunch.

"So, what reunion are you going to?" Guthrie asked. Ian hadn't spoken about it to him yet, and he still didn't know where it was.

She hesitated to say. He sat a little straighter, assuming that his clan didn't get along with whoever these people were.

"Which clan?" he asked.

She frowned at Guthrie.

He set his fork down. "You can't go alone, Calla, if that's what you're thinking. Not after the confrontation you had with Baird and his people last night."

"You know, you sound just like Cearnach."

Guthrie smiled a little at that. Usually, he looked up to Cearnach and appreciated his advice. Though he and his brothers all thought Cearnach had gone a little mad when he went to Calla's wedding, knowing full well that Baird wouldn't like it one wee bit.

Calla finally turned to her meal and said, "I've spoken to Ian about it. I don't want him or anyone else to feel put out that they have to watch over me like I'm a child."

Logan sat taller. "I can go with you instead of going on the hayride."

Calla smiled at Logan and shook her head. "You have fun and let me know all about it tomorrow."

He looked disappointed and glanced in Guthrie's direction as if asking him to talk Ian into letting him go. What was it with him? First, Logan had been sweet-talking Elaine before she was Cearnach's mate, and now he thought he had a chance with Calla? Calla belonged with the grown men.

Guthrie had every intention of speaking with Ian about Calla's plans tonight, but not for Logan's sake. "For your information," Guthrie said, wishing to address her concern about his clan watching out for her, "we feel it an honor to look out for you. Not only that, but Ian got a call from your dad. You didn't tell him you had an accident and further trouble with Baird, did you?"

She frowned at him. "I didn't want to worry my parents. They didn't have to know about it. They're on vacation and needed this break. It doesn't do any good to concern them when nothing truly bad happened." This time she flashed her very heated green eyes at Guthrie.

He'd never seen her riled up in human form. He wanted to smile, but he curbed the urge. "Aye, they're well aware of it now."

"I suppose Ian will keep them informed of everything I do now, even if I don't wish it."

"If it has to do with your safety, aye. Staying with us

means you're part of the pack for now. We look out for our own. We also have to ensure we do what's right by your family."

She turned to finish her meal. "Have fun on your hayride," Calla said to Logan. She smiled sweetly at him, scowled at Guthrie, and headed out of the great hall.

Logan frowned at Guthrie. "Did you have to make her mad?"

"You know Ian couldn't lie to her parents when she might have been hurt."

"Nay, but you didn't need to bring it up."

Then two of the wolfhounds began playing tug-of-war with a bone, and Logan hurried to intervene, as was his job, and move them outdoors.

Suddenly, Guthrie was sitting there eating alone. He wondered how that had happened.

Chapter 4

THAT AFTERNOON, THE SNOW AND ICE HAD MELTED enough to allow the MacNeill brothers and their kin to move Calla's car into the inner bailey, to Calla's vast relief. Thankfully, the car had no major damage, only a slight dent in the front bumper.

Tonight, she had the reunion to oversee, but in the meantime, she would spend some time going over Christmas ideas with Julia. She still couldn't believe Julia thought she and Guthrie had courtship plans. He was just as bossy as Cearnach was with her.

As soon as she entered the garden room to meet with Julia, Calla knew there would be trouble.

And that *trouble* was waiting for her just inside.

Dressed in a white medieval shirt and a muted, ancient blue-and-green plaid kilt of the MacNeill clan, he stood next to one of the floor-to-ceiling glass windows. *Guthrie*.

Calla had no idea why Guthrie was wearing a kilt. Not only that, but he was armed—his sword belted at his waist and a *sgian dubh* in his boot. The carved handle on the knife—that Cearnach had crafted himself—stuck out of the top of Guthrie's boot.

"Come, Calla. I've been gathering some ideas off the Internet." Julia looked warm in her heavy blue wool sweater and a MacNeill plaid skirt, her red hair curling over her shoulders. "We were going to decorate the

Christmas tree in the hall this evening, but since you have the reunion to attend, we want to wait until tomorrow so you can help us, if you'd like."

"I'd love to. Thanks for asking." She really appreciated how Julia included her in pack activities. Calla was excited about the party—the first Christmas event she'd ever planned for anyone—and she wanted to make it just right. But she knew Guthrie would be a royal pain in the arse because he scrutinized all the clan's expenditures and thought spending a lot of money on a Christmas party was unnecessary.

Guthrie raised his brows at Calla as she hurried to shut the glass door and keep the chilling wind out. A light snow was falling in fat flakes outside. But a hot fire glowed in the fire pit as Julia smiled brightly at her and motioned to the dining table where she was studying pictures on her laptop.

Calla assumed Guthrie was there to weigh in on projected costs, but she couldn't help saying, "Are you planning to fight a medieval battle somewhere?"

Calla thought she detected a hint of a smirk struggling to appear, while Guthrie's eyes focused on hers.

"Nay, just the one here," he said. He didn't smile, but his eyes held a spark of mirthful challenge. Calla rolled her eyes. He *had* to be wearing his kilt for some reason other than to annoy her. Unless he was intentionally trying to distract her.

She hadn't overheard anyone talking about the men practicing their swordsmanship today—as cold as it was and with the snow now falling. Though in truth, the men were not fair-weather fighters, and she'd known them to even practice in a light rain.

Julia cast Calla another smile. Ever since the under-wear incident, everyone looked at her and Guthrie differently. When *really*, Calla had taken Guthrie's boxers because he was the only one she believed could handle her teasing—who wouldn't get other notions. And he was the only one of the brothers who was unmated. *And* because she hadn't wanted him to feel left out when his brothers' mates had targeted them.

She knew how it felt to be excluded from parties and social gatherings. First, because she had been a wolf among humans and her father had acted like a rabid wolf when she tried to have human friends—especially a human boy whom her father had threatened to kill if she saw any more of him. Later, she'd worried that the human guy would want to kill *her* if he ever learned she was a *lupus garou*.

She'd hooked up with three lone wolves at various times, and that was another mistake. They were fun, in a singular sort of way. They didn't want to do things around humans or around other wolves. None had been interested in forming a wolf pack of their own, and none had wanted pups. She'd wanted more, like her parents had with her. She'd wanted to join in on parties, human or wolf.

So she'd started her party planner business. She got to attend lots parties and was paid to do it. Most of all, those paying for her services needed and loved her for what she did. It was a win-win scenario.

She sat down at the table next to Julia and readied her pen and pad of paper to take copious notes. She didn't have to look to know Guthrie was still studying her. Her skin prickled with tension like a wolf's would while waiting warily for the attack.

She was used to people watching her as she worked and it had never bothered her. But Guthrie was a different story. He had the most devilish look—as if he was seeing her in a different way. Like he now knew her secret—that she had a crush on him. Which she *didn't*.

She wished he'd go away.

"You could sit down and read a magazine or something," she said, motioning to a few on gardening and castle decor sitting on the coffee table next to the couches.

A little reading nook of Julia's books was also situated nearby, but Calla was certain the armed Highlander *wouldn't* be interested in reading about hot and romantically inclined *lupus garous*.

"It's my duty to offer advice on all matters concerning finances," Guthrie said, not budging.

She should have acted as if she didn't recall he was there because she was so busy looking at the pictures Julia was showing her. But darn it. Her skin felt flushed because she knew he was watching her every move.

"This will probably take a while. Or…better yet, you could leave. We can share the costs of the venture with you later. You can probably talk someone else into donning his sword and fighting with you, and you'd have a lot more fun than standing there." Like a statue. A *very sexy, wolfish* Highland statue.

She shouldn't have said anything, because doing so would feed into the notion that he was bothering her. She'd thought the undercurrent of tension between them had to do with her spending people's money on extravagant parties. Now she wasn't so certain.

His mouth curved up a hair, but he didn't say anything. *Fine*. Calla stiffened a little, intent on ignoring him. If he thought he could keep her from squandering—his words, not hers—the MacNeills' money on this celebration by making her uncomfortable, he was mistaken. Julia wanted to spare no expense on her first-ever Christmas party with her new pack, and Calla was going to help make it the best she could.

She tucked a curl behind her ear and stared at the monitor, trying to concentrate on what Julia was saying. Guthrie moved behind them to observe the Internet pages they were looking at, but he was standing nearest to Calla.

This was even worse! At least when he was standing farther away, she couldn't breathe in his fascinating male wolf scent, a mix of piney woods and fresh air and the fragrance that was uniquely his. And she couldn't help feeling the heat of his body that made hers heat as well.

"Those look awfully—" Guthrie said.

"Like a bargain." Julie raised a brow at Guthrie.

He frowned. "You wanted my opinion from a financial perspective."

Calla shifted her attention to Julia, whose face turned a wee bit red. Julia had asked Guthrie to be here?

Calla marked it down on her pad of paper. "I agree with you, Julia." Calla gave her another site to look at. "These are much more expensive. So the other site's prices are a bargain."

Guthrie snorted. "A bargain would be not spending the money on decorations in the first place."

The ladies ignored him. "Next?" Calla asked, getting into the spirit of this.

"We have to get mistletoe from England, and I was

thinking that these looked good," Julia said, showing Calla the pictures and prices.

"We really don't need that, do we?" Guthrie asked, sounding incredulous.

"Aye," both ladies said.

They considered prices on several sites, while Guthrie folded his arms and shook his head.

"We must have sweet-smelling cinnamon candles to scent the great hall," Julia said, pulling up some pages.

"Surely a couple will suffice. Any more and the scent will overwhelm our enhanced sense of smell," Guthrie said.

"Fifteen, I believe, will work," Calla said.

Guthrie groaned.

Julia smiled.

They had looked at another half-dozen or so Internet pages when Julia asked Calla, "You said you have that party to manage in an hour, right?"

"Aye. I'll be there for a couple of hours," Calla said.

"Good. We can keep poring over ideas for the celebration in between your other commitments," Julia said, as if she had no worry that Calla could pull this off.

"So, have you any idea who will be going with me this time?" she asked Julia.

"Ethan and Jasper and…" Julia looked at Guthrie.

Calla chewed on her bottom lip as she considered his sexy legs. "You can't go dressed like that," she said, determination in her tone.

"Is there a dress code that says I can't, lass?" Guthrie asked, an arrogant brow lifted.

"Aye, there is, if you must know," she said most vehemently. "It has to do with the MacNeills not getting along with the Rankins. Ian warned me. I told him he didn't have to send any of you, but he insisted, even going so far as to say I wasn't going unless an escort did. Well, fine. But keeping the peace with them will be difficult enough if they realize you're there to safeguard me. Wearing your clan's tartan on top of that?" She shook her head.

"They're wearing theirs, aye? So will I wear mine," Guthrie said, no Mr. Congeniality. He was dead serious.

"It's *their* affair. Not *yours*." Calla ground her teeth. "What about Ethan and Jasper?" She hoped they'd at least have better sense and wear something other than kilts.

"Now that they're back in a Highland clan, you better believe they're proud to be part of the family and share it with the world."

Great. One MacNeill dressed in his kilt might have managed to go unnoticed. All three Highland gray wolves in kilts? *Not a chance.*

She folded her arms. "Rankin said they'd provide proper security for me. You don't even need to attend." They hadn't, of course. If they knew she might bring trouble to the event, she could see them canceling her attendance and handling the rest of the affair themselves. Baird McKinley and his kin weren't on the guest list, so she would be fine.

"Nay, lass," Guthrie said.

"You can just drop me off at the manor and come back to pick me up when I'm ready to leave. I'll just call you. I'll be inside orchestrating everything anyway. Baird wouldn't dare crash the party."

"Nay," Guthrie said, being his stubborn self. "Everyone will be celebrating. You need men you can count on who will be dedicated to watching over you."

She let out her breath in a huff. "Fine. You stay out-side in the car, or whatever. You don't go inside. And whatever you do, you *don't* get into a fight with their men. Or *else*." She gave him a dagger of a glower.

He smiled. "When it comes to doing my job, you have nothing to worry about."

She bit back a snort. Doing his job was likely to cause trouble—considering the way he was dressed.

"It's a very regal affair. The men will be wearing Prince Charlie jackets and the like—not…" She consid-ered Guthrie's open shirt, which showed off a hint of his fascinatingly naked chest, sculpted to the max.

"Not…?"

"So…" Her face felt flushed. She didn't know why she was suddenly getting so tongue-tied around Guthrie. He'd never paid any attention to her before, that she'd remembered. "They won't be dressed so—"

"So…wolfishly rugged?" Guthrie ventured.

Her gaze shot up from eyeing his chest to his smiling face, her whole body heating as if she'd gotten too close to the flames in the fire pit.

Julia tried to conceal a chuckle. And was not entirely successful.

"They are not wolves, you know. And you can't wear your sword. It's not a wolf affair," Calla said, ignoring Julia and Guthrie's amusement. "I'm serious!"

Guthrie's smile faded and his wolfish protective self was instantly in place. "The sword is not for a show of force against the Rankin family, but for Baird McKinley and his ilk if they should show."

"Oh, for heaven's sake," Calla said. "They're not going to follow me everywhere I go."

"Maybe or maybe not. If they quit stalking you, they could very well hope we'll become complacent." He patted his sheathed sword. "I will remain armed." He gave her a slight tilt of his head.

"Well, tomorrow I'll be in charge of a toga party. Will you wear a toga for that?"

"I know your schedule," he said.

Which surprised her. He was not her official body-guard. As pack leader, Ian was the one she had to constantly update about her schedule. Endless changes were one of the biggest problems she faced in this business.

"A Highland wolf doesn't wear a toga," he said.

"Right. There's no place to put your sword and *sgian dubh*."

"Besides," Guthrie said, ignoring her comment, "I have work to catch up on, and I believe Ian has selected other men to watch out for you tomorrow."

She felt her face flush again. She shouldn't have assumed Guthrie would accompany her, though ever since she'd finished handling the wedding arrangements at the MacQuarries' castle, Guthrie had been on the list of ten men to watch over her when she was beyond the castle walls. She thought it had been Guthrie's choice, but now she realized Ian had made the selections. She should have known. So why was she feeling a wee bit…disappointed?

She sighed, realizing once again that Guthrie had distracted her when she was *supposed* to be working with Julia on the Christmas celebration.

"I imagine it's about time for you to leave," Julia said, patting Calla's hand as if sympathizing with her.

Calla smiled at her. "Aye, we will get together on this

again as soon as we can. I have all kinds of lovely ideas for games and the like." She glanced at Guthrie. "None require swordplay."

Guthrie shook his head. "Where's the fun in that?"

Guthrie assumed the Rankin reunion would be no big deal as long as none of the McKinleys showed up. "Lass, you have nothing to worry about," Guthrie assured her as he drove Calla to the Rankin manor house.

Ethan and Jasper were sitting in the backseat, both in full MacNeill dress. Calla was wearing a red sweater-dress that made her look soft and huggable, and showed off all her curves. Guthrie shouldn't have cared what she wore, but Ethan had winked at him when he caught Guthrie staring a little too hard, and he'd finally snapped his gaping mouth shut. Even now, her green eyes glinted with menace. Why hadn't he ever noticed how sexy she looked?

He'd always had an interest in her. But after she'd saved Cearnach's life in the river when they were lads, she and her family had moved away. As a grown woman, she'd moved back and gotten involved with Baird. Though she'd also renewed her friendship with Cearnach, and everyone was certain Cearnach meant to mate her. Guthrie and his brothers had allowed them to work on their friendship, even though Cearnach had teased her often enough when she was a young lass.

Then Cearnach had taken Elaine as his mate, and Calla had canceled her wedding with Baird McKinley and moved in temporarily with the MacNeills.

Now Guthrie was running into her all the

time—meeting on the narrow, winding stairs leading to the bedchambers, bumping into her in the kitchen or dining room, or passing in the gardens. And her cheeks continually flamed every time he ran across her and caught her eye. He didn't recall ever seeing her blush so much. Certainly never around Cearnach. He'd been like a brother to her, Guthrie realized.

"You know this is my livelihood. If things don't go well, who do you think will get the blame? Not you and your kin, but me, because I brought you with me," she said like a pissed-off she-wolf, pulling him out of his thoughts.

He smiled. "We'll be fine," he said again, sure of it. What could go wrong? The Rankins and their friends would be busy celebrating, and no one would even notice the Highland wolves serving guard duty on the grounds. "We're only there to protect you if Baird or his men try anything. We have no quarrel with the Rankins."

Which wasn't quite true. The eldest son, Kevin Rankin, had harassed one of their cousins, Heather, at a Celtic festival, and Guthrie and Kevin would have come to blows if Ian hadn't stepped in to stop the fight. Guthrie reminded himself that Kevin was on a cruise and not attending this affair, so Calla should be fine.

He glanced at her sweaterdress, visible with her coat slung over the seat.

He smiled at some of his early memories of her— some of her funny antics as a young lass, like getting a dunking when she caught a trout that was nearly half her size, or playing at sword fighting with one of their wooden practice swords and getting Cearnach in the crotch. That had Cearnach gasping for breath, his brothers laughing, and Calla looking like she would die of mortification. "You have nothing to be worried about," Guthrie said again.

"I still think you should have worn normal clothes. You know, since you're trying not to attract attention."

"We could have worn trousers, aye. But this is a clan affair, and our kin *always* show up at clan gatherings wearing our clan sett with pride. If Ian had pulled the duty himself, he would have done the same thing."

She snorted, and he smiled. "Don't worry. Ethan, Jasper, and I will behave ourselves with the utmost decorum."

Chapter 5

AT LEAST, GUTHRIE HOPED EVERYTHING WOULD BE all right at the Rankin reunion as he drove up to the front door of the five-story, Georgian-style, white-stone manor house. Like some country manor houses built in the late medieval period for gentry families, this one was more for show than defense.

Vehicles were unloading partygoers at the manor house, and then valets were driving them to a gravel car park off to the side of the house.

Trees surrounded the home in a countrified setting, the ones nearest the house sparkling with blue lights. Had that been Calla's idea? At least she hadn't suggested they add Christmas lights to Argent Castle, the plantings, or outer buildings…yet. He could just imagine the extra cost in electricity.

A redheaded man wearing a Prince Charlie jacket and a green-and-blue plaid kilt hurried down the steps, opened the door to the car, and took Calla's hand and kissed it as he helped her out.

Bloody hell. What was Kevin Rankin doing here?

Instantly, Guthrie's wolf half went on offense. He quickly left the car, and Jasper got out and took over the driver's seat, dismissing the man who was going to park the car.

Calla was supposed to be *working* here, not garnering kisses from the son of the man who owned the manor house. Kevin was a rich playboy who thought he was a real ladies' man. From what Calla had told Cearnach, Kevin Rankin treated all women as though they had the hots for him, Calla included. She'd planned this event months ago, so Guthrie hadn't known the man had bothered her initially. If Guthrie had known that, he would have had words with Kevin.

Ethan got out of the vehicle and joined Guthrie, while Jasper drove off to park the car. The business of protecting Calla from Baird and his clansmen swiftly shifted to protecting her from Kevin Rankin. Now Guthrie had no intention of standing outside when she might very well need his help *inside* the house.

Three hulking Rankin bruisers, cousins of Kevin, stared hard at Guthrie and his stepfather, arms folded. They stood on the stairs leading to the entrance of the manor, all wearing the same clan attire. But not wearing swords like Guthrie and his kin. Just the typical *sgian dubh* tucked into their socks.

"We are here to—" Before Guthrie could say "protect the lady," Calla cut him off with a glower.

"They *planned* to stay out here. They're my ride. The manor house is too far out in the country for them to go anywhere and return to pick me up on time." She patted Guthrie on the chest as if to appease him, but it made him feel like he was her dog. Like she was patting him on the head before she left him so he could happily wander around in the yard.

"*I* could take you home after this, *if* you even wanted to go home afterward," Kevin said to Calla, casting an evil smirk at Guthrie.

Guthrie responded with a low growl.

With his human hearing, Kevin didn't catch it, but Ethan and Calla did. Ethan smiled at Guthrie, but Calla shot Guthrie another warning look before she quickly took Kevin's arm.

"Thanks, but I promised to visit with Guthrie's sister-in-law after this affair, concerning Christmas party arrangements I'm working on for their family. Busy season, you know. So Guthrie and his family will drive me home."

Before Guthrie could object to her going inside without him, she hurried into the manor to do her work. Not that the three men standing in his path would have let him or Ethan get by them. Guthrie scowled at her disappearing backside.

One of the Rankin "bouncers" said, "We don't know why you think she needs looking after, but we'll make sure she has a *good* time."

Guthrie didn't like the way the man said it.

Ethan touched Guthrie's arm as if to say that the man wasn't worth fighting. Jasper joined them, and with another scowl in the Rankin men's direction, Guthrie conceded and led his guard detail into the trees surrounding the property. From there, they'd have a perfect view of the driveway and front entryway to watch for any signs of Baird McKinley.

Lights were on in every room in the five-story manor house, and more outside lights cast a soft yellow glow along the driveway and over a carriage house several hundred feet away. Christmas decorations were limited to the blue lights twinkling on a half-dozen fir trees out front.

The light snow continued to drift from the clouds

above, collecting on top of the piled-up snow from the recent blizzard.

Ethan and Jasper were standing farther away, watching the comings and goings. The two men were triplets, like many siblings born to *lupus garou* families. They were dark haired with graying temples, and both were in good shape after having worked with cattle in Texas for years before joining the MacNeill pack. They'd exchanged managing longhorn steer for Highland cattle and worked hard to prove their worth to the pack.

Surprising everyone, Lady Mae most, Ethan had proposed marriage to her. And blushing, she'd accepted. Now Jasper was courting Guthrie's Aunt Agnes. Though Jasper and Agnes were less vocal in their relationship and a lot more into denial that they were courting each other. Guthrie had seen the way Jasper raced to help Aunt Agnes, whether she needed assistance or not, and how she blushed and looked to see if anyone had noticed. Which in a wolf pack usually meant someone had. When he got caught at it, Jasper swore that he was just being Texas neighborly. Nobody believed it for a moment—not when the neighborly part seemed to always be directed at Agnes.

The only thing that the men had had to get used to when they moved to Argent Castle was swordsmanship practice. Not something they'd done much for centuries while living in Texas. Shooting was more their style. But the brothers had been eager to fit in with the family, and Guthrie was glad to have them here with him tonight.

The talking and laughing grew louder as the drinking got under way inside the manor house, the music

becoming just as loud. Guthrie folded his arms, prefer-
ring the solitude of the quiet outside—a wolf's choice
of setting. The chilled breeze whipped his kilt about,
and his senses were on high alert as he smelled the air
currents and checked with his wolf's vision for any
movement in the dark.

All that moved were fir branches waving in the
breeze. The grass was still covered with several inches
of snow, and the sky at gloaming was a cloudy gray. It
was cold, the temperature just at freezing, but he didn't
expect any major changes in the weather.

Ethan glanced back at the manor house. "A couple of
men are looking out the window at us."

"Aye. Just ignore them and watch for any signs of
Baird and his men. We don't want to quarrel with the
Rankins," Guthrie said. As much as he despised having Calla in the house with Kevin, Guthrie had to trust
that she could deal with Kevin on her own for now.
Especially since she had made it clear that she didn't
want Guthrie's assistance.

"That's why we wore the MacNeill tartan, aye?"
Ethan said, sounding amused.

Guthrie shook his head. "If we go to a formal gathering where others are wearing their kin's sett, we do also."

"Aye," Jasper said with a twinkle in his eye. "When
we're invited to the shindig."

Guthrie wasn't about to admit Jasper was right.

"We might not want a fight, but the vultures are
gathering and I warrant they'll be out here picking a
battle with us before we know it," Ethan warned, again
glancing at the manor house.

Snow continued to fall in soft, fat flakes as Guthrie

watched for any movement in the trees surrounding the
ten-acre parklike setting. He and his companions would
see movement in the semi-dark if anyone suddenly
appeared. But it was quiet. He wondered if Baird had
finally given up chasing after Calla constantly.

"Do you think Baird knows the lass's schedule?"
Ethan asked, as if reading Guthrie's mind.

"Aye, I've told Ian that she shouldn't mention that
she's in charge of these affairs, which are being announced all over the place. She insists it's the only way
she can adequately advertise her business." Guthrie
stretched a little to warm up his muscles.

Ethan shook his head.

Behind them, Guthrie heard movement on the steps of
the manor house. Three sets of footsteps. He glanced over
his shoulder. Two were the bouncers from earlier, but the
other was Kevin's younger brother, Ralph Rankin, about
twenty-eight or so and a real hothead. Instead of a redhead like his brother, he was a blond. One of the men was
nearly black-haired, and the other fairer. All three men
were armed with swords now. Being armed and drinking
alcohol was not a good combination.

Guthrie turned his back on the men.

"Why would you be here wearing the MacNeill tartan?" Ralph called out, slurring his words slightly.

He was drunk or getting there, Guthrie suspected. He
didn't turn around to acknowledge them further. Ethan
and Jasper took Guthrie's lead and also ignored the men.

"Drunker than a skunk," Ethan said under his breath.

"Hey! I'm talking to you. What business do you have
being here? Afraid your girlfriend's going to have a go
with one of us?"

"Whoreson," Ethan said this time.

"He's not worth it," Guthrie warned. He didn't plan to cause any trouble for Calla, despite his wanting to take the men to task. He had every intention of keeping his mouth shut and doing his duty. Which was watching out for Baird and his kin. Not dealing with these rowdy, drunken sots.

"Hey! You think you're too good for us?" Ralph continued.

Guthrie smiled. He knew he was.

"Turn around when I'm talking to you."

Guthrie closed his eyes briefly. He'd tried. But he suspected Ralph wasn't going to shut up and go away.

He turned around. "Were you addressing me?"

Guthrie had thought Kevin would make his appearance. Then again, he probably would rather have his brother and cousins deal with the MacNeills and not get his hands dirty. Had they been discussing Guthrie and his family being here and stewing about it all this time?

"No need for you and the rest of your friends to be here," Ralph said, motioning for them to leave like they were annoying bugs. "The lass will be warming my brother's bed tonight."

Guthrie narrowed his eyes. He really had to curb his tongue. Just seeing the way these men were acting, he hated to think that someone inside—like Kevin Rankin—might be harassing Calla.

"Why don't you leave? We'll treat the lass right. We'll take care of her," the black-haired man said. One of Ralph's cousins, but Guthrie didn't know his name.

"We'll wait here for her, if it's all the same to you," Guthrie said. He thought he sounded rather diplomatic, when he would have preferred taking a bite out of the man.

Ralph scowled back at him, probably used to ordering people about and getting his way. "Didn't you hear what I said? Leave. We'll take care of the wee lass. No need for you to stay."

"Aye, I heard. And we stand firm." Guthrie stood straighter, taller, the hair on his arms standing on end, like a wolf's fur would when the wolf was confronted with trouble.

Ralph stalked toward them, his two companions following him. Guthrie instinctively sized them up as they advanced. The black-haired man was less muscled than Ralph, but the other was much bulkier. And all were human.

"Maybe I need to make myself clearer," Ralph said with a drunken swagger.

Guthrie really didn't want to get into a fight with this man and ruin Calla's party. But he never walked away from a battle. Ever. Though he reminded himself the man *was* inebriated.

Ralph and the others closed the distance. When he was well into Guthrie's personal space, Ralph raised his hand as if to shove Guthrie back. Guthrie quickly knocked Ralph's arm away—hard. He imagined the man would be sporting a sore or bruised arm by tomorrow.

Ralph fumbled to draw a sword.

"Don't be a fool, Rankin," Guthrie said. Unless the man was a practiced swordsman, he'd never be a match for a wolf who'd fought in numerous battles early on and had regularly practiced swordsmanship with his kin throughout the years. Both Rankin and his older brother had fought in a mock battle at the last Celtic fest they had attended, so Guthrie knew Ralph could swing a sword, but he hadn't paid close attention to how well.

The man gave him a sloppy, evil grin. "Rusty, eh? Just wear a sword for show, but don't know how to use it? Well, we'll see who the better man is."

Ethan said, "He seems to be itching for a fight. We ought to hog-tie him and take him out back to let him cool his heels a wee bit."

Jasper agreed with a nod of his head.

Though Ethan, Jasper, and their triplet brother, Teague, had been born in Scotland, they'd lived for centuries in Texas, and Guthrie didn't think he'd ever get used to their sayings.

Ralph cursed and finally freed his sword. Guthrie hated to unsheathe his, but he couldn't leave Calla behind and he had to protect himself in case the drunken lout managed to slice at him. He smoothly pulled his sword free of its scabbard.

The man swung at him. With a strong swing, Guthrie's blade connected with Ralph's, hooking it and sending it flying across the cobblestone driveway.

For a moment, no one moved. The aggressors' mouths hung open, stunned. Guthrie and his friends waited, anticipating further violence.

The man turned to his friends. "Make them leave. You're still armed."

The two men drew their swords. Eyeing Guthrie, they didn't approach.

"You don't want to do this," he warned.

That seemed to incite the men. One came at him

while the other targeted Ethan, who had yet to draw his own sword. Like Guthrie, he'd been avoiding a fight.

Just as swiftly as Guthrie had done, Ethan unsheathed his sword.

These men were not as drunk as their fearless leader and lasted a good while longer before Guthrie sent his opponent's sword skittering across the stones to join Ralph's. Ethan quickly dispatched the other man's sword in the same manner.

"*Fight! Fight!*" a few people shouted from the direction of the manor house.

Just great, Guthrie thought. Calla would learn of this.

Sure enough, just as the first man threw a punch at Guthrie, he realized that Calla was already there.

Guthrie avoided the punch and brought his free hand up, jabbing the man in the nose hard. A sickening crunch sounded, and Ralph cried out and held his hand protectively over his nose.

A wee bit too late.

"I *can't* believe you got into a fight with Ralph Rankin," Calla said, furious with Guthrie as he drove her back to Argent Castle.

Ethan and Jasper sat quietly in the backseat, but Guthrie could smell the way they were bristling at Calla's words and knew—because they were there to protect their "guest"—that they were biting their tongues.

"They started it," Guthrie said, not the least bit remorseful. Well, maybe a little because he really hadn't wanted to ruin her party.

"You could have avoided it!" she growled.

"He drew a sword on Guthrie. The sot was drunk and dangerous, lass," Ethan said, angry.

Guthrie hadn't intended to explain why he had fought the man. She had to know he had better sense than to pick a fight.

Calla turned her glower from Ethan back to Guthrie. "You *broke* Ralph's nose!"

"Aye. He had it coming, lass. He said someone was lying in wait to bed you," Guthrie finally said. He hadn't planned to mention that, but it just slipped out, as angry as he still was over the insult.

She closed her gaping mouth. Then she said, "And you *believed* him?"

"I ignored him for a good long while, Calla."

"He did," Ethan said.

Guthrie had lost his father so many years ago that he had never expected his mother to take another mate, but he couldn't have been gladder that the Texas Scot served as his stepfather now.

"I'm sorry, lass. Had there been some other way, I would never have resorted to it," Guthrie said.

"They were *drunk*," she said, as if that made any difference.

"Which made them all the more dangerous," Guthrie told her. "Particularly when they were armed with swords."

"I doubt they had the skill with a sword that you and your kin do."

"True," Guthrie said, "but if a man draws a sword, it's like pulling a gun on another man. You don't threaten someone with it unless you plan to use it."

"He didn't just unsheathe his sword," Ethan said.

"He swung it at Guthrie. Now, lass, a man can't just let that pass."

"You broke Ralph's nose!"

Ethan and Jasper chuckled in the backseat.

"Aye. He threw the first punch," Guthrie said, now wondering if she'd missed that part of the equation.

She let her breath out harshly. "You're lucky he's not pressing charges. And that they're not asking for a refund for my services. Or *you'd* be paying for them."

Guthrie tapped his thumbs on the steering wheel, then said, "Other than that, did the party go as well as you had expected?"

She glowered at him.

He shrugged. "All that's important is that you remain safe."

"Aye, but who's going to keep me—*and my business*—safe from *you*?"

———

As soon as they returned to Argent Castle, Calla stormed toward the stairs of the keep. Guthrie figured he should be glad if Ian told her he would assign someone else to watch over her. He knew he needed to get his mind back on financial reports. So why the hell was he following Calla's sweet, red sweater-covered arse all the way up the stairs?

Calla glanced back at Guthrie. "Where are *you* going?"

"If you intend to speak to Ian about the affair, I'll explain what happened since I have firsthand knowledge. You were inside the Rankin manor house and didn't see most of it."

"You'll give your sweet version of it," Calla said.

"The truth." He motioned to Ian's door, and she knocked at the doorjamb. "May I have a word with you?" she asked Ian, who was sitting at his desk.

Ian hung up his phone and set it down.

"Guthrie broke Ralph Rankin's nose," Ian said, motioning for them to come in and take seats.

Word always spread fast in a wolf pack.

"How did you learn of it?" Calla asked, sounding astounded.

"Ethan called and informed me of what happened. Anytime one of my pack members is involved in a skirmish, it's my business to know."

"Then you know why I don't want Guthrie to accompany me any longer," Calla said, casting him an annoyed look.

"They're not pressing charges, are they?" Ian said, knowing very well they weren't. Ralph Rankin's father was furious with Ralph for getting drunk and then, armed with swords, attacking Guthrie and his men. The old man was just glad no one had been wounded at the point of a sword.

Calla looked more than exasperated. "That *isn't* the point!"

"Calla, in matters like this, I stand by my men, who are there to protect you—" Before she could counter with the notion that they weren't protecting her, Ian quickly added, "and themselves. But someone else is going with you to the party you're in charge of tomorrow."

"Good," Calla said, then with a scathing glance in Guthrie's direction, she brushed past him and out of the room.

"Guthrie, want to close the door?" Ian asked.

Guthrie did, figuring he was going to get a lecture. "What Ethan told you was correct," Guthrie said, taking his seat. He didn't know what Ethan said exactly, but he knew the Texan would have told the truth.

"That Calla's got the hots for you like you have for her?"

Guthrie closed his gaping mouth. Then finding his tongue, he said, "What?"

Ian grinned at him.

Chapter 6

AFTER HANDLING THE RANKIN FAMILY REUNION, PAR-
ticularly following the fight that had ensued during it,
Calla was drained when she retired to her guest bedchamber that night. Thankfully, Ralph Rankin's father,
John, had been incensed with his son's and nephews'
drunken actions. Although more than half of the guests
loved the short display of unscheduled swordsmanship,
Calla didn't believe that was a good ending to her otherwise successful party.

She did wonder if she could have a clan perform
a sword fight, just for entertainment, during a future
Scottish family reunion. The problem was that the only
ones she knew who could do a superb job at it without
injuring their opponents were the MacNeills.

Well, not the *only* problem. She shook her head at the
notion. She could just envision the MacNeills having a
fight with the ones she'd arranged the party for—again.

After taking a long, hot shower, she slipped into bed
and tried to read a book on setting up parties on a budget.
She stared at the pages, not reading or seeing anything,
until she finally gave up, turned out the lamplight, and
closed her eyes. Which conjured up images of Guthrie
in his medieval shirt with his tartan sash crossing his
muscled torso, his kilt blowing in the chilly breeze.

She'd admired his footwork in his brown leather
boots as he had quickly outmaneuvered Ralph, and

she'd watched the way the men's swords clashed and how Guthrie had disarmed Ralph in a flash. Guthrie had looked so confident, warrior-like, and…hell, sexy that she wished he'd been battling with his kin in a friendly practice—not at the Rankin's reunion—so she could have enjoyed it.

Even the women who had raced out to see him fight had been "oohing" and "ahhing" over his physique. Which had made Calla grind her teeth and fold her arms. Aye, she knew better than to actually attempt to stop a sword fight in the middle of it. But she hadn't liked that the women—other than her—were just as fascinated with the Highland hunk.

When one of the women had asked if Guthrie was wearing anything under his kilt, obviously not interested if any of the other kilt-dressed men were, Calla had bit her tongue. She'd wanted to retort that he was wearing briefs—as if she knew—but she'd had her eyes glued to him every bit as much as the rest of the women had, trying to get a peek.

Opening her eyes, Calla gave up trying to sleep and got out of bed. Maybe a glass of milk would help her to quit thinking of what went on at the party.

She threw on a tank top and shorts, a pair of slippers, and a robe, and headed down the hallway to the stairs. Even in the darkened hallway, she could see with her wolf's vision and used the stair railing as she hurried down the curved stone steps.

When she arrived in the kitchen, she found the light switch and flipped it on. The entire keep was quiet, the kitchen spotless. She reached into one of the three stainless-steel fridges and pulled out a carton of milk, then poured herself a glass. After putting the milk away, she took a deep breath and stared out at the frosty garden through the windows behind the kitchen table. Small brass lanterns illuminated the shrubs a short distance from the castle, but the rest of the gardens were dark.

She was about to take a sip of milk when a deep male voice said, "Couldn't sleep?"

Calla squeaked and dropped the glass of milk on the slate floor, splattering milk everywhere. Used to slipping around her house in the middle of the night, she hadn't been prepared for anyone's sudden appearance here.

She wheeled around to see Guthrie grinning at her. "Sorry, lass," he said, not sounding sorry at all but rather highly amused. "I didn't mean to startle you. I'll clean it up."

She glanced at his body. He wore only a pair of black boxers—his bare chest and legs taking more of her attention than necessary. "You're not wearing any shoes. I'll get it."

"It was my fault," Guthrie said.

"I know. It was. But you can't get any closer or you'll cut your feet." She sighed, grabbed some paper towels and wetted them, then began to clean up the mess— milk and milk-covered glass everywhere. Glass hitting a stone floor didn't have a chance.

"You aren't still angry about what happened at the manor house, are you?" Guthrie asked. Seizing some paper towels and ignoring her look of disbelief, he began to help her clean up the mess.

"Guthrie, you're going to get cut." She looked up from his big feet and saw him staring at her robe gaping open. She was wearing a tank top and shorts, for heaven sakes. *He* was nearly naked! She sighed. "I…I think, besides worrying you were going to be charged with assault, I was concerned that the men might have cut you or Ethan."

"You said yourself you didn't think fighting with swords was their strong suit," Guthrie said, drawing closer as he moved in her direction to capture more of the splintered glass.

"Aye, but they weren't just practicing with you, either."

"They didn't stand a chance." Guthrie smiled at her. "You needn't have worried."

She caught his gaze, his green eyes darkened. "Did Ian scold you too much after I left?" She'd been concerned about that too. Afterward, she thought she probably shouldn't have made such a fuss about it.

"He's the pack leader," Guthrie said.

Which most likely meant Ian had chewed him out. "I'm sorry. But it will probably be best if you don't have to safeguard me."

"You think one of the toga wearers would try to fight me?"

She smiled at that. "The Greeks thought of swords as an auxiliary weapon. They were mostly spear bearers. So if you were armed with only your sword and any of them were carrying spears, you'd be in real trouble."

Guthrie chuckled. "Not if they have been drinking, which I'm sure they will be, aye?" He threw out his glass- and milk-covered paper towels and washed his hands.

"What did you ever see in Baird anyway?" Guthrie asked, meaning to sound casual, but his words came out a lot gruffer than he intended.

She paused and frowned a little at him. "Haven't

you ever made a mistake in liking someone? Not really knowing the person as you thought you did? That they're showing you only their good side?"

Instantly, he thought of Margaret Finnegan—the redheaded human who was all sweetness and delight until he told her in no uncertain terms that he couldn't marry her. He'd been clear about it from the start, but she'd had some notion she'd wear him down. She'd called him a stubborn old goat. She had part of it right. The goat part? Not even close.

Still, he'd made a mistake in seeing her for too long, and he paid for it when she'd convinced her father that Guthrie had gotten her pregnant and had to marry her. The problem with that tale was that rarely did a *lupus garou* impregnate a human. So he was all for the paternity test, until she finally told the truth— another guy was the father and *he* wasn't marrying her, either. At least Guthrie was out of the picture on that one.

Calla cleared her throat and cast him a devious smile. "From your nonresponse, I take it you *have* made a mistake in liking someone. Or more than one person—as the case may be."

She waited for him to share. He wasn't about to.

"That wasn't anything recent," he said, wanting to talk about Calla's situation with Baird. Guthrie's former misgivings concerning disastrous female relationships weren't important, as far as he was concerned.

"You know my story," Calla finally said, as if that meant she should be privy to his.

"Nay, I don't, lass. All I know is that you agreed to marry the guy and you finally came to your senses."

"So who was she?" Calla asked, one brow raised. "How long ago was this? It sounds recent to me."

He let out his breath in exasperation. Maybe, he thought, if he explained about Margaret, Calla would open up with him about Baird. He finally said, "Two years ago. She was human and returned to Ireland. I haven't heard from her since."

"That's why our families tell us to limit our contact with humans," Calla said, as if to remind him why he had gotten into the mess he did. As if she needed to.

"They also tell us to watch out for wolves who are not to be trusted," he said.

Her gaze was steady on Guthrie. "Last year, when I returned to the Highlands, to this area, I was again without friends. Sure, I saw Cearnach. But I wanted to date and eventually find someone who would be my lifelong mate." She threw out her paper towel, got a new one, and wetted it. "You really don't like Baird, do you?"

"He's a self-centered bastard, Calla. Didn't Cearnach warn you that Baird would never have allowed you to have any friends if you had married him?" Guthrie didn't know why it perturbed him so much that she would stick up for Baird, not after what he had done to Cearnach and Elaine. "Did Baird know you were Cearnach's friend when you met him?"

Calla's mouth tightened. She looked like she wanted to slug him. "You think the *only* reason Baird had any interest in me was because he wanted to keep me away from Cearnach?"

"Other than that you have an income, your family has money, and you are a single she-wolf…"

She narrowed her eyes at him.

Retreating a wee bit, Guthrie cleared his throat. "I'm just trying to consider all possibilities as to why he is so interested in you. What if it went deeper than just a chance meeting? Like he'd learned you were the same lass who had saved Cearnach in the river so many years ago and that you were friends."

"He was infatuated with *me*, and it had nothing to do with my friendship with Cearnach," she said so vehemently that Guthrie wondered if she thought otherwise but didn't want to admit it.

"But he knew you were friends with my brother when you met Baird, aye?"

"I might have mentioned I knew him and your family."

"In casual conversation, or had he come out and asked you?"

She glowered at Guthrie. "He said he remembered me. All right?"

"From when you had lived in the area before, when you were a child?"

"Aye, aye."

"But you had never met him and didn't remember him."

"Nay. I was young back then. He was probably into doing guy things and really hadn't noticed me all that much. I hadn't noticed him."

"Except that he had seen you and knew you were friends with Cearnach."

"I didn't know he and Cearnach hated each other. Baird acted like he knew him only because he was a wolf with a wolf pack living in the same area. We notice things like that, you know. Cearnach met me trying to fish at the river and then proceeded to teach me how to do it right. Then later, I met you and your brothers. I remember all of you smiling at us, but it was more of a case of the three of you being amused at Cearnach for visiting with a girl."

"Cearnach always liked the girls," Guthrie said.

"You didn't?"

He let out his breath. "We thought he was interested in you as more than just a friend," he said, avoiding her question.

"Seriously?"

"Aye."

"Here I thought *you* were interested in me."

Guthrie felt his face heat a bit. When she smiled, he didn't know what to say. Oh, aye, he'd been interested in the lassie. All his brothers had. She was a bonny lass even back then. But neither he nor his brothers would have interfered when they thought Cearnach was hung up on her. Their cousin, Flynn, long since deceased, was another story. He didn't care about such matters. So even though Guthrie and his brothers teased Cearnach about catching the lass's eye, Guthrie had wished he had seen her first, talked to her first, shown her how to fish first. He was never the glib-tongued romantic that Cearnach was with the lassies. Guthrie still didn't believe he would have captured her attention even back then.

When he didn't comment, Calla sighed. "When I saw Cearnach again, I mentioned to him that I was dating Baird, and that's when your brother went all Highland warrior on me and tried to convince me Baird was a bad person. But Baird had been sweet—"

Guthrie snorted.

She scowled at him. "He'd been great to me. We

hiked, boated, ran as wolves, and swam—it didn't matter what I wanted to do, he always took me."

"He didn't let you go with anyone else, did he? He tried to stop you from seeing Cearnach."

"He thought Cearnach was an old boyfriend. Baird said he wasn't comfortable with me seeing him. I told him we were just friends. Baird said others in his pack didn't see it that way. He was having a hard time believing it too."

Guthrie snorted again.

Looking crossly at Guthrie—which he thought made her appear wolfishly cute, though he was sure she wasn't going for that look—she folded her arms.

Guthrie rose to his full height. "So when Cearnach learned of it, he tried to change your mind because he didn't think Baird was a good match or the person you thought he was."

Calla looked out at the dark gardens. "Aye. Oh, I knew Baird could be controlling, and not just about me not seeing Cearnach. He didn't like it when I had work to do and he felt that I should be with him instead. But I thought if he cared enough about me, he'd change."

"Even at your wedding, he proved otherwise when he had his brothers force Cearnach to leave. It didn't matter that *you* wanted Cearnach there because he was your friend. Baird had to prove he was in charge and you had no say in the matter."

Calla didn't say anything. Guthrie was afraid he'd upset her too much, and she wouldn't say anything more about the matter. They had to know—had Baird only targeted her because she was friends with Cearnach? Had he met up with her on purpose because of a darker intent, or was it just a coincidence? Guthrie didn't believe it was.

"So, you had the whirlwind courtship with him and then…?"

"You've got to realize I'd been living among humans for years. It was refreshing to see members of a wolf pack working together and know that the leader, Baird, was fascinated with me. Cearnach remained a good friend, but we weren't interested in each other in that way. Oh, sure, Baird has his faults, but who doesn't? None of us are perfect. I just assumed that as much as he cared for me, I could live with it."

Guthrie let out his breath. "You don't need to put up with the kind of faults Baird has. The control issues. His constant badgering. His being so manipulative."

Her eyes flickered a bit. "All right, aye. He tended not to care if others got hurt if he got what he wanted. But I didn't see this until the wedding."

"What about your business? Would he have left well enough alone?" Guthrie couldn't see that he would. He suspected Baird would have controlled her business, determining who she saw while she was setting up her engagements, micromanaging her during the activities, and maybe even taking it over so she was working for him. Or maybe even making her quit.

"I told him I wasn't about to give up my business or the way I handled things."

"And?"

She let out her breath in a huff. "He knew where I stood on it. I wouldn't have consented to marrying him otherwise."

"But you suspected otherwise, didn't you?"

"We were getting married. He kept asking me about my finances, my expenses, all about my engagements. But I figured it was because he was interested. That's all. But I have to know. Why do Cearnach and Baird dislike each other? Cearnach would never tell me. He'd just say Baird wouldn't be right for me."

"Do you remember back in 1779 when Cearnach and the rest of us went to the port city of St. Andrews on a buying trip, right before you and your family moved out of the area?"

"Aye. Cearnach promised to buy me hair ribbons."

"See why we thought the two of you were sweet on each other? We learned that the Hawthorn brothers were being hanged at the behest of Lord Whittington, who claimed they had stolen a couple of his merchant ships and murdered some of his men during the battle. We wanted to know if the Hawthorn brothers had any of our merchandise on board that they had stolen from us the previous year—then we saw Elaine."

"The hanged men were Elaine's uncles," Calla whispered.

"Aye. And you recall that we chased after Elaine, though at the time we didn't know her name. Cearnach had been the closest to reaching her when we became embroiled in a fight with men on the street. We discovered later that Baird and his brothers and their cousin were responsible for delaying us. Cearnach lost his hold on her, and she disappeared."

"I remember seeing Cearnach after that. He wouldn't talk about it. He felt something for her, more than just wanting to protect her. I knew it with all my heart. I felt terrible for him, but he didn't wish to speak of it," Calla said.

"Aye. He searched and searched for her. But he never could locate her, and then he discovered she'd returned to America, and he assumed she was safe back at home."

"But she wasn't."

"Nay."

"So…that was the only reason he was angry with Baird? That he and his kin had started a fight and stopped Cearnach from reaching Elaine?" Calla asked.

"Part of it. Some of it was that the McKinleys were vigorously searching to take her into their clan, and whatever their purposes, it wouldn't have been for good. To learn where the stolen treasure was hidden. To force her mating with one of the clansmen to gain her parents' properties. They were all pirates. The whole family. Cearnach later learned that Baird was the one who instigated the whole thing back then. Baird was the one who learned her uncles were there, reported them to the lord, and set a trap for them. Then Baird and his kin went after Elaine. Baird was just as angry that my brothers and I were trying to locate her to keep her safe—from the likes of them."

"Like Cearnach tried to protect me from Baird."

Guthrie nodded.

"Except with me, as far as Baird was concerned, it had nothing to do with pirating."

"Aye, which is why Cearnach would never have mentioned that specific instance to you. You left shortly after that to live in England with your parents, and when you moved back to the area to return to your roots here a year ago, Baird's interest in you would have been for other reasons anyway. Cearnach didn't suppose his mentioning what had happened so long ago would influence you one way or another. You have to admit you stubbornly refused to listen to all his other talks."

She took a deep breath. "Aye. He did tell me about their pirating ways, but that was so long ago, and Baird had been into legitimate businesses for a couple of hundred years or so. I…I'm not sure if what he did to Elaine's uncles would have swayed me for certain, since they also had been pirates, and that was sometimes how their pirating way of life ended. But…Cearnach should have told me. It might have influenced me."

"Aye, lass. I agree." He wished he knew how to stop Baird from pestering her without it coming to a fatal showdown. Guthrie fetched more paper towels and wet them to finish cleaning up the spilled milk so they could return to bed. He knelt down and began to wipe off the milk that had splattered Calla's robe.

Calla instantly grew flustered. Already his kin were talking behind their backs as if the two of them were courting. If anyone caught them together like this…

That's when she heard footfalls. She thought Guthrie would immediately stop washing the splotches of milk on her robe. He didn't. When Duncan walked in and saw Guthrie on his knees at Calla's feet, she knew her face had to be rose red, as hot as it felt. "I dropped a glass of milk," she quickly said, noticing Duncan was dressed the same as Guthrie, only his boxers were navy blue. "Don't come any closer. Your feet are bare. You might get cut."

Duncan looked pointedly at Guthrie's bare feet.

"He wouldn't listen to me and apparently likes to live dangerously," she said, annoyed. She glanced down at Guthrie, still wiping off her robe, and she was certain she didn't have one more spot of milk left on the fabric. "Didn't you get it off already?"

"Turn around and I'll check the back."

Now she knew she had to be flaming red all over. "That's okay—"

"You don't want the milk spots to sour," Guthrie said, sounding determined to humiliate her further in front of his brother.

"I'll…come back later," Duncan said, and he quickly left.

She swore he was stifling a laugh. "*Guthrie*," she said, exasperated, but he put his hands on her hips and turned her so he could wipe off the rest of her milk splatters.

She had dropped the whole eight-ounce glass of milk, but surely she didn't get that much on the *back side* of her robe. His strokes were way too intimate, not just a rough brush-down of the fabric to soak up the milk. And they were way too high, to her way of thinking.

Before she could object, he bent down to wipe off her slippers.

Then he continued to mop up the floor. "I have important business to take care of tomorrow, and whoever Ian sends to watch over you will be perfectly competent, even if the toga wearers are bearing spears," Guthrie said as if he hadn't just completely embarrassed her.

When they were done, Guthrie poured both of them a fresh glass of milk. "Is anything else bothering you? The accommodations are all right? The bed is comfortable enough? The room's sufficiently warm?"

"Aye."

"You were just thirsty?"

She smiled a little, then drank some of her milk. "And you?"

"I thought we might have a prowler in the castle, and I came down to tackle him."

She chuckled. "Right." Then feeling like a mother hen, she said, "Turn around and show me the bottoms of your feet."

He smiled and shook his head, then showed her the sole of his right foot. She washed it with a wet paper towel.

"The other now," Calla instructed.

He obliged. Before she finished, Julia walked into the kitchen, stared at the scene before her, and smiled. "Um, I'll come back later."

"Nay!" Calla said. "I broke a glass and Guthrie insisted on helping me clean it up. Even though he isn't wearing shoes."

"Ah," Julia said, her eyes sparkling.

"Why in the world is everyone making a trip to the kitchen tonight?"

Guthrie only smiled.

Chapter 7

THE NEXT AFTERNOON, AFTER TEACHING THE YOUNGER kids math all morning, Guthrie was called into Ian's office, making him wonder what was up now. He'd really wanted to see how the Christmas party plans were going with Calla and Julia. Well, truth be told, he'd wanted to see Calla again.

He'd missed her at both meals—first, trying to get ready for his class, and at lunchtime, because he'd had a business lunch meeting in town. He hadn't believed he'd have feelings like this about any lass so soon, he thought as he walked up to Ian's office. Every time he heard her sweet voice anywhere nearby, he'd turn to see her. Every time someone mentioned her name, he instantly listened in on the conversation.

When he didn't glimpse her sometime during the day, he wanted to know what she was doing—if she was fine with everything, or if she needed anything. He swore he'd never had such a one-track mind when it came to a woman. He attributed it to her being here, living at Argent Castle, unlike the other lassies he'd courted. If she was still living at her home, he wouldn't be thinking about her constantly. Or so he thought.

He walked into Ian's office, noting that his brother was reading a letter.

"Shut the door, will you, Guthrie?" Ian pushed aside a stack of papers on his desk.

If Ian hadn't been concerned, he would have continued working and just talked at the same time, as he did
when he was swamped with business and the conversation wasn't all that important. Wolves did that—devoted
all their attention to one source if they wanted to see,
hear, and smell what was going on with another wolf.
"Was Calla all right last night?"

Guthrie sat down and smiled. Had Julia told Ian that
he'd been with Calla last night in the kitchen? Or…
Duncan had. Hell, probably both had. "Aye, just a little
spilt milk, but that was it."

"Is there…anything I need to know? Like, do you
want to be on permanent guard duty for Calla?"

"Over spilt milk? Nay." Guthrie knew what his
brother was getting at, but he had no intention of feeding
his curiosity.

Ian considered him, knowing in his wolf's way that
Guthrie wasn't being completely honest with him. "Calla
said she had an impromptu kids' party this morning that
was just scheduled last week. And then she had to set up
the decorations and do whatever else beforehand for the
toga party. So I sent Duncan with some men.

"He was supposed to also go to the toga party. He
had to rearrange his schedule so he could go to the other
activities this morning. You were teaching the kids, so
I didn't want to ask you. But Duncan had plans to take
his mate Christmas shopping. Can you handle the toga
party instead?"

"He's going Christmas shopping again?"

"I understand he and Shelley haven't found everything they need."

Guthrie couldn't see his brother doing all that much

shopping. "You really want me to go to another one of Calla's parties after yesterday's fiasco?" Guthrie asked, surprised.

"Aye."

"I suppose you don't want me to be armed this time."

Ian smiled at him and leaned back against his leather chair. "Leave your swords in the vehicle. You can wear your *sgian dubh* in your sock beneath your trousers in case Baird or his kin show. Do you have any objection to going?"

"Nay, unless the lass doesn't care for the idea. She may still believe I'd stir up too much trouble." Guthrie didn't like the idea that she might wear a toga herself. Then again, maybe she wouldn't. She hadn't worn a Stewart plaid to the Rankin reunion.

Ian chuckled. "Of any of our brothers, you are the least easily provoked. The fight at the reunion was not why I didn't assign you to this job initially. I knew you had financial business to attend to, but then you resolved it at lunch today. I've already informed her that you're heading her guard detail for the party. All right?"

"How did she take it?"

"She was fine with it."

Guthrie eyed his brother, knowing that there was more to it than that. He finally said, "Aye."

"You, Ethan, and Oran will go."

"Was there any sign of Baird and his brothers or cousins following Calla to the party this morning?" Guthrie asked.

"Nay. But I've had Julia talk with her about it. I keep feeling there's more to him stalking her than that he's an alpha wolf who doesn't like to lose."

"That's putting it lightly. Not only did Cearnach convince her not to marry Baird at the wedding, but she's also now under our protection. And we tore into him and his brothers and cousins good the last time we had a confrontation with them. He's more than a sore loser."

"Aye, true. So keep a watchful eye out."

Guthrie rose to leave.

"Are you going to participate in the Christmas decorating party that Julia's scheduled for this afternoon?"

"If I can make it. I've got some other business to attend to."

"All right. Well, it starts in an hour."

Guthrie nodded and left the room. He had no intention of adding to the chaos of decorating the tree. Last year, he'd lost his balance when Cearnach bumped into him while untangling Christmas lights. Guthrie had stumbled onto a cardboard box of decorations, smashing the delicate glass ornaments to bits. He'd felt terrible, though his mother had just smiled at him and shaken her head.

―――※―――

Everyone participating in decorating the tree had gathered in the great hall. Calla was surprised to see a few of the men there. When she spent Christmas at home with her parents, her father would put on the star and hang the lights on the trees out front, but he never helped decorate the Christmas tree, because he thought that was the women's job.

The traditional wassail was being served. In olden times, the Scots would go wassailing by carrying a pewter bowl of hot, spicy, honeyed ale from door to door

to share with their friends and family and wish them
well. They offered well wishes for the crops, the herds,
the trees, the bees, and even the sea for a good harvest.
The MacNeill pack members made their wassail from
apple cider and mulling spices and always drank it while
decorating the tree.

Ian was good-heartedly "supervising" the affair as
he commented on which ornaments should go where.
Everyone was just as good-heartedly ignoring him while
they placed the decorations on the tree exactly where
they thought they should go.

Boxes of glass balls and other ornaments were
stacked everywhere. Four ten-year-old girls were hanging unbreakable ornaments on the bottom branches.
Cearnach and Duncan were stringing lights on the top
branches. Everyone was talking about Christmases past
and the future year. The little girls were talking about
what they wanted for Christmas.

Guthrie was noticeably absent—the only one of the
brothers not in attendance. Calla was dying to ask why
he wasn't there, but then everyone would believe she
had a romantic interest in him, so she tried to concentrate on trimming the tree instead. All of its sides were
visible from some part of the great hall so every section
had to be properly dressed. The tree was mostly bare on
her side, so Calla was having fun filling the branches.

She was getting ready to attach a figure of a longhorn
steer wearing a Christmas hat, compliments of Shelley's
mother's Texas collection—and thinking how fun it was
to see decorations from the various newcomers to the
pack—when she heard Guthrie shouting.

Deep, frustrated shouting. And cursing.

Claws scrambled on the stone floor, boots tromped at a run toward the great hall, and then disaster struck.

Women shrieked and shouted, but Calla was on the other side of the tree where she couldn't see the commotion. But then she saw the twelve-foot tree toppling over—right toward her.

Before she could get out of the way, something hit her hard from the side and slammed her against the floor. Just before the tree landed on top of them. He was on top of her, smelling like the great outdoors, fir tree, and musky, sexy male wolf. *Guthrie.*

"Sorry," he mumbled against her ear, branches framing his head and touching the floor on either side of hers. "I meant to rescue you."

She smiled. "From…the tree?"

He smiled back. "That *was* the idea."

"Logan!" Ian hollered.

"Aye, my laird, sorry. The dogs got away from me."

"So that's what this is all about?" Calla asked Guthrie while they were having their private time under the tree. "Your Irish wolfhounds running amok?"

"Aye. Two of the ladies fell against the tree trying to get out of the path of the dogs. As soon as I saw that, I raced around to this side to ensure no one was back here."

"And…tackled me."

Everyone was moving boxes out of the way, dragging them or sliding them across the floor. Someone got the dogs under control and hurried them out of the great hall, their claws clicking on the floor in their hasty exodus. Ian called on his cell phone for reinforcements from the pack to help lift the tree.

Guthrie lifted his head, smiling at her with a mischievous glint in his green eyes. Despite all the commotion, and to Calla's surprise, Guthrie kissed her. His lips were warm and masculine and tasted like wassail. Cinnamon, apple cider, and oranges. She licked his mouth to enjoy more of the taste and he licked hers back, smiling. Then he deepened the kiss.

Oh my God! She hadn't felt this naughty in forever! The men were going to move the tree soon, and here she and Guthrie would be. Kissing. In front of several members of his pack.

She pushed her arms through the branches, trying to wrap them around his neck. She tangled her tongue with his, his cock hardening against her belly, and she felt deliciously wicked hidden beneath the half-decorated tree.

His hands cupped her face, and he kissed her again. She groaned a little, knowing this had to end soon although she didn't want it to. She shouldn't be doing this. Not with him or any other guy right now. But damn if Guthrie didn't really appeal and it was hard not to give in to the rashness of it. Her eyes were closed with his body pressed against hers, and the tree on top of that. She was burning up—from his kiss.

"Oooooh, I'm telling. They're kissing," one of the girls said, crouching down and peering through the branches.

Calla smiled up at Guthrie. They'd been caught.

"Who?" one of the other girls asked, crouching down beside her to see.

And then all four girls were crowding around to get a peek.

Calla chuckled.

Guthrie said to the girls, "We're under the mistletoe."

The girls looked at the branches. "Where is it?" one asked.

Then the tree started to move as the men began to lift it off Calla and Guthrie.

"Girls," Julia said, "move away, so we can lift the tree without hitting you."

"Aww," one of the girls said, and Guthrie winked at her.

As soon as the tree was lifted enough, Guthrie hurried to get off Calla, then helped her to stand.

"What's mistletoe?" one of the girls asked.

Julia patted her head. "We're ordering some from England to hang over the door, and then you can kiss your mum and dad under it."

Everyone was smiling and looking at Calla and Guthrie. She was certain her face was as rosy as the red poinsettias lining the mantel of the fireplace in the great hall, but she wouldn't have given that kiss up for *anything*.

Chapter 8

GUTHRIE DIDN'T KNOW WHAT HAD COME OVER HIM. They couldn't have moved until the tree was lifted. So what was he to do? She smelled so sweet—a mixture of she-wolf, the citrusy scent of the Christmas fir tree, and the delightful taste of wassail on her lips and tongue... He just had to have a taste or two. He loved how she had kissed him right back. She'd been his captive audience, and she had seemed to enjoy it as much as he had. He just wished that Ian hadn't gotten the men together so quickly to lift the tree.

After the tree fiasco, which was not his fault this time, he couldn't quit thinking about Calla. He realized he wasn't the only one when Ian called him back to his office.

"She asked to see you before you go," Ian said as soon as Guthrie walked into the room.

"About what?" Guthrie asked, frowning and wondering if she had changed her mind about having him go with her.

"The party, maybe. I don't know. I swear, Brother, you look as though you're ready to panic. If you're worried about a woman in a toga getting interested in you, don't wear your kilt. That's all I have. And...have some fun while you're at it. All right?"

Guthrie shook his head. "This is not what I consider having fun." Not when he had to keep Calla out of potential danger.

He left the office and strode to the guest room to see Calla. Her door was open, and she was on the phone, but as soon as she saw him, she motioned for him to come in and smiled a little.

At first he was relieved that she didn't appear upset with him over the kiss, but then he gaped at the toga Calla wore. The silky white fabric was draped over one shoulder, leaving the other bare, with the rest of the fabric falling in sensuous folds that caressed her body all the way to her jewel-sandaled feet.

Forget worrying about Baird harassing her. Between any single men at the party hitting on her and the chill in the air, the lass was in trouble no matter how he looked at it. Or at her.

"Aye, aye, I know the flowers were supposed to be pink, but the bride changed her mind and now she wants purple. So—charge her for it."

She was staring at the floor as she spoke to the florist on the phone, so his gaze stole over her body again. He swore he could even see the shape of her nipples pressed against the fabric when he hadn't noticed them before.

What was she thinking, baring all that delectable body to—he didn't even know what they were—humans or wolves. He assumed humans, but they could be as much trouble as wolves once they began drinking. As evidenced by the Rankin reunion.

~~~

Calla had really hoped Guthrie wouldn't get bodyguard duty while she was in charge of a wild twenty-something, Greek-themed toga party.

She often dressed the part for whatever theme the

party was. Her clients liked it because she fit in better. She really hadn't wanted Guthrie to see her in a toga, especially the way he was eyeing it. She was certain he appreciated it. But as soon as he learned she was wearing it among a bunch of wolves—mostly male variety, she was certain he wouldn't be happy.

She tugged on a coat and said, "I'm all set."

"They're human, right?" Guthrie asked. "The rest of the guests?"

She gave him a small smile. He growled low.

Not good. But, Calla thought, he had to remember that he wasn't there to protect her from everyone. Just Baird and his kin.

Calla thought that Duncan, the youngest of the brothers, had always been the one who wanted to fight first and ask questions later. Cearnach was more one to talk things out, and so, she'd thought, was Guthrie. She'd never seen him like this before, so she wasn't sure what to expect.

When they arrived at a home in a woodland setting, the place was lit up with colorful Christmas lights outside. Styrofoam candy canes were on the front door and reindeer statues in the yard. Someone had had the "cute" notion of stacking one reindeer on the back end of another to make it look like the male was humping the female.

Ethan and Oran snickered. Guthrie bit back a growl. He was afraid this was going to be one hell of a wild party, and he didn't want Calla anywhere near it.

Calla was out of the vehicle before anyone could get her car door, and Guthrie assumed she didn't want him to see what was going on inside. But that wasn't happening this time.

To Ethan and Oran, he said, "You stay outside to keep an eye out for any signs of McKinleys. I'm watching out for Calla *inside*."

His blue eyes bright and red hair mussed by the chilly breeze, Oran smirked. "I'd switch jobs with you in a heartbeat. If she'd stolen my underwear, I'd certainly be sticking close to her."

"Aye, and then you would forget the mission." Guthrie went inside where the music was blaring and a bunch of young professionals were drinking up a storm, dressed in everything from store-bought costumes to plain sheets wrapped around their bodies—their otherwise naked bodies.

He saw more than one male strutting his stuff underneath a sheet and shook his head. There must have been about thirty partygoers, only about a third female. At least half of the males were wolves. None of the females were. Except for Calla.

She seemed to be doing all right without his protection as she directed someone to start playing a game. He admired the way she'd set up the buffet table and decorations, with a festive fire in the fireplace. He had to hand it to her. He was impressed by the way she was managing things.

Then a woman slipped her arm around Guthrie's and said, "Don't know you. And you're supposed to be wearing a toga. Party rules."

"I'm not here as an attendee," Guthrie said, though he suspected the redheaded woman already knew that. "I'm only here to watch out for Calla."

"Is she your girlfriend?"

"Nay."

The woman offered him a beer. He didn't accept it. "I'm Rosalind Brubaker. My brother is throwing the party, so I don't know anyone. Can you help me with one little thing? I've asked everyone, but no one will help me. I have a big chest I need to move, and then you can go back to watching out for Calla." Rosalind squeezed his arm, bringing Guthrie's gaze back to her from Calla. "You have just the right muscles for the job."

"I've really got to—"

"Calla!" Rosalind called out and Calla joined them. "Do you mind if your friend helps me move something? My brother and his friends won't help."

Calla eyed her and then shrugged. "It's really up to Guthrie."

"Good. He says he wouldn't mind." Rosalind grabbed his hand and hauled him to the stairs.

Guthrie glanced at Calla. She was frowning, but not half as hard as he was. He knew Ethan and Oran would watch out for Calla if anyone came to the house that they didn't trust, but he didn't trust the men *in* the house who were getting plastered. He didn't trust this Rosalind either—there was something questionable about her impish expression—but he didn't want to cause a scene. He didn't mind moving a piece of furniture as long as it took only a minute of his time. As soon as he walked into the bedroom, he looked to see what Rosalind needed to have moved. She closed the door with a clunk.

Instantly, his wolfish senses were on high alert. "You wanted me to move something, lass?" he said, annoyed.

"Aye. Me." She pulled her toga down and bared her breasts. They were remarkable, but he wasn't interested.

"All right, enough of this," he said, and with two giant strides, he joined her and lifted her to move her out of the doorway. He jerked the door open, but she grabbed him around the waist.

"Wait!"

"Nay, lass. This isn't going to happen."

A man was just walking up the stairs as Guthrie was leaving Rosalind's bedroom. Guthrie suspected she had not pulled up her toga to respectably cover her breasts when the man caught sight of her. Her brother? Or someone else?

Didn't matter. The man was red-faced and pissed.

"What the hell do you think you're doing with my girlfriend?" He took a swing at Guthrie.

Guthrie immediately smelled that the man was a wolf and had been drinking beer. Guthrie ducked from his fist, but then the man lifted his nose, smelled that Guthrie was a wolf, and began to yank off his toga. *Bloody hell.*

Rosalind squealed, and predictably Calla raced up the stairs to intervene.

"Leave, now," she told Guthrie, grabbing Rosalind's now-naked boyfriend by the arm and shoving him away.

"That's what I was trying to do, lass," Guthrie said. Even though he didn't like leaving Calla on her own, if he didn't have to see another human/wolf party again, he would be satisfied. He just hoped Calla didn't believe he'd wanted this.

When he joined Oran and Ethan outside, Oran said, "You look a bit flustered, Cousin. Any trouble with the Grecian lass?"

Oran was having too much fun with this. "How did

you know about her?" Guthrie asked. "You were *supposed* to be outside."

"There are these things called windows," Oran said. "We saw her pull you upstairs. No windows up there, though." He smirked.

Guthrie shook his head. "The chest that the busty Rosalind wanted me to move was more of the flesh rather than the furniture variety. I should have known. Luckily, her boyfriend wasn't armed with anything more than his bare fists, and he was too drunk to aim them at me accurately, or I would have given *him* a broken nose. Not to mention that the arse was about to shift into his wolf half."

"Bloody hell." Ethan shook his head. "What did Calla have to say?"

Guthrie let out his breath in exasperation. She was sure to be pissed off at him all over again.

"Can't get you out of this one, son," Ethan said affectionately. "Since I didn't see any of what happened this time."

A flash of gray in the woods caught Guthrie's eye. He frowned as he stared at the trees, watching for any sign of glowing green eyes or further movement. "Did either of you see a wolf?"

Ethan and Oran observed the woods. They both shook their heads.

"I'll check it out. Ethan, you guard the door. Oran, you come with me." Guthrie and his cousin took off at a run, and when they reached the cover of the woods, they stripped out of their clothes, then shifted. Nosing around the area where Guthrie thought he had seen the gray wolf, he smelled Baird's scent. Damn him.

The wolf had run off, though, and Guthrie didn't find

any other scents besides Baird's. None of Baird's kin's. Which he thought was strange.

Guthrie and Oran returned to their clothes and changed. They jogged back to the porch where Ethan was anxiously watching for them.

"Baird was there. No signs of anyone else. Either his pack mates aren't interested in getting involved in this any further, or he's going it alone so we don't catch him at it. Sneakier that way."

Ethan said, "Sounds like it. You'd think he'd leave well enough alone."

"Aye, particularly while we are watching out for her. You'd think he'd wait until she was no longer staying with us." Although that didn't set well with Guthrie.

They couldn't keep her at Argent Castle permanently. Not that they wouldn't want to—she was good-natured, helpful, and everybody liked her. But she had made it known that she was returning home after the clan's celebration on Christmas Eve.

He hadn't really thought about it much until now. Sure, he knew she wanted to celebrate Christmas with her parents, but after she'd helped decorate, and he and she had kissed under the tree, he'd had visions of her sitting there on Christmas morning unwrapping presents with the family. With…him.

The notion that she wouldn't be there bothered him more than he wanted to admit.

He watched the woods with Ethan and Oran for another couple of hours until the laughter began to die down inside the cottage. The party must have been winding down. Wrapped in her coat and a long woolen scarf, Calla finally exited the cottage. With her red hair hanging loose and caught in the cold breeze, she looked frazzled more than anything else, but Guthrie was damned relieved to see her. Though he was certain she was going to be angry with him.

He hurried to get the car door for her.

A half hour later on the way home, she still hadn't said anything. No one had, and it was killing him not to get this over with. After another silent quarter of an hour passed, Guthrie finally said, "Well?"

She started chuckling.

He stared at her for a moment, then looked back at the road. He would never understand women. "Why did you not tell the lass you needed me for something else?" Guthrie asked, semi-annoyed.

"I didn't know what she had in mind," Calla said.

Guthrie snorted.

"I *didn't*," she insisted. "I don't know the family. And you didn't *have* to go with her."

"If a lassie asks me to help move a piece of furniture, what am I to say? Nay, I might hurt my back?"

She began to laugh.

"I thought you'd be angry over the whole mess." Even though it appeared she wasn't—only highly amused, at his expense. He was glad for that. He'd much rather she be entertained than angry.

"You didn't stay with her when she bared her breasts," Calla said.

"How come I missed that?" Ethan grumbled jokingly.

"You think my mother would have wanted you in the middle of that?" Guthrie asked, being serious.

Oran laughed. "Nay, she would have been furious even if Ethan hadn't been involved in any of it. Me, now, that's a different story. I'm unattached," he said, smiling at Calla.

Calla had thought the whole thing was so funny that she hadn't realized Guthrie was still waiting for her to scold him for *this* party debacle. When Rosalind had thrown herself at him, Guthrie's expression had been priceless, especially when he saw Calla coming up the stairs.

The part about Rosalind's boyfriend even considering going wolf on them was *not* funny, however. It had taken a hell of a lot of fast talking to convince him to stand down and behave. If the man had shifted in front of the human guests who came to see the commotion, the wolves would have had to turn them all. What a catastrophe that would have been. Thankfully, the man had just snarled at his girlfriend and then returned to the party.

Calla assumed that was the end of that relationship. Speaking of which, Calla had overheard Rosalind telling Guthrie that she didn't know anyone at the party. She hadn't known then that Rosalind had a boyfriend, but she had wondered what Rosalind was up to. Calla hadn't wanted to make the decision for Guthrie, but she was pleasantly surprised with the one he made. What was most endearing about Guthrie was how much he worried that Calla thought he *had* wanted a romp with the woman. Rosalind had known very well what she wanted, and that was Guthrie, the only man at the party not wearing a toga.

Calla chuckled again, and he glanced her way, his brow furrowed. She grinned at him, and he shook his head.

Chapter 9

WHEN THEY ARRIVED HOME, ETHAN GAVE GUTHRIE A slight nod, as if saying he would tell Ian what had happened with regard to Baird so that Guthrie could speak with the lass alone. Guthrie was certain that Ethan would also tell Ian about the half-naked woman. He and Oran were grinning so broadly that Guthrie was convinced they'd both ask Ian to ensure that Guthrie was *always* in charge of the guard detail for Calla. *And* that Ian always picked them to go with Guthrie when he had to watch over her.

"Calla, can I speak with you for a minute?" Guthrie asked, opening the door to the keep for her.

"About?"

"Let's go someplace more…private. The study? Or the garden room?"

Her body tense, she looked a little wary. "The garden room will be fine."

They walked through the keep to the kitchen, but before they reached the door, they discovered Cearnach and Duncan eating pork sandwiches at the table and drinking mulled wine. Both stopped talking to acknowledge Guthrie and Calla with smiles.

"How'd the party go?" Duncan asked, smirking.

Duncan couldn't have heard what had happened at this party yet, so Guthrie assumed he was still amused about the reunion fiasco—as if anytime that Guthrie went to one of her scheduled events, he'd cause trouble. Even if that *had* been the case so far.

Her brows raised, Calla said, "I'm sure Guthrie is dying to tell you about it. You'll most likely find it as entertaining as the other." She moved outside into the cold.

Guthrie's brothers grinned broadly at him. "Not another sword fight, eh, Brother?" Cearnach asked, sounding like he was dying to know what had happened this time.

Guthrie shook his head, then followed Calla out the door. When he closed the door behind them, she said, "You know they'll learn about it shortly. They're probably already calling Ethan or Oran to discover what exactly did happen."

Guthrie looked down at Calla's impish expression as he walked her down the path to the outdoor garden room. She was enjoying this a little too much.

When he looked down at the toga caressing her ankles, he realized he should have asked if she wanted to change into something more comfortable first, or at least something he wouldn't be staring at so hard once she removed her coat. He had to admit she looked damned hot as a Grecian woman.

He opened the door to the garden room, glad to see it was deserted. He turned on the light, then closed the door after them. After taking her coat and wool scarf and hanging them on the coatrack, he started a fire in the fire pit to warm the place.

"I need to speak with you about Baird," Guthrie said.

"Why do you want to talk about him again?" she asked, suddenly sounding wary.

"I saw Baird in his wolf coat watching the cottage to-night while you were inside orchestrating the toga party."

Calla's eyes widened a bit. Then she shook her head and walked over to a rack of wine and motioned to the bottles. "Want something to drink?"

"Sure. Anything that you would like is fine with me."

She handed him a bottle of merlot.

He removed the cork and poured each of them a glass.

"Aye, so I wondered again if there is some other reason why he keeps stalking you."

"I…I don't know. Was anyone else with him?"

"Nay. His pack may be disillusioned with him over chasing after you and not resolving the issue. If you have any other notions why he won't leave you alone, let us know."

"I will." Calla took a seat on one of the soft moss-colored sofas that wound around the fire pit.

The Celtic gold embroidered pillows had been replaced with Christmas ones—the Santas on them wearing the blue and green kilt of the MacNeill clan. The scent of Christmas spice filled the air, making Guthrie think the ladies had been there earlier, burning their cinnamon-scented candles. He was trying to figure out whether to sit closer to Calla and be able to better breathe in *her* sweet scent, which would be a mistake, or to sit farther away and have a better view of her toga, which could be just as much of a mistake.

He sighed and took a seat across from her. "What do you have planned for tomorrow?"

She took another sip of her wine and set her glass down on the coffee table. "I'm going with Julia, Heather, and a few other ladies to pick up Christmas gifts."

She slipped off one sandal and then the other. He glanced at her toga, thinking about her removing it next, although he shouldn't have allowed his thoughts to stray in that direction. She pulled her bare feet up on the couch and tucked them beneath her. Then she lifted the plaid throw over her lap. He wished he was curled up beside her.

"Who's watching over you?" he asked.

She shrugged. "Ian always sets the guard schedule."

Guthrie hadn't heard anything about it so he assumed Ian had assigned someone else to watch them. Still, if Guthrie had the free time… "When are you going?"

She hesitated to say, as if weighing the reasons he'd ask.

"I have to teach the older kids math in the morning," he said, hinting that he'd go with her if the time was right.

She smiled a little. "If you want to come with us, we'll go after you're done."

Guthrie warmed at that, but the warm feeling he got from her reminded him of something. He backed off. He had to give her time to get over Baird. No more doomed-from-the-start rebounds for him. He and Calla really had to just…be friends for now. He had to try harder to remember that when he was around her.

"Like you said, it's up to Ian," Guthrie said. Even if Ian had selected another team to watch over her, Guthrie could go, just as extra muscle. Looking comfortable now, she lifted her glass and took another swallow of wine. She sighed deeply. "I'm really tired and I guess it's about time to call it a night."

Guthrie wanted to kiss her. After the night he'd had

with Rosalind's unwanted display of bearing her breasts
and Calla's own amusement because of it, plus the wine,
the fire, and the way Calla looked so damned appealing
in that slinky toga, he wanted to kiss her.

They both finished their wine, then she rose to her feet
and he stood. The kiss they had shared when they were
pinned under the tree…that was different. They'd had an
audience of girls. Though he hadn't expected that. Most
likely some of the adults had also seen something of what
was going on. That kiss had been impulsive, when he
never was that way, ever. But there he'd been, lying on
top of her, unable to move off her, breathing in her sweet
scent, feeling her soft curves, becoming aroused, and
well, it just…happened.

Here, they were alone. The reason for wanting this
kiss was something entirely different.

He was used to analyzing the pros and cons of a financial situation, deliberating any alternative courses of action.
This had nothing to do with money, but still he found himself evaluating the situation like he would in considering an
investment. Because in a way, kissing her again indicated
that he wanted to invest more in the relationship.

Calla knew just what Guthrie wanted—to kiss her as
if they'd been on a date, which they hadn't been. Just because they'd shared some wine and talked a little about
past relationships earlier, that didn't mean anything,
although she was feeling relaxed and comfortable with
him. And she felt sexy in her toga. That didn't mean
they should kiss or anything. Probably shouldn't. Yes,
she was certain they shouldn't.

So why was she eagerly waiting for him to do
something?

Rebound, she kept reminding herself. She wasn't going to encourage him in any way—not by mannerism, speech, or eye contact. Nothing. And then he smiled. And she smiled back.

And that was it.

They quickly closed the distance between them, though she didn't remember moving. But she must have because she wasn't standing next to the sofa any longer and their lips were melded together as if they were meant to be that way. The wine on his lips and tongue tasted as divine as he did. His hands were on her bare shoulders, holding her in place while he worked miracles with his kisses.

He swept his mouth over her jaw and down her neck, and licked the hollow of her throat, making her tingle with his touch. Standing next to the fire, she was burning up, scorched inside and out by his sensuous kisses. His warm mouth stroked across her bare shoulder, his hands holding her still, lest she melt onto the sofa. She felt ready to collapse, and she was afraid of where this might lead.

Wolves could not have sex without mating for life. It was a condition of their wolf nature. It wasn't a moral issue, but the natural order of things, an inborn trait, a way to continue their *lupus garou* species, just like strictly wolves continued theirs.

Yet, damn, if she didn't want to take this all the way with Guthrie. Not to mate with him, but to satisfy a sexual craving she couldn't deny. They were both breathing hard, their hearts pounding, their pheromones kicking each other's into higher gear—and she knew she had to stop this. He was getting close to brushing his mouth against her breast, her nipples surely visible beneath the silky gown, as aroused as she was already.

She should have reminded him that she was tired and going to bed, yet she barely breathed as his warm breath caressed her breast.

He brushed his cheek against her aroused breast and she touched his head, her fingers tangling in his hair. Her breath hitched as she waited for him to take her nipple in his mouth. The feel of his warm face rubbing against it, the silky fabric of her toga sliding over it made her wet for him.

She kept telling herself they couldn't go too far, yet she wanted to pull down the top of her toga, letting it fall over her gold braided belt, to bare herself to him.

His hand cupped her breast and he moved his mouth back to hers, his thumb sliding over the nipple, teasing it. His tongue pushed between her lips, and she sucked him in like a ravenous wolf, making him moan. She ground her hips against him, wanting to feel his arousal. His cock was as hard now as it had been when he'd been pressed against her under the Christmas tree. Despite knowing they shouldn't indulge in the fantasy, she didn't want to stop—couldn't stop.

His thumb was doing wicked things to her nipple, just as she moved wickedly against his erection.

Then he pulled away and she wanted to scream, "Don't stop!"

His green eyes were cloudy with lust, his look un-readable otherwise, and she thought for a moment he was worried about taking things too far. But then he looked down at her breasts, leaned down, and licked a nipple through the fabric of her toga, and *oh my God*, she thought she would come right then and there. She'd never experienced anything so erotic in her life.

He pulled down the shoulder-less part of the gown and massaged her bare breast with his big hand, while he suckled her other nipple through the fabric.

Somehow he'd maneuvered her back to the soft sofa.

The next thing she knew, he was pulling her gown off the other breast and then his mouth was again on it—the sensation of his tongue and mouth touching her flesh too pleasurable for words.

He paused, taking her in with his hot-blooded gaze, then held her face in his hands, his touch tender.

He was waiting for her to tell him how far she wanted to take this. Surprised, she hesitated. She was used to Baird lunging right ahead, even if she wasn't quite ready.

With Guthrie, she wanted this. She appreciated how he took her feelings into consideration and allowed her to set the pace and boundaries. She should have pulled up her gown, smiled sweetly, said her good night, and vamoosed back to the safety of her guest bedchamber.

Instead, her fingers seemed to have a mind of their own. The next thing she knew, she was pulling off his wool sweater and he was helping her. He tossed it onto another part of the sectional sofa, and then she helped him off with his shirt.

Chest to chest they began kissing again, her hands on his back, his on her arms, sliding, caressing, enjoying the intimacy. She ran her hands over his hard muscles rippling beneath her fingertips.

It didn't take long before he leaned her back onto the sofa, his leg wedged between hers. Keeping most of his weight off her, he kissed her mouth with ardent enthusiasm, their breathing heavy, his tongue and hers passionately dueling.

His hand swept down her leg once, twice, his warm fingers sizzling against her skin, sliding the silky fabric up her thigh, making her feel erotically sexy. He took deep breaths, smelling how wet she was for him, how much she wanted him. It could only turn him on more—wolf that he was. He slid his hand down her thigh again, except this time he pulled her gown up slowly, seductively, his hand brushing it up so that his touch against her skin continued to scald her.

He ran his hand over her bare thigh, stroking higher. She already ached for completion, and if he didn't finish what he'd begun, she would never forgive him. *Ever.*

Then his hand slid between her legs. Her breath caught. At first, he cupped her mound and began kissing her mouth again, as if he'd captured her and she was his. Without warning, he pressed two fingers into her wet sheath and she nearly came unglued.

"Oh, God, yes," she breathed out, and then he nibbled on her lip, her ear, her chin, stroking her at the same time that he rubbed her sweet spot and alternating that with inserting his fingers into her. She felt the building crescendo, the peak so close that she wanted to race to the top. And then it happened—the sweet, wondrous climax hit, and she shattered into a million glorious, sated pieces, crying out with pleasure.

He was still kissing her when he began to unzip his pants. They couldn't have sex—even though she desperately wanted to. Oh how she wanted to feel him buried to the hilt deep inside her, thrusting, feeling his own pleasure, but…they couldn't. Not as *lupus garous*. Not unless they had decided on a mating. Which, of course, they had not. And this *wasn't* supposed to be happening in the first place. But she wouldn't have put a stop to it for the world.

He suddenly stopped what he was doing, grabbed the throw blanket at her feet, and tucked it under her. What *was* he doing? Too eager to know, she stroked his trousered legs.

He studied her for a moment, came to a decision, and yanked down his pants, then reached for her hand. He squeezed her fingers around his aroused length, guiding her to stroke him. They could do this, she thought with relief and a measure of excitement. She loved being able to give him pleasure too.

She stroked him, their tongues dancing. He groaned at her touch. She loved how he kissed her, continuing the more intimate connection between them. She'd already primed him so much with their kissing and then her coming that he quickly came.

For a moment, they breathed in each other's scents, their hearts beating pell-mell, their skin moist with perspiration as they came off their exhilarating sexual high. She wished they could cuddle and wake up together in each other's arms, as much as she knew they shouldn't and couldn't.

But now, she didn't know what to say or do—and felt a little uneasy. He seemed to feel the same way as he studied her back, but didn't say anything. He leaned down and kissed her lips sweetly, and she fought the impulse to wrap her arms around him and hold him tight—which would indicate she didn't want to let go of him or the moment.

She kissed him back lightly, her hands gently stroking his arms in a way that wasn't possessive or indicating she wanted to stay with him longer. Just a nice ending to an otherwise awkward moment.

"I guess it's really time for bed now," she said and instantly felt her skin warm, as if she was referring to going to bed with him now.

"Uh, yeah." He moved off her, grabbed his shirt, and cleaned up, then pulled up his pants. At the same time, she worked on getting her toga back in place. He pulled on his sweater, gazing at her, not looking away as if he was ashamed. He was analyzing the way she was feeling like a wolf would, smelling her scent and watching her expression. Yet he looked a little worried. Was he concerned that they had done this? That he shouldn't have? Or maybe he was bothered that he had come so fast and couldn't hold on any longer.

Her emotions were all over the place, and she didn't want to overthink what had happened between them. They'd just needed a release. That was all. They'd both been available—convenient. Nothing more than that. She refused to feel any remorse for what had happened between them here tonight.

He got her coat and helped her into it. She wanted to say something about it not meaning anything and not to regret it. But she didn't want him to think she was saying that what they'd done meant nothing to her.

"Calla," Guthrie said as they stood at the door. He didn't say anything more, like he wasn't sure what to say.

She smiled, though her smile probably didn't appear very genuine. She didn't much feel like smiling. "Thanks for the nice evening and the chance to unwind.

I always need to do so after a big event." God, did that sound like she had sex with a guy just to unwind after a party? And that she did it regularly? Feeling mortified, she felt her face heat, but she didn't want to say anything else and make it worse.

He studied her for a moment as if judging or attempting to judge how she was feeling. But he left it at that and escorted her back to the keep in silence.

That was the hardest part, she thought. She immediately thought of what Baird would have done in a situation like this. Which was truly a case of not looking forward but looking back, and she couldn't afford to do that. She had to remind herself that Baird was not Guthrie, and vice versa. That Baird wanted to mate with her from the beginning, so he'd eagerly attempted to push a mating whenever they were together. And she remembered how much she had stalled him by saying she was too busy to see him when sometimes she had not been. But she'd needed her space. And she hadn't been ready.

At the same time, she hated that she couldn't let go of the feelings of uncertainty with Guthrie. Yet she had to. For her own sanity.

She glanced at his shirt wadded up in his hand, his solemn look. She had the fleeting hope that no one would be about when they entered the keep. If anyone was, they'd know just why Guthrie had taken his shirt off in the garden room when he was alone with her out there.

As soon as they walked into the kitchen, Calla noted how quiet the place was. The light had been left on—probably for them. She was used to everything being quiet in her carriage house. But because many people lived or worked here, she heard conversation taking place in one room or another all the time, except for late at night.

The sound of footsteps headed for the kitchen instantly disquieted her. She wanted to tell Guthrie to hide his shirt behind his back, but she couldn't. That would be like saying she was ashamed of what they'd done, and truly she was anything but. She would cherish that special time forever, keeping the toga party and the aftermath as one of her most treasured memories.

Julia entered the kitchen and smiled at Calla, who felt that her instantly heated body had flushed and given her away—par for the course for a redhead.

To Calla's surprise, Julia said, "Can I have a word with you, Guthrie, in a moment?"

"Aye, of course." He looked miserable.

"If you'll meet me in the library, I'll be there in just a few minutes. I wanted to get a cup of hot chocolate first." She glanced at Calla. "Would you like some too?"

"Nay, thanks. I'm headed up to bed." Calla looked again at Guthrie. She wanted to say something to Julia, worried that the female pack leader intended to tell Guthrie to watch his step with Calla. Then again, maybe Julia needed to speak with him about pack business.

Calla quickly excused herself, thinking maybe Guthrie would still walk her to her room, but he only said good night. Calla knew then that he felt he'd made a mistake with her. As Calla headed toward her chamber, she hardened her resolve to not attempt to get serious with anyone for a good long while. She wasn't up to going through a repeat of what had happened between her and Baird.

Was Julia going to lecture Guthrie about it? That was bound to make things even worse.

Chapter 10

GUTHRIE SAT IN THE LIBRARY IN ONE OF THE COMFORT-able reading chairs, his shirt still crumpled in his fist. He should have dumped it with his dirty laundry before he met with Julia. Not that he could hide anything even if he'd wanted to. Julia could already smell that he and Calla had enjoyed some intimate time together.

He suspected he knew what Julia was going to say when she arrived with her cup of hot chocolate. He wondered when she'd taken to drinking that instead of the hot lavender tea she usually had at night.

He sighed. Julia walked in, shut the door, and joined him in the sitting area. Once she was seated, she said, "I know that both you and Calla are highly attracted to each other. It's obvious to everyone."

"Aye, and I've already decided I need to back off a wee bit with the lass," he said, wanting to get this over with.

"Good. I worry about you."

She looked so serious that his jaw dropped. "Me?" he asked incredulously. Calla, yes. What was there to be concerned about with *him*?

"Guthrie, I know you say the deal with your ex-girlfriend, Tenell, was over and done with when you broke up. But...well, the rest of us saw it differently. You'd invested so much time and energy in the relationship. We know you were seriously thinking she was the right one for you."

Guthrie frowned. When Tenell had gone back to her

old boyfriend, that had been the end. Guthrie had returned to working on the clan's finances, and life went back to business as usual.

"I'm afraid…I'm afraid you might be feeling the effects of having a rebound relationship."

Bloody hell. Where had Julia come up with that notion? Did everyone think the same?

"Me?" He couldn't help sounding shocked. "Calla's the one you should be concerned about."

Julia nodded. "I am, of course. But it's different for each of you. Calla is moving forward. Aye, though she's been cautious of forming new long-term relationships, which is for the best. This business with you might well be the same thing for her as you're feeling. A need to set aside the loneliness you're experiencing now that Tenell is no longer in your life."

"You can't be serious. She left and I forgot about her."

Julia let out her breath, a habit Ian had when he felt one of his brothers wasn't listening to him. It appeared she was picking up her mate's habits.

"All right, lass, how did I act that made you and others believe I am feeling melancholy about breaking up with Tenell?"

"You quit eating."

"I wasn't hungry."

"You're always hungry," Julia said, frowning at him. "You withdrew from anything to do with activities involving couples."

"I was busy with financial dealings."

"Right, but you locked yourself away for days to conduct business. You don't normally do that." She arched a brow in challenge.

"I needed the quiet time. Sometimes distractions can make me lose my concentration when I'm trying to make important financial decisions for the pack."

"Your door is always open, Guthrie. Admit it. Just like Ian's is, no matter what."

He ground his teeth and folded his arms. Did *everyone* think he'd been upset about the breakup?

"You're in denial."

He stubbornly refused to agree with her. He *wasn't* in denial.

"You skipped sword practice a number of times, even though you love to do it. In fact, anything you enjoy doing, you stopped participating in—fishing, running as a wolf, boating, everything."

"I…was…*busy*."

"You slept later than you normally do. Missed days of breakfasts and skipped them entirely."

"I had stayed up too late."

"You had gone to bed early."

He almost smiled at her tenacity. "Anything else?" As if that wasn't enough.

"You missed engagements and you *never* do that. You are one of the most punctual and levelheaded of your brothers, but you were snapping at anyone who touched on the sensitive subject of the ex-girlfriend."

"I did not."

She let out her breath again. "You refuse to talk about it to anyone. If it was no big deal, you'd joke about it or something. But you've buried the whole situation instead."

"This is about your writing, isn't it?" he asked, since Julia was a romance author.

"Huh?"

"You analyze people to make up stories, even if you're making a big deal out of nothing."

She smiled and patted his leg. "Suffice it to say that I worry about you." She finished her hot chocolate.

"Well, I thought *you* were involved in the seating arrangement in the great hall for an earlier meal," he said, raising an accusatory brow. "And that my brothers and cousins are conspiring to get me together with the lass."

"It's true we've all enjoyed seeing that you and Calla are…hitting it off. I don't think any of us believed that the two of you would progress to this point so… quickly." She cast him a wee smile. "I just think for your sake, you might be a little more cautious." She rose from her chair and he stood. "'Night, Guthrie."

Before she could leave, Guthrie said, "I understand you and the ladies are Christmas shopping tomorrow."

"Yes. You're not on the guard detail," she said.

"Aye. I'll just go along and stick close to you."

He expected her to say he couldn't go because he needed to be more…circumspect. Instead, to his surprise, Julia actually offered him a radiant smile. Then she took her leave and he wondered what that discussion had really been about. He knew he could live another hundred years and still not understand the workings of a woman's mind.

Calla had just settled into bed and was reading a little more of the book on parties on a budget when someone knocked on her door. Guthrie? Here to apologize? She ground her teeth and got out of bed. She grabbed her robe and put it on, then cinched it. If he apologized, she was going to give him a tongue-lashing.

When she opened the door, she found Julia standing there instead, all smiles. "I'm sorry to disturb you when you probably had already gone to bed, but…could we talk for a moment?"

Oh, great, now Julia was going to lecture *her* at this hour? Calla let her in and closed the door, forming the explanation she'd wanted to give Julia earlier. Before she could start, Julia said, "I'm worried about you."

An hour later, Julia bid Calla good night. She was surprised by what Julia had told her—that Guthrie had seriously considered mating with another woman and was in total denial that the breakup had affected him. All the things that Julia had brought up concerning Guthrie had been the same for Calla—the sleeping in, the lack of appetite, the unwillingness to speak about Baird with anyone. She'd thrown herself into her work, found herself unable to concentrate on her business, and missed meetings with clients. She'd locked herself away in her home, not wanting to go anywhere or do anything beyond work-related activities—while telling others she was too tired.

She'd been worried that she might be headed for a rebound situation with Guthrie. She felt awful that he was experiencing that instead.

Calla curled back up in bed with her book, sure that her decision to put some space between her and Guthrie was the right one. She would not lust after Guthrie's hot kisses or give in to his heated gazes or think of him as anything more than a friend like Cearnach was. But she and Cearnach had never kissed. Well, once when they were young. She'd found it much like her mother or father kissing her. He'd certainly never turned her furnace up to blazing. She'd never blushed around him, ever, that she could recall. Even now, just thinking about the way Guthrie had touched her so intimately, she was hot and interested all over again.

She vowed to just be friends, though. Maybe when he'd had sufficient time to get over his breakup they might court each other. Sometime in the future. She set the book aside and turned off her light. Tomorrow, Calla would pay a surprise visit to Guthrie's math class to show him they really could be just friends.

With that thought in mind, she smiled and closed her eyes. And immediately envisioned Guthrie suckling on her nipple. She groaned.

There wasn't any way that she could see him in the same light as she saw Cearnach.

Ian wrapped Julia in his arms, snuggling with her, kissing her hair, and cleared his throat, suspecting why his sweet, little American lass had to slip off to get a cup of hot chocolate so late at night. Last night, she'd done the same thing, only she'd never gotten her hot chocolate and had come straight back to bed. When she told him about Guthrie and Calla and the spilt milk, he couldn't help but laugh.

This evening after the toga party, Guthrie had escorted Calla to the garden room to talk about Baird, according to Ethan. His poor brother. Ian could just imagine how Guthrie would have reacted to the bare-breasted woman. Ian wondered how he would have responded, had it been him in the same situation. Especially if he'd been worried about how Julia would take it.

Guthrie and Calla hadn't returned to their rooms before he went to bed. He hadn't heard any indication they were moving about. Then all of a sudden, his sweet mate had to return to the kitchen for her cup of hot chocolate again.

"Did you see Guthrie and Calla?" Ian asked, hoping they weren't breaking more glasses of milk down there.

"Aye."

He kissed the top of her head. "And?"

When she was this quiet, she was up to no good.

"They went to bed."

"You're not trying to matchmake, are you?"

"Me? Never."

He chuckled. She was.

The next morning, Calla asked Julia where Guthrie would be teaching the older teens. When she got there, she found a room set up with three rows of tables and chairs. Guthrie's back was turned to her while he was writing on the white board, and she slipped into the class. Several of the students turned to look. Logan, who was sitting in the front row, grinned at her.

She smiled and took a seat at the last table. Either the kids were really eager to learn math, or Guthrie had made them all sit up front. Julia had told her that he was teaching the kids about savings and investments, and she'd been curious to hear what he had to say.

He seemed to be in a really chipper mood—even more so when he turned to see her sitting in on his class. She smiled.

He smiled back at her, a wolfish look that said he was up to some mischief. Gone was any indication that he'd been worried about what occurred between them last night. She was glad to see his good humor return.

"Maybe Miss Stewart can share her experiences of being an entrepreneur," Guthrie said, motioning to her to come to the front of the class, "since we're talking about earning money and setting aside savings and the like."

Her face had to have flushed as hot as it felt. She wouldn't have minded talking to the kids, but not as a teacher would. She didn't have anything prepared for this. She was about to shake her head, smile, and politely decline when Logan said, "All right!"

Guthrie grinned and the other kids began to cheer her on. Probably anything to get out of discussing what Guthrie had been talking about. Not to mention that whatever she said wouldn't be test material.

She rose from her seat, tilted her chin down at Guthrie to say she'd pay him back, and then walked to the front of the class. She thought he'd just stand there, like she was his pupil and she had to give a speech. But he went to the back of the class and sat down like he was one of the students, grinning at her.

What in the world had Julia said to Guthrie last night that had made him so...*cheerful* again?

She took a deep breath. "Most of you probably know that I have a party and wedding planning service that I started some years ago," she said, loosening up as she started to talk about what she loved to do. "One thing I want to make clear is that even if you don't make a whole lot of money at your job, if you really love your work and you make enough to live off it comfortably, that's worth more than making one hundred times the income at a job you absolutely hate. My dad taught me that and I completely agree."

The kids looked like they couldn't believe anyone would work for a tiny bit of money if they could make huge amounts. Guthrie raised his eyebrows too. Logan's hand shot up.

"Aye, Logan?"

"But if you make all that extra money, you can spend it on all kinds of fun stuff and then it makes the job worthwhile."

"What is it that you love to do more than anything else in the world?"

"Work with the dogs."

"Aye, good. What is it you hate to do most of all?"

Logan glanced at Guthrie, and she hoped math wasn't what he was thinking of. Guthrie bowed his head to Logan to encourage him to speak freely.

"Um, my dad is the armorer for the clan. He keeps all the weapons in good shape and makes the new swords for those of us who are coming of age." Logan wrinkled his nose. "I hate the firing of the weapons, working with metal all day. I mean, I do it to help my dad out, but what I really love to do is work with the dogs."

She smiled. "Okay, good example. So let's say you could earn a hundred times more working at the armory than you could working with the dogs. Which would you rather do?"

His friends grinned at him.

"Well…the question isn't fair."

"How so?"

"I have to do both and I don't get paid for either."

Everyone laughed.

"Okay, so if you don't get paid and you had a choice?"

"Working with the dogs. I do what I have to when I work for my father, but I can't wait to work with the dogs every day."

"He's our future veterinarian," Guthrie supplied.

"Really?"

"Aye," Logan said proudly. "But...I'll still help my dad when he needs me to."

She smiled. "Well, that's just fine. And that proves my point." At least she hoped it did. "All right. So with my business, I've managed to move from one location to another and still am able to gain new clients. Word of mouth has been really important. If I have a successful event, then people who attend the event spread the word, and before I know it, I have several more engagements scheduled throughout the year."

"What if you have an unexpected sword fight at the party and then one guy," Logan said, looking back at Guthrie, "socks another in the nose?"

The other kids laughed.

"Well, it *can* be a disaster," she said. "Or sometimes something good can come of it."

"Like?" Guthrie asked, sounding both amused and interested.

"Like how a future client asked if I could schedule a reunion for a family later next year, only they would like me to set up a *sword-fighting* demonstration. I thought if Ian was agreeable, some of his men might like to put on this show."

"For free?" Guthrie asked, brows raised.

"Of course not. I would charge more, based on Ian's suggestion, well, and yours, being his financial advisor. The extra proceeds would go to the MacNeill pack."

"I want to do it," Logan said, and several of the teens eagerly volunteered to help.

She laughed.

"Moneywise, how well *do* your parties do?" Guthrie asked, probably directing the lecture back to the math side of the business since this *was* a math class.

"All of you have learned about percentages, aye?" Calla asked the students.

They groaned.

"Okay, well, you want to make a high enough profit— income less expenses—to make the venture worthwhile. You have to include all the costs—getting there, your time involved, the cost of goods and services, et cetera."

"And do you?" Guthrie asked.

She had the feeling he wasn't asking just to teach his students something, or because he was the financial manager of the pack. This was more personal.

"If you consider making ninety-five a good income for the year, aye."

"Ninety-five pounds?" Logan asked, looking as though she was crazy.

"Thousand. Ninety-five thousand pounds. Which, for anyone who knows anything about U.S. dollars, is close to one hundred and fifty thousand."

That got everyone's attention, even Guthrie's. He gave her a small smile.

She gave them all kinds of suggestions for how they could start their own businesses, save money, and even invest it. Then she had an idea. But she couldn't propose it to Guthrie since he wasn't in charge of the pack.

"That's all I have. Any questions?" she asked.

Guthrie looked like he was dying to question her about something, but the kids didn't have anything else to ask. "Thanks to everyone for listening to me."

She moved to the back of the class and saw by the clock that the class was about over. She'd fully intended to pay attention to Guthrie while he taught his class and not take it over herself.

Guthrie said to his students, "You have homework on page 131, the first thirty problems."

She was glad she was no longer learning this stuff. Her father had been a real taskmaster.

Groans followed, and then Guthrie dismissed the class.

Before she could leave, Guthrie said, "You were smiling so brightly that I wondered what you were thinking of."

"That you give great math classes." She smiled when she said it. "See you in a few minutes for Christmas shopping."

She hurried out of the room, but before she went to get her purse and jacket, she dropped by Ian's office. She had to know something about Guthrie. "Come on in," Ian said. "Shut the door if you'd like."

She shut the door and took a seat in front of Ian's desk. "If it's not too personal, I was curious as to why Guthrie seems to always be obsessed with money. Not that we shouldn't keep costs down. But he appears overly concerned about it."

She thought that the way she earned her money might be a sticking point with Guthrie. If so, there was no sense in even considering trying to make something of a more…permanent type of relationship with him. It would always be a sticking point between them.

Ian leaned back and said, "You know Elaine's uncles were…privateers in the eighteenth century, aye?"

"Right. Or pirates, depending who was on the business end of their swords," Calla said.

"Aye. How well I know that. But since Elaine joined us, we refer to them only as privateers. One year, her uncles stole our ship and merchandise. We had to make do with very little food that winter. All of us were concerned, but Guthrie took the whole business more to heart than most and ensured that all food was rationed out so that no one starved that winter. You understand we were only sixteen at the time.

"Since then, he has taken over the finances and done a fine job of it. He's always been very conscientious about costs and expenditures. A short while ago, we had a big mess with stolen investments. He's always been one to forgo anything but necessities when disaster strikes. And he's good at coming up with ways to bring money into the clan to help us make do."

"And now?"

"After securing our stolen funds, we're doing well or we couldn't have hired you to help in preparing a grand celebration for Christmas Eve, which as you know, isn't as big a deal for the Scots as it is for the Americans. So this is important to me—for Julia's sake, and the others who are of Scottish heritage but have lived for so many years in America."

Calla sighed. "I wish Guthrie would enjoy some of the festivities. He's much too serious." Except for last night. She was still surprised at herself—and him—for taking it that far. She'd never done that before with any man she was only just getting to know.

Ian gave her a small smile. "I'm sure he's enjoying himself even if he isn't letting on."

"How would you know that?" She was hoping Ian hadn't realized… Oh, brother, Julia had probably told him what she and Guthrie were up to in the garden room—and it hadn't all been just talking about Baird.

"He's asked to be put on permanent detail to watch over you."

She closed her gaping mouth.

"I can't imagine any other reason he wishes to, unless he wants to enjoy himself for a change."

She…couldn't believe it. "Okay. Um, well, you know I have that masquerade ball to go to and I…" She wanted Guthrie to go with her—not as a bodyguard, but as a date. She had intended to ask Guthrie, since he seemed more cheerful this morning. But what if Ian had already put him in charge of her bodyguard detail?

"Aye," Ian said, his dark eyes watching her. "Is there a problem?"

"I was supposed to go with Baird. We would have been mated wolves by then."

"I see."

She wasn't sure Ian did.

"We'll have extra guards watching out for you in case he shows up."

"Okay, but…"

Ian was frowning, probably figuring something was really wrong with the situation. She let out her breath. "Well, it's just that I needed an escort."

"All right. Cearnach, Duncan, and Oran will go as your bodyguard detail."

"And…Guthrie?"

"He'll be free to be your escort." Ian smiled at her.

She rose from the chair. "Thanks so much, Ian. I'll… give him the good news a little later."

"Aye, lass. I'm sure he will be delighted."

"Only if he dances," she said, then smiled again and said her good-byes. She was only taking a wolf who would dance with her, so she really, really hoped Guthrie loved to dance.

Chapter 11

GUTHRIE WAS STILL SMILING ABOUT CALLA'S COMMENT that he gave a great math class, not quite sure how to take her. He was feeling much better since he'd had the talk with Julia last night. He'd stubbornly resisted the notion that she had been right about his actions since Tenell had gone. But after giving it a lot of thought that evening, he had to admit Julia had been correct—about a lot of things.

He'd caught Julia's eye this morning, and she'd smiled at him as if she could tell he'd changed. Hell, he hadn't thought he was that transparent. Good thing he didn't play card games.

Just coming to grips with his feelings about breaking up with Tenell had made him feel so much more light-hearted, and he really was ready to move on. At least he thought he was. The talk had made him aware of some rebound relationship pitfalls to avoid, like comparing Calla to Tenell or to the Irish lass before that. The key to the situation was determining whether one of them wasn't ready for a real commitment to a relationship. Not in a mating, as it was for their kind, but in wanting to see just each other, forget their pasts, and move forward. Start anew. Fresh.

He could do that. Could Calla?

Calla had sweetness and spiciness, a sense of humor, and intelligence that he liked. In the future, they might even have something. If, *in the meantime*, he could keep his hands off her. If he couldn't, he knew he'd just want more. She was too appealing for his own good.

No matter how much Guthrie told himself he needed to take it easy with Calla, every time he saw her, his damn heart started beating faster, and his pheromones kicked in. He immediately took note of what she was wearing and tried to capture her scent.

If anyone had asked him what anyone else was wearing, he'd have been hard pressed to answer. But Calla? A pale blue sweater that set off her strawberry blond curls and a pair of dark blue pants and snow boots. Even so, he envisioned her still wearing the white toga…and after, when she wasn't wearing it.

She might need more time to come to grips with her relationship with Baird. Or even to see if she was interested in more of one with Guthrie. Like she had said, she needed to unwind after the party last night and it didn't mean that she was ready for anything more serious.

Guthrie had even made the effort to find seating away from Calla this morning at breakfast. But as soon as he had taken the seat next to Duncan, Heather vacated the seat on the other side of him and Calla took her place. It had to be a conspiracy to test his resolve.

If he didn't know better, he'd think the lass was attempting to court him. When he was trying to maintain some distance.

Guthrie drove Calla, Julie, Elaine, Heather, Shelley, his Aunt Agnes, and his mother into the town of Druie in their minibus that could seat as many as fifteen pack members, and they all chatted away about the places where they wanted to go. All but Calla. She was as quiet as she'd been at breakfast, but she caught his eye in the rearview mirror and gave him another of her elusive smiles.

Hell, if she kept it up, they were going back to the garden room or, better yet, her guest room or his bedchamber for a repeat of last night's extracurricular activities.

He parked a way out so they could stroll along the sidewalks and search for the presents they wanted to pick up for Christmas. He stuck close to the group while four other pack members kept eyes on them from strategic points as the group moved to see the sights. He half listened to their conversation while keeping an eye out for Baird or any of his kin.

He and the ladies paused to watch a heavily tattooed man with a shaved head as he demonstrated swallowing a sword. Despite the chilly winter breeze, the sword-swallower was dressed in a kilt and no shirt.

Guthrie observed the feat, thinking the man had to be damn cold but could not be a wolf—no wolf would risk being found in wolf form with tattoos and raising dangerous speculation. In any event, Guthrie thought the man should have had more respect for both his sword and where he placed it.

His mother said, "If anyone in our family did that, Ian would make him leave the pack."

Agreeing, Guthrie smiled at her. The ladies went into shops of all sorts while Ethan caught his eye every so often and gave him a nod from across the street. A man dressed in a ten-foot-tall reindeer costume walked on stilts in the crowded street as shoppers huddled together, talking or sauntering into the next store, several carrying packages.

Six reindeer pulled a sled carrying the jolly old elf himself to his Christmas throne where some of his helpers waited for him. Women and kids were already queued up to see him, including some of the MacNeill wolf pack's younger children waiting with their mothers to see Santa and receive a small toy from him.

When the ladies came out of another shop, Calla got a call. "This is Calla Stewart's Party and Wedding Planning Service, Calla speaking. How may I help you?"

She got the calls all the time from prospective clients, but as soon as her forehead wrinkled, Guthrie drew closer to see what the matter was.

The other ladies waited with her, but she waved them on and they entered the next shop. Calla stopped walking and Guthrie stayed with her. He reminded himself it could be nothing, like a bride changing the colors of her flowers again.

Until Calla said in an annoyed way to the caller, "Baird."

Calla often received calls from unknown numbers that led to party dates, so she hadn't hesitated to answer the call. But when she heard Baird's voice on the other end of the line, her heart beat faster. He'd never tried using an unknown number before. Now every time she got a call like that, she'd suspect it was him and wouldn't want to answer it. *Damn him.*

"Calla, don't hang up on me," Baird said, his voice gruff, not conciliatory. She wasn't sure if it was because he had to get the words out before she did hang up on him, or if he was still angry with her for not getting back together with him.

"Hear me out. I've only been trying to see you because the"—Baird paused as if he was biting back a curse word—"MacNeills won't let me speak with you. I just want to talk and clear the air between us. I'm sorry about what happened to Cearnach and Elaine. I really believed, and still do, that Cearnach was trying to break us up. I thought he had the hots for you. So I was wrong about that. I realized that as soon as he mated with Elaine. But he was still trying to break us up. You've got to see where I'm coming from."

"Baird…" Elaine noticed Guthrie moving closer to her and looking like he was ready to give Baird a piece of his mind—or more, if he could reach through the phone and connect physically. "I already said I wanted to end this business between us amicably. We're not getting back together. Cearnach's been my friend for longer than I've known you.

"Despite his concern that you weren't right for me, he came to the wedding to congratulate me on the marriage, and he behaved himself. I told you I had invited him. You and your brothers and cousins had to retaliate by destroying his vehicle, stealing Elaine's rental car, and leaving them to fend for themselves as wolves in the light of day as they made their way back to the castle. Both Cearnach and Elaine could have been injured or killed. So no, we can't work things out between us. You'd never let me have any friends who weren't of your choosing."

"Calla…"

"Nay, Baird. Find someone else. It's over between us. Just…let it go and quit following me everywhere."

"They won't always be watching you," he warned and ended the call.

Her skin crawling with unease, Calla glanced around at the crowded street and sidewalks, looking for any sign of Baird, phone to her ear as if he was still there. She knew the MacNeills would not like what Baird had said to her.

She finally slipped her phone into her pocket, forced a smile at Guthrie, and said, "Got to catch up to the other ladies." Before Guthrie could question her about Baird, she quickly stepped into the shop to join Julia.

"Another engagement or one that you're already handling?" Julia asked, but then she frowned at Calla. "What's wrong?"

"Nothing," Calla said.

"Don't tell me that. Your face has lost most of its color and you're upset. Who called?"

Calla should have figured she couldn't get anything past another wolf. "Baird. I'm so sick of this, Julia. But I have no idea how to get him to stop bothering me."

"Did he threaten you?"

"He said that I wouldn't have the MacNeills to watch over me always. Just an idle threat. I mean, what can he do about anything? He can't force me to marry him."

No longer in the mood for shopping, Calla hated that Baird *did* have the power to upset her like that. She really didn't think he would do anything more than keep trying to make up to her once she left Argent Castle. But still, she'd been having fun, and now her thoughts were centered on him. And she hated it.

Julia patted her arm. "What do you think about this color for Ian?"

She loved how Julia knew she was distressed and tried to get her mind off Baird. "The blue sweater would be perfect for him."

Despite the distraction, Calla kept trying unsuccessfully to think of a way to resolve this issue with Baird. As she and the other ladies headed outside, Guthrie's eyes were focused on her. He looked so concerned for her and she so appreciated him.

No matter how much she told herself that she had to wait to court someone again, damn it all, she didn't want to wait! So what if Guthrie and she weren't meant for each other? Life meant taking chances. And if he was still hung up a little on an old girlfriend? She could take his mind right off her and she would, she thought.

She walked over to him. He was looking sternly at her, like he expected her to tell him what Baird had said. She took Guthrie's arm and wrapped it around her waist, looking up at him and raising her brows. Did he want to do this, or not?

He was frowning, but he tightened his hold on her, so she assumed he did want the closeness. "Life's too short," she said and smiled up at Guthrie.

She was going to enjoy her outing with the ladies and one hunk of a Highland wolf bodyguard. She looked to see where the other ladies were headed for their shopping.

They weren't. They were all smiling at her and Guthrie.

"What?" she asked as innocently as she could. "Are you finished shopping?"

There was a collective shake of heads and the ladies

continued smiling as they turned and considered the next shop they planned to go to.

Guthrie leaned down a little and said with a rough and interested voice for Calla's ears only, "Does this mean what I think it does?"

She smiled wickedly up at him. "That…we're courting? Aye."

He gave her the most devilish look back, and she thought it meant that he was seriously considering returning to the garden room tonight. But they needed to start slow, she thought, to ensure they were really ready for this dating business. Nice and slow and easy.

She strolled along with him, trying to window-shop and enjoy all the Christmas decorations. While before she had wanted to listen to the ladies' conversation, all she was truly aware of now was Guthrie's arm wrapped around her, his warm body heating hers in the cold winter breeze, and how much she loved being close to him like this.

She noticed that Guthrie was still watching people, looking for any sign of trouble and playing his bodyguard role even though the other men were also, yet he seemed relaxed with her, his hand firmly on her waist just beneath her jacket. As much as a wolf as he was, she shouldn't have been surprised.

"Was your hand cold?" she asked him.

He grinned down at her. "Yeah, but you're heating it right up."

She smiled. The ladies motioned to the Wee Highland Tearoom for lunch. Guthrie began to pull away as if he was going to let the ladies have their luncheon together without joining them, but Calla wasn't having any of it.

If they were going to court, this was their first unofficial date. She took his hand and led him inside the dining facility, with its antique furniture and porcelain teacups and teapots of every kind either on display or in use. The baked goods and sweet treats scented the air with strawberries, toffee, and lemon, making Calla's mouth water and her stomach grumble.

And, of course, Guthrie *had* to hear. He chuckled.

The ladies split up to sit at two tables since many of the tables seated only four. Julia and Heather sat with Guthrie and Calla. Clotted cream tea was soon offered with sandwiches, oven-warmed scones with jam and cream, toffee pudding, strawberry jam tarts, and lemon curd tarts. Julia loved Scottish fare, but she was always looking for something chocolate to go with her meal.

Calla was happy with toffee pudding and caught Guthrie smirking at her as she licked her spoon. That made her blush anew.

Guthrie had just finished eating his scone when he got a call. "All right. Thanks." He said to the ladies, "Ethan spotted one of Baird's brothers and a cousin in town. It doesn't mean anything sinister. They could be here like anybody else."

"Did they have bags like they'd been shopping?" Calla asked, feeling suspicious.

"Nay, just…strolling along the street like tons of other Christmas shoppers."

"Your men aren't following them, are they?"

"Nay. Their mission is to stick close to us. They know not to split forces."

"Good." Yet Calla's skin prickled with apprehension.

"What if they've been following us for some time, and they purposely let Ethan and the others know they were?"

"It doesn't make any difference," Guthrie said.

But it did. What if they saw Guthrie's arm around her waist? And they reported it back to Baird? Which they would. What if he became really incensed that first Guthrie's brother was trying to talk her out of marrying Baird, and now Guthrie was making the moves on her—and she was all for it? Well, worse, she actually had encouraged it!

"Lass," Guthrie said, watching her expression, "what did Baird say to you?"

"That your family wouldn't always be there to watch over me."

Guthrie's face reddened a bit in anger, his eyes narrowing. "Fine. He wants a fight, he's got it."

She didn't think Guthrie meant he was going to just have a sword fight like he did with Rankin and his cousins, but a wolf-to-wolf battle. If Baird didn't give up his pursuit, it wasn't going to be combat practice.

"I don't want it to come to that," Calla said.

"I understand, Calla. We don't take situations like this lightly. But it can't go on like this."

She nodded. Then let out her breath on a sigh. She couldn't always be looking over one shoulder, worried that Baird would become bolder if the MacNeill wolves weren't there to watch her back. She resolved to learn if Baird wanted something more from her, as Guthrie suspected. Much as it hurt to admit, she couldn't believe that Baird had just been that infatuated with her. Not any longer.

But her infatuation with Guthrie…that was something else entirely. Which reminded her.

"On a different subject, I've talked to Ian about this and…" She paused. She had already made the effort to show she wanted to court Guthrie, but she wasn't sure he was game for what she had to ask him next. And she really hoped he was. "Next week, I'll be attending a masquerade ball."

Guthrie's brows rose. "*So*…is this a masquerade party you're in charge of?"

"Nay, not this time. I'm attending, as in strictly for fun. No work, no planning. Just arriving and partying."

His mouth quirked up a bit at that.

"But I have a problem."

"Aye? Your bodyguard detail—"

"Nay. Not about them. I…need a date." She absolutely hated to mention the next part because she was certain Guthrie wouldn't like to hear it. But she couldn't help it. "I was supposed to be attending with my mate."

He frowned at that. "You were invited as a couple?"

"Nay, I was invited, and I could bring a guest."

"That means you now need an escort."

"Aye. That's what I was trying to say. I couldn't attend without one." She brushed off the sleeve of her sweater in an imperious way. "It just isn't done."

He leaned over and whispered, "Humans?"

"A mix."

"Like at the toga party," Guthrie said, folding his arms.

"It shouldn't be a problem for you if you don't offer—"

"I *didn't* offer."

"If a toga-wearing woman doesn't ask you to move her…things, then it shouldn't be a problem," Calla continued in a teasing way. "And there's going to be dancing. So I need a partner who *loves* to dance." She raised a brow. She wasn't going to make it easy on Guthrie. Courting her had conditions.

"So, can you dance? Logan said he'd take me," she added, as if that would sway Guthrie. Not that she wanted to take the teen instead. She fully intended to dance the night away. Though she hoped Guthrie would want to be her dance partner all night long.

Julia laughed and shook her head. Calla had forgotten that she and Heather were sitting there soaking up their conversation.

"Logan? He's not going anywhere with you. You attract danger. He wouldn't be prepared for it. As to your question, aye, I dance. What about the costume?"

She felt as though they were negotiating a party that she was planning for a client. "Anything, except that you can't wear your kilt or everyone will know you're a MacNeill. It's a masquerade ball so no one is supposed to know who you are."

"You had this all planned, didn't you?" Guthrie asked, looking highly amused.

"What do you mean?"

"You dump the fiancé and find someone else to take you to the party."

She laughed. "Aye, it worked, didn't it? I can find someone who will dress incognito and dance all night with me. Right?"

He smiled.

"And who will appreciate the venture," she added, emphasizing this wasn't a mission and he was to just enjoy himself.

She loved the way the skin crinkled beneath his eyes when they lit with merriment. Or…maybe wolfish intrigue. Like his idea of fun was something a little hotter than just dancing at a ball. But if he passed this test? She'd know she was on the right track with Guthrie.

———

Even though Guthrie sensed Calla was nervous about spotting two of Baird's kin nearby, he admired the way she was attempting to get beyond Baird's harassment by bantering with Guthrie about the ball. The ball she was supposed to go to with her *mate*, which Guthrie thought was significant.

So what if Baird's cousin and brother had seen her in town with the MacNeills and being cozy with Guthrie?

"We're courting, remember?" he said, and her look of worry lifted. If they were going to court one another, *everyone* was going to know about it. Guthrie wouldn't hide the fact when they were out in public. If it pissed Baird off, so be it.

Guthrie had suspected all along that with the way Baird continued to hassle Calla, he wasn't going to let go of her ever. That meant dealing with this situation with extreme prejudice. The problem was that Calla had loved Baird once. If it came to having to eliminate him because he became a danger to Calla, could she forgive Guthrie?

The ladies were getting ready to leave and Guthrie slid his arm around Calla's waist, intending to show the world they were doing this. "You don't need to ask anyone else to go with you to the masquerade ball, lass. You have your dance partner already."

Chapter 12

LATER THAT AFTERNOON, CALLA GOT TOGETHER WITH Julia to discuss Christmas party plans, but she also had another thought she wanted to run by Julia. Calla's parents had been lone wolves, having their own pack of sorts, but not coexisting among a large pack like the MacNeills'. She found it fascinating to learn how the MacNeill pack homeschooled its children.

"So you teach writing and English, Guthrie does math, and Shelley is the botanist in the group. What about Aunt Agnes?" Calla asked as she sat down to have tea with Julia.

"She's the family historian so she handles history classes. Lady Mae teaches about proper etiquette for boys and girls. Heather is responsible for literature classes, while I share my writing techniques. As for the men—Cearnach handles pet care. Duncan is the weapons instructor and trains in everything from archery to swordsmanship. Ethan and his brothers teach about bovine care, and Guthrie covers math topics, including showing the little ones how to identify bills and coins, and the older ones money management. You missed the class he offered this morning, but he has a class with the older ones again on Friday morning, if you want to drop by and listen in."

"Actually, I made it to his morning class on earning and saving money, and it got me thinking. I was wondering if the kids could be involved in some kind of a craft bazaar so they could earn money for Christmas. Rather than their parents giving them money to buy gifts, they could earn their own. Then when they went shopping, the value of the money would mean so much more to them."

"I love it! A whole bunch of us are great with crafts. I'm certain we can even get a lot of the adults to help supervise and spread the word about the bazaar to all the kids in the pack. Maybe even have a food booth like they do at Renaissance fairs in the States."

"I know Ian doesn't like to have outsiders visit the castle, but what if we opened it up to everyone? We could charge a small fee to see some of the castle and its grounds since it's never open to the public. Do something really special for a weekend before Christmas. We've already decorated everything."

Julia took a deep breath. "Guthrie wanted to do something like that to help make money after the theft of the pack's investments, but Ian said no. He had fits just having the human film crew here for the production of that Highland movie, though the MacNeill clan needed the money. Even so, he wouldn't agree to opening up the castle to the public. But if we were using the funds for some worthy cause, maybe Ian would agree."

This was going to be the best Christmas ever, Calla thought. If they could pull it off.

———

Later that afternoon, Ian called Guthrie into his office. "Have a seat, why don't you?" Ian said.

Guthrie sat down and wondered what *this* was

all about. He wasn't used to his brother calling him into his office continually like this, unless he really needed to discuss something in private that was of the utmost importance.

Ian looked eager to share some bit of good news. Had someone found a way to put Baird off for good? That's the news Guthrie would love to hear.

"Julia asked me to allow a Christmas bazaar to help fund college tuition for the kids in the clan."

Guthrie couldn't believe she'd asked.

"She wants to open the castle to the public for a special Christmas viewing, since we're going all out decorating and celebrating the holiday this year," Ian continued, as if this was an everyday occurrence and he had no problem with it.

"You said nay, aye?" Guthrie said.

Ian cleared his throat and leaned back in his chair. "You know how I hate opening the castle up to outsiders."

"Aye. Which is why you said nay, right?" Guthrie asked, folding his arms slightly defensively, since all *his* ideas about doing something like that after they lost money in a scam investing scheme had met with Ian's strong disapproval. Guthrie thought it was a great concept, but how did Julia sway Ian this time?

"After Calla sat in on your class, during which you were teaching kids how to be responsible with money and savings, she came up with the idea and shared it with Julia. She said if it hadn't been for what you were teaching our children, she wouldn't have thought of it."

Guthrie was surprised to hear Calla would say that, since she hadn't arrived in time to hear his lecture!

"Many of the adults would be eager to participate,"

Ian continued. "If Cearnach still wants to, he can sell some of his *sgian dubhs*—since the hand-carved handles are so popular. Duncan could teach swordsmanship, at a price. Some of the men might be willing to set up archery competitions for a small entry fee to participants. We could have Ethan and his brothers give hayrides, like riding in Santa's sleigh or some such thing."

Guthrie smiled. "You are *serious*?"

"Aye, Brother. Just agree to it because I'm not in the habit of groveling, and then you can be in charge of it all."

Guthrie couldn't believe this was his brother, his pack leader, speaking. Aye, he was all for it. But since Calla had suggested it, shouldn't it be her show to run? She was great at setting up parties. And he didn't want her to think he had taken over something that was her idea. "Me? I thought Calla—"

"Nay, she will help coordinate some of the activities for the children, and Cearnach, being second in charge, can help to manage some, but you will be responsible overall for everything to do with the money—how it will be spent, advertising the affair, collecting money, and setting it aside for the tuition fund." Ian waited, then smirked. "Don't look so shocked, Guthrie."

"Is that all?"

"Aye." Ian frowned. "You will do it, won't you?"

Guthrie smiled. "Of course, just like I wanted to before, except I'd never considered quite this grand an affair. I'll keep you informed about the expenses and the like."

Aye, Julia had influenced Ian to do many things he had never allowed before, but Guthrie couldn't wrap his mind around this. Especially since Calla had proposed it and given him the credit after *she* had spoken to his class! He suspected this was her way of getting him back for having her talk to the class in place of his lecture.

After their meeting, Guthrie went to look for Calla and soon found her in the kitchen sneaking a scone. She nearly dropped it when she heard him approach.

"Hungry?" he asked.

Her face flushed beautifully.

He lifted the remaining one off the platter and took a bite. "As long as Cook doesn't catch us in here, we're fine."

She smiled, looking a little guilty. "I'm used to grabbing a bite to eat on my own schedule."

"Most of us sneak one a time or two. So, you liked my class on saving money, eh?"

Her eyes widened fractionally.

"Ian said you proposed having a festival of sorts to Julia."

"Aye, but she has to have Ian approve it, and he doesn't ever open the castle to the public."

"He did this time."

"Are you serious?" she asked.

"Most assuredly, and I'm in charge of finances for the affair. So, shall we set up a plan for expenditures? We need to figure out the amount it would take to recoup our losses, then how much will serve as a profit."

They heard someone coming, and Guthrie grabbed Calla's hand. "Let's make plans in the garden room."

"Wait. We need paper or my laptop first. Don't we?"

He smiled. "Aye." This early, he couldn't get away with kissing her in the garden room, or more of what had happened last night.

In the garden room, he and Calla brainstormed fast and furiously all the events they could have. Periodically, Guthrie stopped to call a pack member to see if he or she could be in charge of one activity or another. After a few hours, they'd made all the plans and contacted everyone to carry them out.

"That worked well," Guthrie said, satisfied that they had been able to work out Calla's grand schemes in a cost-effective way. Though he knew it would take some effort to make the event run smoothly, the pack members worked well together and he knew they could do it. If it was a success this year, they might be able to do it again next year, and they'd be able to plan it even better. He grabbed a bottle of wine. "Want some to celebrate?"

"Aye. I think we really accomplished a lot in the short time we worked on this."

"We did." And so well together. Between the two of them, they had some great ideas from festivals they'd attended, plus his knowledge of his own pack's strengths and her experience. Most of all, working with Calla was a real pleasure. He could see how well she planned her parties and other social gatherings, how he'd been wrong about her apparent frivolity. She actually had a real business sense when she figured costs and revenues. She was just as thorough and detailed as he was. He admired her for all of it.

They sat together on the sofa this time, enjoying their wine, but he couldn't quit thinking about Baird and his involvement in this business with Calla. He didn't want to bring it up again, but after Baird had called and threatened her, and with his men still in the area, there had to be something more to this.

"Calla, I'm certain Baird's angry because you stood him up at the wedding, and female wolves are a rare commodity. So he can't easily find another she-wolf for a mate. Not only that, but he's an alpha—the lost honor and pride in losing you after you said yes has to be killing him. His men are probably talking behind his back about how he couldn't keep his woman. And I know he's got to be furious that we've taken you in—given his kin's history with the MacNeills."

"But?"

Guthrie frowned. "It just seems like this goes further than an obsession over the woman he loved and lost."

She shrugged. "I have a steady income. Some men might find that handy. But I live in the old carriage house behind my parents' place so I don't have any properties to call my own, if Baird was hoping to add the manor house to his assets."

"Your parents have no other children, though, and everything—including their manor house and any other investments they have, their hotels even—would go to you, right?"

"Sure. But he's not someone who thinks about money a lot."

"You mean like me?" Guthrie asked.

She smiled a little. "I never heard him talk about finances. We just never discussed them. Though I did talk to Robert, his pack financial manager, for tips on good investments."

Guthrie grunted. "I hope you didn't invest in anything his cousin was in charge of."

She rolled her eyes. "Nay. I was just asking to see if he knew something I didn't."

"Do you have money? Investments?"

"Sure, I've got investments. Just because I spend large amounts of other people's money doesn't mean I spend *my* money like that. I've saved up a lot of change. But like I said, it's not anything Baird and I ever talked about."

"Having kids?"

She raised a brow. "I assumed he wanted kids. But nay, we never actually talked about it. Still, it's a natural inclination wolves have."

"Did you plan to live with him or…"

"We were getting married," she reminded Guthrie.

"Aye, lass. But were you planning on moving in with him?"

"We hadn't really agreed on anything."

Guthrie raised *his* brows this time.

"We were going on a two-week honeymoon, and then he had to go out of town on business. So I assumed we would stay at either my place or his until we got a place of our own."

Setting his empty wineglass on the table, Guthrie let out his breath.

"What?" she asked, sounding exasperated with him.

"How could you agree to marry him without nailing down all the details?"

She shrugged. "I assumed we'd figure it out."

She finished her wine and set her glass on the table. "What about you?"

"What about me? Do I want kids? Aye."

She smiled.

Seeing her amused expression, he asked, "What's *that* look for?"

"You're good with kids. I can see you helping out at a children's birthday party."

"Not dressed as a clown, nay. Otherwise, aye, I could help. As to the finances, if you need help with investment tips, I'm all yours." He meant for more than just investments. "So, did we cover all the topics?"

"Last night," she began hesitantly, "you seemed upset, but today…"

"Today, I feel like you do. It's time to move on. As long as you're agreeable, lass."

"But last night…" she said again.

"Julia made me appreciate some things about my past relationship with Tenell. And after I gave it considerable thought, I realized she was right. Once I came to the conclusion that it was truly time for me to move on, I knew I was ready. When I decide something as important as this, I don't waste time."

Just then she looked so sweet and kissable that he took her soft sweater-covered shoulders in his hands and began to kiss her cheeks, her eyes, her lips. Even though she had more clothes on than she did last night—jeans, a sweater, and boots, nothing like the slinky toga—she was just as seductively appealing.

He swore he wouldn't go as far with her tonight. Not when they were in the initial courtship phase, but wolves didn't usually take months to come to a decision. Aye, they mated for life, but if they really felt the heat between them, the compatibility of likes and dislikes about life in general, the sense of caring, protectiveness, and desire, they didn't wait a year to mate. That made him think she'd had doubts about Baird all along, even if she'd denied them to herself.

There wasn't any way that Guthrie could court the lass for a year without taking her for a mate well before that.

This…was exactly what Calla had been looking for in a wolf all her life. The heat, the fervor, the common interests, the need, and the mutual respect they had for each other, a wolf that was as close to being right for her—she thought—as he could be.

"Kids," she said against his mouth.

He smiled against her lips.

She looked up at him.

"Aye," he said and plunged his fingers through her hair as he tongued her mouth with hot, passionate enthusiasm—as if he intended to work on having kids with her right that very minute. Which had her smiling, though she had no intention of going that far this soon.

But when he lifted her sweater, pulled down her bra, and began suckling a breast, she was rethinking the waiting scenario.

He moved her onto her back on the sofa, his body between her legs, his mouth still enjoying her breast, his tongue doing wicked things to her nipple. She swept her hands up and under his shirt and sweater, feeling his back muscles exquisitely bunched for her tangible exploration. She loved the way his jeans-covered cock rubbed against her crotch, turning her on, making her wet and ready for him. The delightful smell of his raw, male wolf sex stirred her female scents to mingle with his. When he claimed her mouth in a searing kiss, his green eyes darkened, his posture, expression, and the delightful smell of him telling her that he wanted so much more.

She was burning up for him, wanting him to ease the throbbing between her legs. He moved then and began to unbutton her pants and slide the zipper down. She so wanted to go all the way, but she said, "Just dating, not mating," reminding him in case the way she was reacting to him, to this, was telling him another story.

"You're killing me," he said and pulled off her jeans in a hurry.

She caught the pained smile he gave her. She thought she could make him come at the same time as last time and rubbed his cock through his pants, but then he slid his hand down her panties. When he began stroking her and kissing her, she only managed to slide her hands down the back of his pants and cup his firm buttocks.

His fingers stroked her fervently, dipping into her wet sheath and then circling her nub again. She was powerless to resist him, to resist this deep-seated draw between them. She'd never felt this strong of a pull before. Putting on the brakes was killing her as much as it was him.

He was rubbing himself against her thigh, claiming her with his scent, even if he couldn't plunge his cock into her and permanently mate with her yet. He kept up the strokes, the pressure, the heat, the urgency, until she was shouting his name in a passionate, totally unguarded way. Which she had never done in her whole life.

She thought to help him come, like they'd done last night, but instead, he stiffly reached for her pants and handed them to her as he leaned down for another, much sweeter kiss.

"What about—" she said, about to ask about *his* needs.

He only shook his head, his voice husky when he spoke. "When it's time, lass."

She frowned a little at him, then pulled on her pants. "When it's time for…?"

"For us."

A mating. She sighed. "You aren't going to make me feel guilty about this, are you?"

He chuckled. "Does that work?"

—∽∾—

For a whole week, a great flurry of activity descended on the castle and surrounding property as clan members readied Argent Castle and the grounds for the big weekend bazaar, activities, and tour of the keep.

Guthrie continued to court Calla as much as he could, getting together with her to discuss plans, sitting with her at meals, trying to keep their relationship as "sweet" as possible to allow her time to get more used to him. Although being anywhere near her made him think of being with her alone and for a more intimate purpose. But as soon as they were alone, she made excuses not to go as far—kissing, cuddling, and a lot of fondling, and then she'd put on the brakes again.

This had been the longest week of his life. Not because of all the work to get things ready for the celebration, but because of the way he and Calla were left wanting after their intimate exchanges.

Calla called on associates she'd dealt with in her business over the years and was making a lot of progress toward organizing tour groups on short notice. The biggest draw was that the castle had never been open to the public. The only time the clan had allowed humans into the place was during the filming of the American Highland historical movie. Guthrie hadn't even considered that aspect, but Calla had and was very good at seeing ways to market her expertise.

One of the things she brought up during their meeting was the public interest in a behind-the-scenes look at where the movie had been filmed.

"We could have some of the pack members who played bit parts in the movie reenact a couple of scenes, including the one in the great hall," Calla had said when presenting the idea to Ian and Julia.

"As long as they stay well away from the Christmas tree, or there'll be hell to pay if anyone knocks it over," Julia warned. That reminded Guthrie of rescuing Calla under it—and the kiss they had shared.

The night he was to escort Calla to the masquerade party, Guthrie dressed in a traditional leather kilt, remembering his promise not to wear his MacNeill plaid. Even though it irked him not to wear his family colors with pride, it was their first real social gathering to attend as a couple. He was really looking forward to it, wanting to show she was with him, as a male wolf would with a she-wolf he was courting, and wanting to get away from the castle for a bit.

The bad part was that Baird and his kin were still a threat. Instead of taking this as a perfectly lovely social event where he and Calla had nothing to do but enjoy themselves, he still had to watch their backs.

Cearnach slapped him on the back and grinned. "You look a wee bit anxious, Brother."

Guthrie frowned at him, not knowing what he meant.

"She'll be impressed with your attire for the event. And Duncan, Oran, and I will watch your backs so that you can enjoy yourselves."

"Aye, thanks," Guthrie said, but he knew he wouldn't be able to completely enjoy himself while he was protecting Calla.

Even so, Guthrie couldn't help really anticipating what she'd wear to this event, after the toga she had sported before. When she arrived in the great hall, she was stunning in her forest green, Elizabethan-inspired velvet gown, perfect for a Christmas masquerade. The cut on the bodice showed the swell of her breasts, the trim waist and full skirt adding to the sexiness of her figure. Most of her hair was secured in an elegant twist on top of her head. Some of her red-gold curls framed her face, making him want to pull out her hairpins and see her hair cascade to her shoulders in soft waves.

The other ladies were all admiring her gown, touching it like he wanted to touch her. She caught his eye, her gaze instantly sweeping over him. That made him stand a little taller, like a wolf who wanted to impress her with his build. What was there about her that made him want to both please and tease her in a fun-loving way?

Her mouth curved up some, and he thought she either approved of his attire or was amused by it. Maybe a little of both.

One of the ladies handed her a red velvet hooded cloak. *Little Red Riding Hood.* This big, bad wolf in a leather kilt wanted to eat her all up.

He joined her and she ran her hand over the soft leather kilt. Now that made him want to growl with interest. "A leather kilt. No one will recognize you," she said.

"Do you like it?" he asked, wishing their audience would go away.

She touched his soft cream-colored sweater. "Hmm, aye. We will go together perfectly. No clashing of colors." Then she handed him a black-feathered mask.

He frowned at it. No way would he wear anything of the sort.

"It's a masquerade ball. You *have* to wear it," she insisted.

"I've got it," Oran said, hurrying into the great hall. "I wore this at a party once. Makes the men stay away from you and your woman, and it intrigues the lassies if they don't have a man." He handed Guthrie a black and silver helmet with an ominous-looking vented face guard.

It was a fantasy kind, unlike true Roman, Norman, or Saxon knights' helmets. Like the large scaled metal on a knight's arms, the helmet had large scales from the top of the head to the back. He liked it—but he wasn't wearing it.

"Nay. I need to see you—every bit of you—at all times. Too easy for someone to blindside me," Guthrie said to Calla.

She shook her head.

"Besides, it looks more like something an armored knight would wear, not a leather-kilted Highlander," Guthrie said.

"As long as you dance with me all night," she reminded him.

"It will be my pleasure, lass." He smiled. He danced as well as any other man who did so in good form, even though dancing all night was not really his thing. Still, he wouldn't have allowed anyone else to take her. Especially when she'd thrown down the gauntlet to see if he'd bite.

Oran, Duncan, and Cearnach went as her guard detail because if Baird had the nerve to show up, with or without backup, they wanted to ensure he didn't get anywhere near her. As part of the masquerade, all the men were armed with their *sgian dubhs* and swords. Oran dressed as a pirate, but he had a black leather mask to cover his eyes. If he weren't on guard duty, Oran would steal some wench away from an unworthy bloke, Guthrie had no doubt. Duncan and Cearnach wore their MacNeill kilts—the ancient muted variety—so most wouldn't know they were the MacNeill brothers. There was no talking them into wearing anything else, but he had noticed that Calla didn't try very hard with them. Like Guthrie, they would not wear masks.

"They'll insist you wear some kind of masks when we arrive. They will have loaners if you don't have something else you'd rather wear," Calla warned them.

"Nay, Guthrie is right. We need to keep our sight, smell, and hearing unhampered," Cearnach said. He patted his sword. "We'll go without."

"The real challenge won't be us getting into the ball without masks," Guthrie said, "but getting you into the car with all those skirts."

His brothers and cousin were laughing hard as Guthrie tried to tuck her all in. He loved the feel of her, all soft and curvy, and her dress was just as soft. He couldn't wait to hold her close and dance with her.

"I can do it. I can do it," she said, but he was having way too much fun.

Chapter 13

WHEN CALLA AND GUTHRIE AND THEIR GUARD PARTY arrived at the country manor house, which was a couple of hours away, vehicles were already sitting in a gravel car park. The MacNeills had intended to get there early so their guard detail could watch for the new arrivals. Men and women were gathering at the door or leaning off balconies to get a look at the newcomers and their costumes. Many of the women wore lavish gowns, but a few were in other kinds of costumes. Most of the men wore masks and tuxes, so the MacNeill brothers stood out in their kilts, and some of the female guests looked quite intrigued.

Calla groaned. "Here you thought you had to protect *me*," she said to the brothers.

Oran said, "Here I thought being a roguish pirate would sweep the ladies off their feet. I should have known better and worn my kilt."

Even though Oran smiled interestedly at the costumed women, Calla knew he would do his duty and watch out for her. She wished he could just relish the party. Though she had to admit, he looked like he was already having a great time. Cearnach and Duncan were much more circumspect, checking over the crowd, mostly looking at the males and smelling the air like Guthrie was, trying to pick up the scents of the wolves over the humans.

"You know that if there's even a whiff that Baird and his kin are here…"

"Then we'll go home at once," Calla said. "You already warned me. But we just got here. Let's enjoy ourselves for the time being. All right?"

She would kill Baird and his kin herself if they ruined this evening for her. And she wasn't *normally* a violent person. Though she did have her moments.

Everything looked so spectacular—the lighting outside and the white lights on several of the trees. The Hightowers even had mistletoe hanging over the front doorstep. One lady was eagerly waiting to "greet" someone who stepped under it with her. She was dressed in a vampire costume, the black collar stiffened, the skirt high on the thigh, with a fringe of red lacy underskirt peeking around the edge. Her black hair was piled up on her head with a red rose poking out of the curls. A black velvet choker sported red jewels dangling from the necklace as if they were drops of blood.

"I'll take care of her," Oran offered, as if he had to protect them from the fangs of a vampire.

Oran took hold of the woman's shoulders and kissed her, deftly moving her aside as he did it so Guthrie was able to escort Calla inside. Calla laughed at Oran.

The foyer was decorated in antiques and Santas in leather, iron, cloth, wood, porcelain, and just about every other material. A butler hurried to take Calla's red cloak as a woman about Calla's age, who was dressed in a sexy werewolf costume—gray fur ears, furry wristbands, and short miniskirt with a gray bushy tail—greeted them. She *was* a wolf! When she smelled that Calla was one too, she smiled brightly at her.

"Come right this way," she said. "I'm Ivy, daughter of Northrop and Adeline Hightower." Before Calla could introduce herself and her escort, Ivy said, "And you must be Calla, the party planner extraordinaire." Calla hadn't met Ivy before, but she'd planned a party for the Hightowers a year ago, which was why Calla had been invited to this affair. They'd told her they would have had her plan this one too, but it had been in the making for two years with a different party planner that they hadn't been happy with.

"I've heard through the grapevine"—Ivy glanced at Guthrie—"that one hot guy escorted you to the toga party. *And* got an eyeful of Rosalind doing her usual thing."

"You know Rosalind?" Calla might have been surprised, but she often got referrals from one party and ended up meeting many of the same people at new parties.

"Sure. These parties are often for all of the same people. I couldn't go to the toga party because I was trying to get ready for this one. I wished I'd seen it, though. The Rankins' parties are always mixed…"—Ivy lowered her voice—"mixed wolf-human affairs. Not that Rosalind and her brother realize it. Rosalind told me she met some guy Calla was dating. And *you* must be him."

"Aye, one and the same." Guthrie bowed his head a little in acknowledgment to Ivy.

"You know, everyone's *supposed* to be wearing masks," Ivy said, but since she wasn't wearing one either, Guthrie figured she'd let it slide. Ivy turned back to Calla. "You were coming with a fiancé, last I'd heard."

Immediately, Guthrie stiffened beside Calla.

Calla wanted to squeeze his arm to tell him she was all right with talking about it. "Aye, change of plans."

Ivy gave her a big grin as she led them into the great hall where refreshments and hors d'oeuvres were being served. Several guests were loitering beside a very tall, skinny tree decorated in Santas and bows, listening as a band played Celtic Christmas music.

"So what happened? You called off the wedding?" Ivy asked.

"Aye. It wouldn't have worked out," Calla said, though she didn't want to talk about it here and now. She was here strictly to revel in the party atmosphere.

"Not with you being an alpha, it wouldn't have."

Calla suddenly felt strong vibes that Ivy wasn't just idly chitchatting.

"You…know him *well*?" Calla asked, concerned that Baird might actually come to the party. Especially if he'd been friends with Ivy and her family. He'd never mentioned anything about knowing Ivy when Calla had talked to him about attending the masquerade with her. She wasn't worried for herself if Baird showed up, but she was afraid he would pick a fight with Guthrie. Or his kin would with Guthrie's kin.

"I dated him right before you must have started seeing him. I met with him on a seal boat trip out of Dunvegan Castle."

"Baird acting like a tourist? Not in this lifetime," Guthrie said. "If he'd been out hunting the seals, then I could envision it."

Calla suddenly felt queasy. "I met him there too," she said. Guthrie looked at her suspiciously and she explained, "I was just starting up my business here. I had some free time on my hands and thought it would be fun. I didn't think anything of him being there. Just two single wolves running into each other. We saw nesting herons, Arctic terns, and sea eagles."

"So you had a camera with you?" Guthrie asked.

"Well, aye. Don't all tourists?"

He snorted. "Did Baird?"

"Nay," she admitted. "I supposed not all tourists have them." Or Baird had not been a tourist. Which meant Baird had suckered her right in. That reminded her of how lonely she'd been, wishing she could find a wolf to do that kind of thing with.

Ivy laughed. "You would make a good detective with Scotland Yard, Guthrie."

"Was he with his kin or alone? I swear he rarely goes anywhere alone," Guthrie said.

"Alone," Calla said on a sigh. "He acted like he was totally smitten with me. You can't know how flattering that was for a change. In retrospect, I realize he never went there afterward. With me or with others—not that I know of, anyway."

"He has a friend who works there," Ivy said. She lowered her voice conspiratorially. "Since Baird met you the same way, his friend probably let him know that there was another single she-wolf on the tour. I think the guy who schedules the tours is a distant relation. I suspect he asked you the usual questions—is this for a group purchase, single visitor, ever been there before? What is your age—to see if you are eligible for a discount. What is your job, for the same reason."

Calla shook her head in disbelief.

"A girlfriend of mine, who is single, booked a tour with them for a group," Ivy continued. "Once she said that she was making arrangements for a group, the booking agent didn't need to know more. He didn't ask her age or occupation. Just the credit card number that the charge would go on.

"To sweeten the deal on the seal boat tour, the booking agent gave me a discount for having my own business. At the boat dock, Baird was acting interested in the birds when I smelled that he was a wolf. He was obviously alone, no other wolves on the tour, and he seemed really interested in the tour. Not in me. I liked that he didn't know I was a wolf yet. Ha! As if."

"What do you mean?" Calla asked.

"Did you have to book your tour a week in advance?" Ivy said.

"Yes…?" Calla answered with increasing unease.

"I think it's because then Baird would do some investigation of his own. Or have one of his minions do it. And I fit his type exactly: I am single, have well-to-do parents who aren't with a pack, and I was lonely—a rebound from another relationship," Ivy said.

That sent warning bells ringing.

"Oh, and I'm a successful dress designer, which makes me think that he likes women who are financially secure on their own."

"You're kidding," Calla said, knowing she wasn't. How far had he gone to learn about her? If she had used a dating service, he would have known something about her right off, but she would have known some things about him too. It wouldn't be as one-sided, as underhanded as this.

"So we're on the boat, and he's still upwind of me and acting like I don't exist, and that makes me want to meet him. Wolf curiosity, you know. Plus, I was alone and I thought it would be fun, knowing he'd tell me if he was mated right off," Ivy said. "Well, he was so sweet and thrilled to meet a fellow wolf. We hit it off and—"

"Don't tell me," Calla said, glad she'd dumped his butt. "He took you to the Seaside Café afterward."

"Yep, close by and owned by a cousin. One big, happy family. We were easy pickings. God. He comes along and sweeps me off my feet. Told me I was just the one for him. But I wasn't. And I told him so. What about you?"

"The same. Only I wore rose-colored glasses for longer," Calla said, annoyed with herself all over again. How could she have been so naive?

"Longer than a year?" Ivy asked. "He was pushing for a mating forever. I actually stuck it out for a year, just about. I was busy with my business. We had fun when we got together, but he didn't want me to associate with my old friends." Ivy shrugged. "I have several girlfriends and business associates, and I wasn't about to give them up just because he didn't like them. What about you?"

"Same with me. It was about a year. I was always scheduling parties, heavily involved in my work. I was so busy that there were weeks when we couldn't find the time to get together. And he was constantly pushing for us to marry so he could at least be with me at night—he said."

Calla heaved a sigh, noticing that even though Guthrie was listening to everything they said, he was also keeping a watchful eye out for trouble.

"He's not coming to the party, is he?" Calla asked.

"He wouldn't be welcome. But he might try to patch things up with you."

"Didn't he try with you?"

"Oh, at first, aye. Once he set his sights on you, I didn't have any more trouble with him."

"You mean he was stalking you afterward too?"

"I wouldn't call it stalking exactly. We would run into each other at some of the same pubs and other places. Hard not to."

"Until he met me, aye?"

Ivy bit her bottom lip as she seemed to ponder the notion. "Hmm, you're right. I didn't see him at any of the usual places after he began seeing you. He must have been taking you to different places. He probably didn't want you to meet the old girlfriend." Ivy smiled. "I think he's more hung up on you than he ever was with me. Maybe it's because I called it quits before we agreed to actually marry. Even so, that had to have hurt his big ego, not to mention dealing with his pack over it.

"With you, he was so close to making the commitment—at the altar even, and you walked out on him. Now that has to be the ultimate slight. Probably also because Cearnach helped sway you to not marry Baird, and now you're staying with Cearnach's family." She gave Guthrie a smile that said she knew there was more to it than Calla just *staying* with the MacNeills.

The musicians began to play a waltz.

"I've got to greet my guests. Why don't you get some refreshments, mingle, and dance?" Ivy glanced at the other men with them.

"Bodyguard detail. Baird has been stalking me," Calla explained. She introduced Guthrie's cousin and brothers.

"And thank you, Ivy, for telling me all this," Calla said, grateful to know the truth, even if it hurt.

Ivy sighed. "Maybe Baird will find another woman to harass." She smiled at Oran, who was grinning at her.

"I'm single, and I love your wolfishness," Oran told her right away.

Calla wasn't sure if he was talking about Ivy's wolfishness as in real wolf or the costume.

"I've never gone on a seal trip, but I wouldn't see the birds and seals anyway if I took *you* out on the boat," Oran added. "And I had no idea you even existed before today."

Calla laughed.

Ivy chuckled. "Then you can come with me."

"Bodyguard detail," Guthrie reminded his cousin with a stern look.

"He can stand near the front door, but not under the mistletoe," Ivy said, with a small smile curving her lips. "I saw that kiss you gave Geraldine."

Oran's cheeks turned a little red, though he laughed it off and offered his arm as if he were a gallant, swashbuckling pirate, which, for fun, he was. The two of them left the great hall, Ivy's faux-fur wolf's tail wagging behind her.

"Sounds like Baird's been doing this kind of thing with women for a while," Guthrie said, slipping his arm around Calla's waist and pulling her to the center of the great hall where others were already dancing. "I've wanted to do this forever."

He didn't even wait to pull her close. As soon as she was in his arms, she was firmly against his chest, and she briefly thought of her velvet gown turning into crushed velvet. Though the way he'd packed her skirts into the car had probably wrinkled the fabric a bit already. She couldn't help noticing how eagerly he had helped her. She had to admit, Guthrie had been hilarious—trying to stuff the billowing gown and underskirts into the small car, his hands "inadvertently" pressing against her thighs.

In his arms, she loved the feel of Guthrie's hard body against hers, the way he smelled wolfishly excited to be this close to her, the way he seemed to want to be with her and only her. Which reminded her of dating Baird. She didn't think Guthrie was anything like him personally, but the intrigue was the same.

But she didn't *want* her next relationship to be like her last one. She needed emotional support for the last disastrous relationship, not a commitment to someone new. She thought Guthrie knew that too. He'd been pulling away from her in an attempt to keep things on a more even keel, not having unconsummated sex on the sofa around the fire pit again.

So, *this* didn't mean a whole lot of anything. Just an alpha male wanting to get close and personal. Nothing that screamed—*I want you for an eternity*—as in a wolf mating.

If her experience with Baird had taught her one thing, it was that a male wolf would do anything to mate, and she wanted to make sure she was settling down with the right one this time. She-wolves who were born to *lupus garous* were fewer in number, so she had to remind herself that she was a precious commodity. She laughed at herself over that.

She'd never been popular among humans when she

was younger. It had something to do with growling at them when they angered her, or wanting to bite one guy who had started seeing someone behind her back. That was one good thing about being a wolf—she had smelled the other woman on him. Biting him had not been an option. No way had she wanted to turn the jerk and have him as her responsibility.

She hadn't been around her wolf kind all that much. The few she had known were either mated, just friends, or hadn't appealed in the least.

So she was going to just enjoy this with Guthrie—the way he held her close, moving to the music nice and easy, their bodies melded together—as a fun way to get back into the swing of dating.

He kissed the top of her head, and she felt the pang of wanting something further and tried to ignore it. Just this, nothing more. Not kissing again, tasting his sugary tongue and hot, sexy mouth like when they'd kissed beneath the toppled Christmas tree. Not breathing in that musky scent that said he wanted to go beyond where they should go. That feeling was only natural—given the way they were holding each other close and rubbing their bodies together. She attempted to ignore the feel of his growing arousal pressed against her.

She shouldn't have looked up at him to see if he wanted more.

He wore the most devilish smirk as he looked down at her—as if saying he *knew* she wanted to go further. That she couldn't hold out forever.

She smiled a little at him, giving him the go-ahead. *Just plain sexy fun*, she thought. And he leaned down to kiss her. His lips didn't start with anything soft—just like he hadn't started the dance by keeping a distance between them and then slowly moving in closer to her. He seemed hungry for the kiss, like he was starved for affection. She shouldn't have, but she soaked in the heat and hotness of his kiss, growling a little with satisfaction.

When he heard her growl softly, he didn't smile, but plunged his tongue into her mouth, as if her need screamed to be met and he had to satisfy his own rampant urges.

His tongue stroking hers garnered nearly all of her attention, except for the way he rubbed against her, his soft leather kilt unable to hide the swell of his erection as he slid it against her velvet-covered belly. Her nipples were already hard with the way she was pressed against his firm chest. Her insides seemed to liquefy—melting to his practiced touch.

After seeing all the women in costumes that barely covered their knickers, she had wondered if she should have worn less, rather than more. But Guthrie seemed to love having all her velvety softness in his grasp, and she loved feeling hot and sexy in his arms. She didn't need to dress scantily to entice the wolf.

His clean, male, musky wolf scent intoxicated her. His large hands stroked her velvet-covered buttocks as if he couldn't get enough of touching her...or the gown. So wrapped up in him, she no longer heard the music playing—or if the waltz had ended and changed to something else. Or saw if anyone else was in the great hall. Or smelled anyone nearby. Guthrie filled all her senses.

His tongue licked the seam of her mouth again, seeking entrance. And she let him in again, knowing they should stop this public display of affection in case anyone was watching, but she didn't want to. His tongue stroked the inside of her mouth and her tongue— powerful, overwhelming, eager. She was so wet. So ready for him, if they had intended to take it that far.

At that point, she wanted to go home with him. What had happened to keeping this light and amicable and not so hot and heavy?

She pulled away from him to catch her breath, her heartbeat drumming hard, her breathing labored. Okay, so Baird had never made her nearly come with his kisses, but she thought it prudent to put some space between herself and Guthrie, to get to know some other wolves… first. Before she got too involved and said *I will* again. It wasn't that Guthrie wasn't right for her—as far as she knew—but that she'd made such a mistake with Baird, thinking the same thing.

Besides, she knew she was vulnerable, a natural aspect of loving someone and having to end the relationship. With Baird continuing to harass her, she couldn't completely let go of that situation, either.

"Are you all right?" Guthrie asked, and she realized, damn it, that her eyes were filled with tears.

See? Calla chastised herself. This was the problem. She *had* loved Baird, even now that she knew he probably hadn't loved her. But she couldn't help feeling the aftereffects of the disastrous end to an almost marriage and mating.

"Aye, aye."

"Did you want to get something to drink?"

"You're not trying to get out of dancing, are you?" she asked with a smile.

"Not on your life."

She sighed and snuggled close as he continued to dance with her. The problem with seeing other male wolves was if the wolf became thoroughly interested in the she-wolf, he wouldn't want her to see anyone else. Even if she wasn't certain the match was a good one.

Then she would be right back to being with another wolf like Baird.

"I'm a little bit…" She began to say "needy," but she didn't want to ruin the moment. "Well…" What then? "I hate to say…" That she was confused? That she needed more time? What if she didn't? What if Guthrie *was* just the kind of wolf she needed in her life?

Oh, hell, her parents would have fits. Not that they didn't like the MacNeill family, but she could see them both shaking their heads at her, telling her it was too soon. To wait. To date a bunch of male wolves until she found the right one. If Guthrie turned out to be the right one, he'd wait for her to make up her mind, wouldn't he? But every time she was with him, she didn't want to wait. *Oh, damn it all.*

He cast her an elusive smile as if he could tell he was turning her thoughts inside out. That she was already hung up on him, a great deal.

"We'll just dance," she said, determined that was all there would be between them. For now.

"All right by me," he whispered against her cheek.

Wondering if she might dance with someone else, she looked around at the other dancers. She had no plans to date any more humans. She wanted a mate. Sighing, she couldn't tell which of the males were wolves unless she went up and smelled them or asked. Some of them looked halfway interesting, like the vampire across the room who bowed his head slightly to her, or the guy in the three-cornered hat with the plumed feather poking out of it, looking like he was one of the Three Musketeers. He winked at her.

She suddenly felt self-conscious. Did they think she was easy because of the way she'd been dancing with Guthrie? Kissing him? Looking as though they needed to get a room?

"You wanted a dance partner who was willing to dance with you all night long," Guthrie whispered into her ear as if he was speaking seductively to her, almost like he was telling the other men she'd chanced to look at that she was taken. "*One* dance partner," he said.

She smiled up at him and wrapped her arms around his neck. "Don't you think I should dance with others a little? What if there is a she-wolf here that could prove intriguing to you?"

She was serious. Even though she didn't want to give this up, she didn't want to spoil Guthrie's chance to have fun if he saw a woman he'd like to dance with. Even someone like Ivy with her short skirt and swinging wolf's tail. What if Calla was only filling some craving for him too?

From what Calla had gathered, Guthrie was always helping with one thing or another, and he didn't seem to take a lot of time to just enjoy life's little pleasures.

"*You* asked me here. If nothing else, I'm protecting you," Guthrie said.

"Ah." The bit about protecting her again. Not that he was just hot for her body like she was for his. Darn it. "The kiss was just…?"

He smiled.

"For show?" she offered, since he wouldn't say.

"What do *you* think?"

"I think I'm getting in way over my head."

He chuckled. "Probably."

She was. She'd known it the moment he kissed her under the Christmas tree. She could fret about this, worry that he wasn't the right one for all eternity, and still not get him out of her system, she thought.

"Did you want to cool down a bit and get a drink?"

"Why? Are you hot?" She meant because they had been dancing so close and the crush of people around them was making the room hotter. Not to mention that her gown was warm and his wool sweater had to be too.

He grinned at the question. "Am I?"

Smiling, she shook her head in amusement. "Yeah, but I'm not talking about *that* right now. Let's get a drink and then we can dance some more afterward."

They hadn't even made it to the refreshment table when they heard the clanging of swords in the front foyer and a woman's scream.

Chapter 14

IMMEDIATELY, GUTHRIE'S BLOOD SURGED WITH adrenaline, making him ready for battle. He recognized that Oran was engaging someone from the way his sword struck the aggressor's weapon, and the speed and force with which he struck. Guthrie desperately wanted to see who was fighting Oran, but he kept Calla by his side and out of harm's way in case it was a ploy to draw him away from her. He wasn't about to leave her behind, and he wasn't going to take her into the fray.

He glanced around to see if anyone else was carrying a sword. One man dressed as a World War I soldier in a khaki kilt, service dress jacket, and low boots. The man dressed as a Musketeer had one too, but he was gone.

Guthrie heard a sword hit a wall and drop to the wooden floor in the foyer. People who were watching the sword fight clapped. Cearnach came into the great hall and motioned to Guthrie that all was clear.

"I wonder what that was all about," Calla said as the music started again.

"Not Baird or his men or he would have been..." Then Guthrie saw him, clear as day, dancing with a woman in a gold gown and mask.

"What?" Calla asked, turning to see what he was staring at.

"Baird's here, dancing over there. Whoever was

fighting with Oran must have been a diversion for Baird to get in."

Calla's breath hitched. The man wouldn't leave her alone. But Guthrie knew they couldn't fight him here. Baird had to know that too. Most likely, he was showing her that she couldn't stop him from getting close and bothering her—not even with the MacNeills guarding her.

"And his two brothers and two of his cousins are here, dancing with other women," she noticed.

"Aye." Guthrie was about to tell her that they had to leave, as he'd first intended if Baird and his men showed up, but he really was trying to do this courtship business right. "Do you want to go?"

She frowned up at him. "Are you trying to get out of dancing with me all night? Besides, Ivy said he wasn't welcome. She might ask him to leave herself."

Guthrie smiled at her, got her a glass of mulled wine, and once he had his whisky, they stood watching the dancers for a moment. He conferred with his brothers and cousin about leaving, but aside from the initial sword fight, the McKinleys didn't seem to be causing any more trouble or making any moves in Calla's direction. Besides, to an extent, he agreed with her. He wouldn't normally allow another wolf to run him off, not when they had every right to be here.

When they finished their drinks, he returned to the dance floor with her.

Baird and his kinsmen were dressed like pirates, with full-sleeved shirts, black masks, black trousers, and boots. Since the whole family had been a bunch of pirates, Guthrie didn't think they were masquerading at all.

He soon closed his arms around Calla and held her soft, velvet-covered body against him, wishing they were at Argent, somewhere a lot more private.

"Calla," he whispered against her ear as he moved slowly with her, all his senses taking her in—her delightful she-wolf aroma, the scent of strawberries and sweet wine; the feel of her, warm and soft and such a perfect fit against his aroused body; the beat of her heart; and the whisper of her warm breath on his neck as she glanced up at him.

"Hmm…"

"I'm really having a difficult time with…this relationship stuff."

She rested her head against his chest and wrapped her arms around his back. "Hmm."

"What I mean is that I know you put on the brakes with Baird and dated him for a year before you agreed to mate him, but…"

Calla nodded.

"The thing of it is, I can't wait that long."

She looked up at him, her expression mildly amused. Vixen.

Didn't she know how hard this was for him to talk about? "Every time you look at me—like that—every time we touch, every time we kiss…I want so much more. Don't you?"

She grinned up at him. "Oh, aye, but it's just a lustful need. If we see each other longer, we won't feel the pull so strongly. Don't you agree?"

"Nay."

She smiled wickedly at him. "Okay, tell me you didn't feel the same way about the girlfriends you seriously considered mating. In the beginning, you were dying to fulfill some sexual need. It's only natural."

He didn't say anything, just tightened his hold on her as she swayed to the music with him. This—with Calla—felt different. He couldn't explain why he felt so…tied to her, but he did. Didn't she feel the same way about him? Or was he projecting how he felt about Calla onto her?

"Aye," she finally said, her cheek snuggled against his chest again.

"What?"

She looked up at him and smiled. "That's the way I feel about you—like I can't get enough of you. Like I want to take this further. When I was with Baird, I always had a closed-in feeling, like he was in my space, smothering me. Pressuring me. Not giving me the freedom I needed."

She sighed. "I never would have been able to work with him on a project like the one you and I are coordinating—together. I never was able to discuss my work with him. He wasn't interested. He acted as though my *job* was a hobby. If he had some function to attend, he wanted me to go with him. He would become extremely annoyed if I had other plans.

"Oh, he tried to couch his irritation, which showed he did care for me to an extent. I worried that once we were mated and I was his pack mate, he might insist that we attend all social gatherings together—despite what I had planned and how important it was to me."

Guthrie rubbed her back gently.

"Well," Guthrie said, mulling it over, "if you really want to dance with someone else tonight, you are free to do so with my blessing," he said.

She studied him for a moment and then smiled. "I don't believe that. You'd be all growly and scare the potential dance partner away."

He laughed.

"But thank you for saying so. I love how you're *trying* to respect my boundaries, and I respect yours. We complement each other. So, as to that aspect, I think we're more suited to each other than with anyone I've ever dated. That's saying a lot. To me, a relationship isn't based just on sexual compatibility. It has to be based on…well, just so much more."

"I agree. And I want to share so much more with you."

She smiled at him. "Oh?"

He smiled back.

"Hmm," she said.

They ignored Baird and his men, though Guthrie assumed Baird would try to get a dance with Calla. He was a pack leader who had planned to come to this masquerade with Calla, and he seemed to have something to prove to his kin and to himself.

When he did come to ask Calla to dance, Guthrie said, "Nay, Baird. Leave the lass alone. She's already said she wants nothing more to do with you, and she's already found a replacement."

She looked up at Guthrie, but he wasn't taking his words back.

Baird smiled a little at Guthrie, then said to Calla, "You thought *I* was controlling. He won't even allow you to decline a dance on your own behalf, if you wish it."

"He said exactly what I would have told you if I'd gotten to it first. So no, I won't dance with you."

"You're making a mistake," Baird said.

Guthrie made a move toward Baird but stopped short before he threw the man out of the ballroom, while Calla tightened her hand on Guthrie's arm. She smiled sweetly at Baird, then pulled Guthrie away.

Guthrie ground his teeth. "You know how much it bothers me that I can't do anything about him. If we were not here, among all these people…"

Calla sighed. "Forget him. I'm with you and I'm not interested in dancing with anyone else tonight." She held him tight against her soft body.

In that instant, he felt the anger seep out and realized just how good she was for him.

Calla was certain that if she had been dancing with Baird and Guthrie had tried to butt in, Baird would have been furious. But instead of doing something about it himself, he would have had one of his brothers take Guthrie to task. She'd been worried that Guthrie would continue to be angry about it, but when he acted as though all he cared about was her and dancing with her the rest of the night, she loved him for it.

At one point, she saw Ivy watching Baird and wondered why the woman hadn't had him thrown out. Maybe she was afraid to make a scene in her home. Her parents might have said to leave the situation alone unless Baird and his kin caused trouble.

She noticed that Oran disappeared for a time, and then so did Guthrie's brothers. When the party was winding down and Calla's feet were hurting enough that she was ready to call it a night, they said their good-byes to their host and hostesses, and then headed out to the car.

Duncan was standing next to it, arms folded and looking fierce.

Her feet hurt so much that she was walking slower than normal. Guthrie glanced down at her. "Are you all right, lass?"

"If I could, I'd take off my heels and…"

He didn't hesitate to scoop her up in his arms and carry her the rest of the way to the car. She chuckled. "I should have said something before this."

"Aye, you should have."

"I didn't want you to say anything about how I made you dance with me all night long and how it was my fault that I didn't stop when my feet began to hurt."

He kissed her cheek. "Lass, any way that I can hold you close is welcome."

"You know," she said, wrapping her arms around his neck, "you keep talking like that and—"

He grinned at her.

She let out her breath. "I just think we should be cautious about committing to anything too quickly."

"Aye," he said and held her tighter.

She really didn't believe he agreed with her, but she adored the way he carried her out to the car, kept her tucked in his arms, which warmed her in the cold breeze, and agreed so sweetly.

"Were you guarding the vehicle?" she asked Duncan as Guthrie pushed all her skirts into the car and then got in next to her.

"Aye, lass. We took turns."

"Because of Baird?" she asked.

In the backseat, Guthrie put his arm around her and pulled her close. She rested her head on his shoulder.

"Aye. We didn't want to find that they had moved our car or slashed the tires or anything," Duncan said. "*Again.*"

Calla was happily tired and glad to have been with
Guthrie and his kin at the ball. They had so much to do
tomorrow, and they'd been working such long hours,
getting ready for the big weekend of festivities, that she
fell asleep on the trip home. She woke the next morning,
buried under the covers, sleeping in her underwear in
the guest chambers with her beautiful gown spread out
over a chair.

After she dressed in her long Stewart plaid skirt and
sweater, she hurried to join the others who were preparing to open for the big day. Argent Castle was abuzz
with excitement. The weather had warmed up to fifty
degrees, and the weekend tour and gift-selling bazaar
was open for business.

Heather and Julia were giving tours of the castle.
Duncan and some of the teens were offering swordsmanship lessons for young and old alike, though the
swords were only practice ones the kids used in training
and play.

As much as Ian didn't like opening the castle to
strangers, Calla noticed him smiling and could tell he
enjoyed seeing his people so happy, all dressed in their
plaids, some of the ones tending craft and food booths
sporting Santa hats. Calla's red-and-green Stewart plaid
stood out among all the blue-and-green MacNeill kilts,
but she was having a ball.

Ethan and his brothers were providing hayrides
in faux Santa's sleighs—the red wagons decorated in
battery-operated sparkling lights—to the pastureland to
visit the Highland cattle.

Tables were set up for eating or for the kids to create paper crafts. Some were gluing paper clothes to a

Scottish bagpiper boy, choosing from a kilt, jacket, tam-o'-shanter Scottish cap, boots, and bagpipe. Other kids could color their own tartans or create cotton-ball lambs on a paper plate. Some of the clanswomen helped children create reindeer like the ones that ranged freely in the Cairngorm Mountains, the children's painted hand-prints used to print antlers atop brown paper cutouts.

A bagpiper was playing on the ramparts, surveying the archery competitions, sword-fighting demonstration, and face painting. Cook and some of her assistants were selling scones, fruit cakes, bannocks, Scottish black buns, and venison stew.

Over by the stables, Calla tried playing the game of quoits, in which iron rings are tossed at an upright pin, much like pitching horseshoes. But after her toss landed the ring impossibly far from the iron pin, she decided she was better at setting up the games than playing them. She saw Guthrie watching her, arms folded and smirking. She would have asked if he could do better, but she didn't dare, certain he could.

Ian had nixed the notion of having a kissing-under-the-mistletoe booth. Even though the wolves had tougher immune systems than humans, he didn't want any of the *lupus garou* females in his pack kissing a bunch of strangers—human or otherwise.

Guards were posted along the wall walk as a deterrent in case Baird and his kin attempted to sneak into the castle posing as guests. The guards were armed with swords and crossbows, not that they meant to use them. To the tourists, the weapons were just part of the show. They took pictures in the inner bailey with the guards, who looked fierce with their swords out and holding their

Scottish targes, the shields scarred from sword fights, both in ancient times on the battlefield and modern times on the playing field.

Kids and adults alike visited the Irish wolfhounds in their enclosure where the dogs had room to run and play. Logan was happily in charge of that. Though since the wolfhounds were included in the cost of admission, Ian was paying for Logan's time so he could earn enough to buy Christmas presents for his family, like the kids who were selling crafts.

The tour only included certain rooms in the castle, the kennels, the stables, and the gardens. The reenactment of the fight scene in the great hall had been a great success, and Calla was glad no one had gotten close to knocking over the Christmas tree.

Calla and Guthrie were in charge of all the events overall, and Calla thought everything was going splendidly. She couldn't thank Ian enough for allowing the fair and Guthrie for making her an equal partner in the venture.

Calla noted that Guthrie was also taking part in some of the activities—and looking like he was having just as much fun. She observed him giving lessons to a lad who was taking a shot at archery.

She smiled to see Guthrie offer encouragement to the boy, who looked to be about preteen, but when Guthrie caught her eye, she felt her cheeks flush. He motioned her over when the boy had finished his five chances at archery. Guthrie didn't have any other takers at the moment, though Cearnach was helping a lad of about ten or so take aim at another target nearby.

Calla joined Guthrie but hesitated to take the bow. "I've never used a bow before."

He raised his brows in challenge.

"Oh, all right," she said under her breath. How bad could she be? *No worse than at quoits*, she suspected.

Guthrie moved in closer to her, not like the way he'd shown the lad how to shoot. First, he said, "We have to determine which of your eyes is dominant. Make a triangle with your thumbs and two index fingers. Hold your arms straight out and look at the target in the distance through the triangle. Then bring the triangle back to your face. Whichever eye your triangle frames is your dominant eye."

He watched her as she brought the triangle partly over her nose and it veered off a little more to her left eye. He smiled.

"Did I do it wrong?"

"Nay, your left eye is more dominant." He handed her a bow. Standing behind her, Guthrie placed her right hand on the bow, his touch warm, inviting, and not in the least bit teacher-like. His face was so close to hers that he looked like he wanted to give her a kiss along with the lesson on archery. His mouth curved up again, sexy, hot, and interested. "I told you it's hard to see you as just another pretty lass."

Smiling, she shook her head. "Keep saying such things and you might just change my mind."

"You mean to mate with me, aye?"

She rewarded him with a smile, but nothing more.

"I won't give up trying." He kissed her ear, then slipped his leg between hers and guided her left foot over so that her feet were shoulder width apart. Somehow she didn't think he would do that with anyone else he was instructing, either. He placed her right hand on the bowstring. "Now, pull back." She did, and then he said, "You want to use your back muscles, not your shoulder muscles. Your shoulder should be low and relaxed." He ran his hand over her shoulder and down her arm to her elbow. "Your elbow should bend a wee bit, so that it's not locked in place."

She was trying not to chuckle at the way he was touching her. She just hoped that anyone watching saw her trying to concentrate on his instruction—and not the way his touch was turning her on.

"Now it's time to nock an arrow," he said.

He helped her nock the arrow on the string and prepare to shoot with one finger above the nock point and two fingers below.

"You want to shoot with just your fingertips on the string. Extend the bow arm out in front of you, and draw back with your right hand. Bring the string all the way back to the corner of your mouth, and release. Your fingers should roll quickly out of the way of the bowstring to keep it from influencing the flight of the arrow. And then you release."

She said softly to him, "You don't teach everyone to shoot this way."

"Nay, only a very special student."

"I don't think I can hit anything with you being so close." Guthrie chuckled.

"I'm serious.

"Aye." But he stayed beside her. "I haven't been close to you all day, and you have no idea how hard that's been."

She laughed. "You've been busy."

"Watching out for you, aye." Then he continued the

lesson. "Some like to release their breath and then shoot. Some close one eye. Others prefer to keep both eyes open. It might take a few tries to adjust for the wind and learn to sight the target properly. Okay, let's get ready to do this." He helped her pull the string back, his fingers on the tips of hers.

"Ready. Release."

She let go of the string and watched as the wind carried her arrow to the right of the target. The lad had at least hit the edge on two of his tries.

"Good," Guthrie said, as if he really meant it.

"Guthrie, I missed the target completely."

"Aye, but you have never done this before, right?"

"Nay, never."

"Aye, so it takes practice. When you shoot the next arrow, you'll be able to adjust your aim and better compensate for the wind."

She let out her breath. "Aye." She'd love to do this when Guthrie wasn't watching her. That was a first, since she normally wouldn't have cared. Yet with him, she didn't want to look like a failure. Not that she was easily discouraged.

She tried again, only without his help. She wasn't sure what she did, but the next thing she knew, the arrow fell at her feet. Overheated with embarrassment, she picked up her arrow and tried again. This time, she *way* overcompensated and came closer to hitting the target to the left of hers.

Cearnach and his archery student glanced at her and grinned. "I liked your target better," she said to them, though her arrow was a foot away from hitting their target.

"Next one will be a perfect shot," Guthrie told her.

To her chagrin, Cearnach and his charge both waited to see how far off she was this time. She released her arrow and it nicked the top of her target. Cearnach and the boy clapped.

She felt her skin warm considerably with mortification.

Guthrie smiled. "You did it!"

"It didn't even stick to the target."

He laughed. "Aye, but if you aimed a wee bit lower, it would have hit the bull's-eye."

That made her think of him hitting the bull's-eye with her—making her come apart under his exquisite touch.

"I'll give you private lessons later," he whispered in her ear, his lips brushing a kiss there.

She didn't believe he was talking about archery. "Who removed my gown last night?"

"Ah, lass, everyone had gone to bed already, and I didn't think you wanted wrinkles in your gown."

"So you did."

"Aye. I would have given you a foot rub, if you had awakened."

"Hmm," she said. "Next time we go dancing, I'll take you up on it."

"You've got it."

He glanced behind them as footfalls approached. "Seems I've got a lineup of lassies wanting lessons."

Four ladies about her age were smiling brightly at him. "Ah, so I see. Thanks for the lesson. Have fun." Calla smiled sweetly at him, trying not to show her jealousy. When did she begin to feel so possessive of him?

She handed him the bow and stalked off to a food

booth. She had not even made it halfway there when Guthrie caught up with her. She glanced back to see that Oran had taken his place at the archery range. "Too many lasses to handle?"

"I was only interested in teaching you how to ply a bow and arrow," Guthrie said. "Only…you."

—⁂—

After all the guests had left and the MacNeills had finished the meal that night, several of the pack members gathered around the den in front of a fire.

"I would like to propose a toast," Julia said, "to thank Calla for her brilliant idea and for helping change Ian's mind about opening the castle and estates to outsiders."

"I thought it all turned out really well, but everyone in the pack has to take credit. Everyone did a marvelous job and I think we all had fun," Calla said.

Julia took a seat next to her. "Guthrie is upstairs in his office, figuring out how much money was made. Ian's with him. He has asked if you and Guthrie could be in charge of this again next year."

Before Calla could respond, Heather added, "I've never had so much fun in my life."

Aunt Agnes agreed. "With more time to plan next year, we could have the children put on a puppet play, and we would have time to make more crafts."

"I'd love to offer cards made with dried flowers, if I'd had more time," Shelley said.

"Cook told us she'd prepare more food." Elaine motioned in the direction of the kitchen. "She and her assistants are in the kitchen now making food for tomorrow. She said their cakes and scones sold out quickly."

The rest of the conversation centered on the day's activities—what worked and what could be improved— and Calla hadn't heard of any trouble all day long. Best of all, Baird and his wolf pack had stayed away.

Ian joined them in the den with Guthrie. "After all sales less expenses were calculated, we made more than twenty-five thousand pounds to be put toward a college fund for the older teens," Ian announced, sounding as proud as he could be.

Everyone clapped and cheered.

"Both our own people and numerous guests asked me throughout the day if we could do this as an annual Christmas event," Ian continued. "As you know, I'm not happy with having humans invading the castle at any time, particularly when we have wolves who are more newly turned and some children who are not good at keeping their shifting urges in abeyance around humans."

Everyone looked expectantly at him.

"But, as successful as it was, and as much as everyone wanted to do this again next year, we will."

Everyone agreed.

Ian looked directly at Calla and said, "*If* you agree to help organize it. Guthrie said he couldn't do it without you."

"Of course," she said, smiling. It would cut into the time she spent working on her own engagements, but as successful as this one was, everyone would do something similar next year, and she wouldn't need to spend quite so much time on it. And maybe she could pass out business cards to potential clients who would like her to help set up such events for them.

"All right, if that's it, we will have a busy day tomorrow," Ian said, taking Julia's hand and saying their good nights.

Most said their good nights after that and headed off to bed. Heather yawned, stretched, and smiled at Calla. "I'm so glad you're staying with us. Never in a million years would Ian have agreed to anything like this if you hadn't suggested it. We'll have more time to advertise next year, and it'll be even better."

"I thought it was truly wonderful," Calla said. "I'm certain news of the fair will spread by word of mouth. When people start sharing pictures on all the networking sites, that will help to get the word out too."

"Aye, I agree." Heather glanced at Guthrie. "Well, good night. Have to get my beauty rest to give tours again tomorrow. At least Flynn's ghostly spirit didn't bother anyone. Maybe he realizes how important this is to the clan."

Heather took her leave.

Now just Guthrie and Calla were sitting in front of the glowing fire. Calla was tired, but she felt relaxed and happy to be here and didn't want to retire to bed just yet. In silence, she watched the flames flickering. She assumed Guthrie was as well. Until she cast a glance in his direction and saw him watching her.

She suddenly felt as though she was sitting way too close to the fire.

He moved to the love seat and sat beside her, heating her all the more. Because of the small size of the love seat, his hip and thigh were pressed against hers, but he didn't make any move to act more intimately.

"I have you to thank for making it all happen," he said.

"It was your class that gave me the idea."

"The one that you taught?" he asked, sounding thoroughly amused.

"Aye, but it gave me the notion."

"I think you should teach more of my classes if that gives you such great ideas."

"Then you would be out of a job."

"I think we need to teach them together," he said, a brow raised.

She thought he was talking about a mating. She wasn't ready to go there.

She laid her head on his shoulder and wrapped his arm around her. "We can't keep doing this, you know," he said very seriously.

"What's that?"

"Keeping everybody in suspense. Everyone is waiting for the big day."

She raised her head and looked at him, wondering if he meant the Christmas celebration.

"Us. A mating. I think they're dying with anticipation as much as I am."

She laughed.

Chapter 15

THE NEXT DAY, IAN PULLED MORE MEN AWAY FROM other duties to watch for McKinleys. If Baird was going to try to see Calla, this was the last day the castle and its properties would be open to outsiders. It was easy to lose track of people when so many of the pack members were busy, and the crowds were even thicker today. Calla suspected it had to do with everyone showing off the fun they'd had at the castle the day before on blogs and other networking sites.

She noticed that Guthrie was more watchful of the visitors today, and more watchful of her. A time or two, a man had caught his eye, and Guthrie had lost sight of her as she helped some kids with crafts.

After hours of working, she finally had to go to the bathroom. No way was she using one of the port-o-potties meant for the public outside the castle walls, so Aunt Agnes—who insisted everyone call her that, not just her nephews—told her to go inside. Calla figured she didn't need to tell Guthrie personally. She needed a little privacy, after all.

Guthrie saw Calla headed to the keep and watched her progress as he joined his aunt.

"She went to use the bathroom, Guthrie," his aunt said before he could question her. "Och, for heaven's sake, leave the poor lass alone for a few minutes."

Guthrie saw Logan, phone to his ear, speaking

quickly and running toward him. The boy should have been with the dogs, but he was ashen and frowning.

"Had to go to the bathroom. Saw Baird come in through the servants' gate. I didn't have a weapon to stop him. I tried to get hold of Ian, but then I saw you," Logan hurried to say.

"Where'd he go? Baird? Where'd Baird go?" Guthrie was already running toward the keep, his heart racing.

"Inside the keep."

"Damn him."

"Aye." Logan glanced back as they heard someone running to catch up to them. "Your brothers and Oran are coming."

Guthrie would kill Baird if he harmed Calla in any way.

———

Calla had just washed up in her bathroom when she heard the lock to her bedroom door snick closed. She frowned. Guthrie couldn't have come to see her. Not with all the activities going on. Not right now.

She opened the bathroom door and saw Baird standing by her bed.

"What are you doing here?" she asked, her heart drumming against her ribs. *How in the world had he gotten in?* Her skin felt chilled. She hoped now that Guthrie *would* come to check on her.

"My life isn't worth living if you don't come back to me, Calla," Baird said, truly sounding like he was pleading.

She couldn't believe it. He was either the greatest play actor there was, or on some level, he truly believed what he'd said. Neither made any sense.

"You need to leave right this very minute." She

hoped she could talk him out of this madness. "If Ian and his people find you here…"

"You don't understand. I can't leave until you agree to be my mate. Stay here if you like and plan the MacNeills' Christmas party…but please come back to me. Just say you'll be mine."

Please? She'd never seen him behave in such a way. Groveling. If his pack members saw their leader begging before her, she figured they'd kick him out of the pack.

"Baird, you have to leave. I don't know what your game is, but Ian and his men—"

She heard the men running toward the door. Her heart was already pounding hard. Baird didn't even look away from her. He had to be crazy!

Guthrie shouted at the door, yanking and banging on it, sounding as though he was ready to break it down, but the door was solid oak. They would need a battering ram.

"Open the door, Baird. We'll allow you safe passage if you leave in peace," Ian said, his voice commanding.

"Calla, are you all right?" Guthrie shouted.

"Aye, Guthrie. I am." She begged Baird, "Please, do as Ian asks. They'll honor their words." Baird ignored them completely, a wild look in his eyes that scared her. She was afraid he planned to hurt her if he didn't get his way. She didn't see that he was armed. He'd probably figured that if the MacNeill men caught him with weapons, it would go worse for him. But he could still hurt her with his bare hands.

She assumed that talking him down wasn't going to work. The problem with wolves was that they watched a person's slightest body movements—eyes, muscles twitching, changes in stance, mouth—and could assess what someone was about to do. So as soon as she tried to slip into the bathroom and slam the door closed, he was there in a heartbeat, his hand shoved against the door, his foot in place before she'd managed to get the door closed. He hit the door so hard that she jumped back to avoid it striking her.

Immediately, she began tugging off her sweater and kicking off her boots. But she only managed to get that far before he crossed the floor and grabbed for her. "Nay, damn it, Calla. I don't want to hurt you. But I will if you attempt to shift."

She was still wearing her long skirt and bra. The skirt would hamper her wolf's hind legs, but nothing would obstruct her bite. She figured that if she shifted, he'd have no other choice but to back off and give up.

Unless he shifted too.

At least that was the plan, right before he slammed his fist into her temple.

Oran had run to get the master key to Calla's bedchamber while Guthrie and his brothers listened, trying to figure out a plan.

Ian tried to call Baird on his cell phone. Baird ignored the ringing, but now they knew he had the phone on him.

Calla and Baird weren't talking or fighting any longer, and that had Guthrie worried.

"He wants her," Ian said, trying to reassure him. "He's not going to jeopardize that by hurting her."

"I don't believe it," Guthrie said. "Baird had to be desperate to come here like this and get stuck in such a dangerous predicament. There's no telling what he meant to do."

Oran raced down the hallway with a set of keys jangling. Ian tried the master key on the door and unlocked it, but the door was bolted. There was no budging it.

"Get a couple of axes," Guthrie said to Oran, who ran off to get them. "Baird, open the damned door!" Guthrie turned to Ian. "It's too quiet in there. What if he forced her out the window?"

"Bloody hell," Ian said, and called someone on his cell as he motioned for Duncan and Cearnach to go around the back side of the keep where her window looked out over the gardens. "Jasper, get some men to Calla's guest-room window *pronto*. Baird might be escaping from her room that way."

Guthrie prayed that Baird wasn't taking Calla with him that way. Fear consumed him. Everything was too quiet.

Then they heard movement in the bedroom.

"Calla!" Guthrie shouted, his skin sweating with worry.

"I'm coming," she said, sounding weak, as if she was in pain.

Guthrie growled, wanting to kill Baird in the worst way.

Ian called Cearnach. "Calla's coming to the door. Baird must have left." Then he made another call. "Oran, forget the axes. Calla's opening the door."

The bolt slid open and Guthrie pushed the door slowly, not wanting to hit Calla with it and worried that Baird had injured her.

She was sitting on the bed, holding the side of her head and dressed only in a bra and her skirt. He helped her to lie down and covered her with a blanket, while Ian stalked to the open window and shouted down to someone below, "Baird's not up here."

Cearnach shouted, "Not here, either."

"Gather men together to check all the grounds," Ian said.

Logan kept cursing himself for his mistake. It wasn't his job to guard the back gate, and he didn't know whose job it was, but if he'd been wearing a sword, he would have stopped Baird from going after Calla. He didn't know what else he could do once he saw Cearnach and Duncan headed for her back window and Oran returning to the keep with two axes. Logan was supposed to go back to the dogs, but he couldn't until he knew Calla was all right.

What if Baird had already escaped?

Logan hid next to the tower that he was fairly certain Baird would hurry past if he managed to escape Calla's room. Seeing no movement in the woods, Logan stripped out of his clothes, then shifted. His heart thundering, he stayed out of sight on the other side of the corner tower. His ears pricked in the direction of running footfalls headed out the back gate. He saw Baird bolt for the woods, but he waited. Once Baird disappeared into the trees, Logan took off after him. Baird continued racing through the woods so Logan followed, making sure Baird didn't catch sight of him. Baird didn't look like he was armed, but knowing him, some of his kin would be nearby, and they could be well armed or in their wolf coats.

Logan had stopped, hidden in the fir trees and watching, when he heard other men hurry to join Baird—one older brother, one younger, and one cousin. The cousin, Robert, said, "If we don't get Calla back, we're all dead men."

"Tell me something I don't know," Baird said. "What the hell do you think I've been doing?"

His brother Vardon said, "We should have grabbed her when we were at her home. You had the perfect opportunity."

Baird gave him a dirty look and stalked off, the men following.

"Trying to grab her when she had nearly reached Argent Castle was too late," Robert said. "Hell, we nearly had a damned wolf fight over it."

Logan heard the slightest movement behind him and jerked his head around. Guthrie, in his wolf coat. He'd nearly given Logan a heart attack.

Guthrie narrowed his eyes at Logan, telling him he shouldn't be out here like this. But there were four men, and if they attacked Guthrie, he would need Logan to even up the sides.

Guthrie turned his head to listen to the conversation. He wanted Logan to return to the keep at once, but he didn't want to alert the McKinleys that he and Logan were listening as the men stalked through the woods, heading for the road where they must have left their vehicle. They were moving fast, undoubtedly afraid the MacNeills would give chase, but they wouldn't. They still had the fair visitors to watch out for, and they had to ensure that no more of Baird's men had slipped inside the castle walls.

"Hell, he's still sweet on her," Vardon said. "Still trying to smooth things over with her. When are you going to figure out that's not going to work?"

"I want her to be my mate, damn it! Someone who would love me like she did until the bunch of you screwed things up when you went after Cearnach," Baird said.

"*You* gave us the go-ahead. No way in hell would we have gone against your orders. You were in agreement all along *until* Calla learned of what we'd done and dumped your arse," Vardon said.

Guthrie didn't hear either the other brother or the cousin agree. Seemed like Vardon was the only one who could say what he did to the pack leader and get away with it.

Guthrie wondered what they meant that they had been at her place. She wasn't supposed to have been alone at any time. He thought she had dropped her parents off at the airport and gone straight to Argent Castle. She hadn't said a thing about what had happened between Baird and her before Guthrie and his kin rescued her from the McKinleys in the blizzard.

And the business of them worrying that if they didn't get Calla back they were dead men? What the hell was that all about? It explained why Baird was so eager to drag her back to the pack, beyond personal obsession, but why? Guthrie was afraid that the more desperate the men became, the worse it would be for Calla.

The men didn't say anything more on the way back to their vehicle. When the car drove off, Guthrie and Logan loped back to the castle.

After shifting and dressing, Guthrie returned to Calla's guest room.

Ian was standing guard over Calla, who was covered in a couple blankets and looking sleepy.

"Aunt Agatha came up to see to Calla, and the doctor will be here any minute," Ian said and added, "Are you all right, lass?"

"Aye. He just knocked me out and escaped before I could turn into the wolf. He didn't want me biting him, which under the circumstances, I would have done if I'd been able to shift."

Ian's cell rang, and he excused himself and stepped into the hallway.

"What did he say to you?" Guthrie asked, still puzzling over the conversation the men had in the woods. Though they'd heard some of the shouting going on in the room before this, some of it was so absurd that he wanted to hear her take on it. He stroked her soft hair, still furious with the way Baird had injured her.

"The usual. He wants me back. But it has me worried. This is how a desperate man would act. I swear he was actually pleading for me to go with him. I've never seen him act like he was truly afraid of what would happen if I didn't agree."

Guthrie shook his head.

She closed her eyes.

"Nay, stay awake, Calla. The doctor will check you over, but we have to be sure you're all right."

"I'm fine. I have a roaring headache, but I'm fine otherwise."

"Why would he want you so desperately that he would risk his life coming here to convince you to go with him? It was madness for him to do this," Guthrie said. "I overheard Robert McKinley saying that they were dead men if they didn't get you back."

Her eyes widened. "You went after him? Alone?"

"Logan was with me. I saw Logan racing to reach the woods and figured he was chasing after Baird on his own. I had to go after him so he didn't get himself killed. Baird met up with his men, three of them, and we listened in on them. They were all anxious and headed through the woods to their car. They didn't know Logan and I were following them."

"He said his life wasn't worth living if I didn't go back to him. But it sounds like more than just Baird's life is at stake," Calla said.

"Baird's brother Vardon was really chewing him out. Sounds to me like their pack is rethinking having chosen Baird to be their leader. That could make a man desperate enough to pull something as stupid as this," Guthrie agreed.

Ian stepped back into the room and asked Calla, "Is there anything else you can remember?"

"Just…well, it seemed kind of odd. He said that he didn't mind if I stayed here through the time I'd planned, if I'd just agree to be his mate."

"Hell," Guthrie said. "I can't imagine him ever making such a concession for you."

Ian agreed. "He's desperate all right. From what both of you have said, it seems like a pack-driven concern. There must be more to it."

Aunt Agatha quickly entered the room. "I hope you're going to talk to Logan. He's telling the other lads he tracked the men down until you arrived, Guthrie."

"Great. If you're all right…" Ian said to Calla.

"Aye, I'm fine. Go talk to the boys."

"If the men don't kill Baird, I will," Aunt Agnes said, slapping a wet cloth in Guthrie's hand. "Take care of her." Then she winked at Calla and left the room.

They all watched Aunt Agnes make a hasty retreat, no one saying a word. Calla guided Guthrie's hand to her temple where the injury still throbbed. "Cold compress on head injury," she said.

"Aye," Guthrie said and gently laid the compress on her head.

Ian said, "I'm going to check with our men, learn who was supposed to be at the back gate and how Baird got in, and talk to the lads. I don't want them thinking they can just run off and do this kind of thing again."

Calla looked relieved when Ian left. Guthrie squeezed her hand, but when she started to close her eyes, he reminded her, "Nay, lass. Keep your eyes open."

She made a face at him and he smiled.

"Vardon said they should have grabbed you when you were at your home. You never mentioned that when we came to rescue you from them in the blizzard."

"I was supposed to drop my parents off at the airport and come straight here. My dad had his times way off. I was in a rush to get them to the airport and had no time to finish packing to come here straight from the airport. My dad is never rattled like that."

"Baird is *not* forcing you to return to him," Guthrie said, taking her hand and kissing her cheek.

She smiled a little at him. "Tell me something that I *don't* know."

Later that day after Calla had napped, she smiled to see Guthrie sitting in one of the chairs in her guest room, watching her.

"You haven't been there *all* this time, have you?"

"Aye. As your soon-to-be mate, I'm protecting you."

She smiled. Her head was still tender, but she felt much better, her *lupus garou* genetics kicking in to heal the mild injury more rapidly than a human's could. "So what happened while I was sleeping?"

Guthrie came to sit on the bed next to her. "Logan was upset that he wasn't able to stop Baird before he got to the keep and injured you, so he waited in his wolf form, watching the back gate and lingering there in case Baird managed to escape."

"None of the humans saw him shift or wearing his wolf coat, did they?"

"Nay. Ian spoke with him and told him how dangerous that could have been, both if any of our visitors had seen him and if Baird had confronted him. Even though Logan insisted he had bigger teeth than Baird at the time, so he would have been fine."

"Yeah, but there were more than one of them. He should have known that. They could have seen Logan. Killed him. He's just lucky you followed him."

"Aye. The kid's a good tracker, though. He stayed out of sight and downwind of them. But Ian counseled him soundly—and the other boys also because they were eating Logan's story up."

She frowned at Guthrie. "What could Baird and the others with him have done that they need me back so badly?"

"We don't know. His brother Vardon said they should never have listened to this scheme of Baird's. We just have to figure out what scheme that is."

Chapter 16

At dinnertime, Guthrie had asked if Calla wanted to eat in her room, but she declined. She wasn't really even hungry, but she wanted everyone to know she was fine. She took her place beside Guthrie in the great hall, beginning to feel like that truly was her place, as many times as she'd sat there now. Many of the pack members came to wish her well and apologized for not taking better care to see that Baird was stopped, word having quickly spread throughout the pack. She was trying really hard not tear up at all the kindness they'd shown her.

Guthrie was talking to Duncan about one of the sword reenactments, simulating a movie scene, when her phone rang.

She glanced at the caller ID. *Baird?* She couldn't believe it. Then again, if he was facing serious backlash from his pack because she had left him, she could understand it to some extent.

Her temple throbbed as if in sympathy. She ignored his call and turned the phone on vibrate. He called again. And again. She couldn't quit thinking about what he'd said—that he couldn't live without her. She had thought he meant he couldn't live without her because he cherished her so much, but the conversation that Logan and Guthrie had heard seemed to imply that Baird and his kin really would be dead without her.

No matter what he'd done, she wasn't going back to him, ever. He'd dug his own grave.

Still, curiosity overwhelmed her. She hated this. Hated that he wouldn't let her go. When the phone rang again, she leaned over to Guthrie, who was still speaking to his brother, and said, "I've got to take this. Be right back."

He looked up at her questioningly and saw the phone in her hand.

"I've got to take this call. Be a couple of minutes." Then she hurried out of the great hall, noticing that a number of eyes were on her. She stalked through the kitchen to the door that led outside.

As soon as she stepped outside, she realized she should have grabbed a coat. "What do you want, Baird?" she asked, standing in the cold. Maybe if she just talked to him, she could get him to tell her the truth about what was going on with him and his pack. And how that involved her.

"I want you back. I've told you so and I'll keep telling you so."

"You have to be crazy! After you struck me?"

"I didn't want to do that to you, Calla. You know I never would have if I hadn't needed to protect myself."

"You thought I'd—"

"Bite me? The thought crossed my mind when you were stripping out of your clothes and I assumed you had no intention of making love to me." He paused dramatically. "I've been quiet up to now about this, and I didn't want to mention it to you because it's not your fault, but I've run into a bit of a financial problem and—"

"That's why you wanted to marry me?" she asked, furious. So it truly did have nothing to do with wanting her for a mate.

"Nay. That's not all, love," Baird quickly said. "I still want you. But you see, I've got to call in a substantial loan and well, if you came back to me, I wouldn't have to do it."

"So you *do* need my money." She couldn't believe it! "Did you borrow your pack's money without their knowledge? And someone has learned of it, and you're in deep trouble?" A pack leader couldn't just take the pack's savings and do whatever he wanted with them.

"Nay. Hear me out," he said, sounding irritated. "If I call in the loan, I'll have plenty of money. But it's not about that." Again, he hesitated.

"If you don't need my money, I don't understand what this has to do with me." Or his pack wanting him dead.

"Just this, love. If you don't agree to be my mate, I can't hold off on this any longer." He waited for a heartbeat. Then when she didn't respond, he said, "Just don't expect much in the line of Christmas presents from your parents this year." The phone clicked dead in her ear.

Her thoughts were swirling. What did Baird mean by that? Her *parents* had borrowed money from him? Her heart skipping beats, she immediately tried calling her father, but she punched the wrong button in her haste and had to try again.

"Calla?" her dad said.

"Dad, I got a call from Baird. He says he needs to call in a loan he lent to—"

"That *bastard*. He said he'd wait until we could get our finances together."

Her skin chilling with anxiety, she felt her stomach twisting into knots. "Why did you borrow from him? I thought you were doing well." She realized then that over the past year she'd been so busy getting her own business operational, with the move and all, that she hadn't paid attention to how it was going for her parents. They'd always done well with their hotels, so she'd never given it any thought.

"With all the renovations we made to the two hotels, and the economy in such a downswing, we've lost a lot of money. The banks wouldn't loan us any more funds and we have to finish the renovations. You were marrying Baird. I got to talking to him about our financial situation—he was pushing for a fancier wedding than we could afford—and… Well, Calla, I didn't want to say, but Baird paid for the wedding and helped finance the rest of the loan we needed for the hotels. We figured we could pay him back within ten years, since you were marrying him and he would be family. Everything was fine until…"

She let out her frosty breath in the chilly breeze. She was getting too cold and had to go inside. "Until I walked out on him at the wedding."

She felt horrible. She headed back inside the keep, glad to see no one about, and hurried up the stairs to her room, shutting the door behind her. She was so cold. She couldn't shake the chill she felt from having stood out in the wintry weather and the chill she felt from the mess her parents were in. The hotel business was their life, having started with an inn and pub eons ago. They'd been so proud to own a more modern hotel and then expanded to two and had even planned to venture into a couple of bed-and-breakfasts. She felt terrible for them. She would do just about anything to keep them from losing it all—but she *wouldn't* mate Baird.

"It's not your fault, Calla. Baird insisted on the best money could buy for your ceremony. It was a way to show off to the pack how wealthy his in-laws were. He was delighted he could help us out. I have to admit we were thrilled he did too. He said the money came from funds he'd saved separately from the pack's money, so it was his own to do with as he wished. He assured us he knew we could pay it all back to him in time and offered a reasonable interest rate, better than the banks could offer, though we couldn't get any more loans from the bank.

"But when the marriage didn't go through, we were afraid he'd try to use the loan as leverage to get you to return to him. We'd rather lose everything we own than see you mated to him. We had to use our own investments to pay for what we have already done. The manor house is mortgaged to the hilt. Cost overruns and lost profits made the burden more than we could handle."

"I think he must have used the pack's money without permission."

"*What?*" Her father sounded as shocked as she was that her parents had borrowed from Baird.

"Guthrie overheard Baird's cousin saying he believes that the pack is going to kill them over something. What else could it be about? Baird said if I went back to him, he wouldn't have to repay the loan because my business's income would be added to their pack's finances, and the money you owe and all your properties would all be under their jurisdiction. But without my mating Baird, the pack wouldn't get my income and you could possibly default on the loan, meaning it's not a good financial investment for them."

"Bloody hell. He lied to us then."

"Most likely." She let out her breath. "I'm not going back to him, no matter the mess he's gotten himself into. How much money did you borrow?"

"A half million."

She about had a stroke.

"We thought business would pick up after the renovations, but we have to finish off what we started."

A half million?

"All right. I've got some money saved, and I'll see if I can take out a loan based on my earnings. I doubt I can take out that much, though. What if we sold the carriage house? I could move back in with you and Mum at the manor house."

"He wants it all now, Calla. He's desperate to get you back."

"Because he knows he's running out of time."

Her father didn't say anything.

"I'm…courting Guthrie MacNeill. That's one reason Baird is running out of time for me to agree to mate him. If he was truly afraid his wolf pack had learned he'd spent their money without their permission, there is that too." She assumed her parents would be upset with her and tell her to wait until she was more over this situation with Baird. In the background, she heard her father tell her mother that she was dating Guthrie.

Silence.

"Dad, are you still there?"

"Calla, this is great news. When can you get married?"

"Dad?" Her father had to be crazy! She could just imagine going downstairs, joining Guthrie, throwing her arms around him and saying, *"Hey, let's get mated because I need to borrow a half-million dollars from you and that's what mates are for, eh?"*

"If you marry Guthrie, his pack would take us in as family and—"

"Dad, nay!"

Silence.

Then she heard her parents conversing in the background and waited.

"We're trying to come up with some money through our relatives here," her father explained.

"In Ireland?" Calla asked.

"It was the last thing we could come up with."

"Why didn't you tell me?" She was certain her distant relatives would want a partial interest in her parents' properties in exchange for a loan.

"We didn't want you feeling it was all your fault or that you were obligated to return to him."

"I have some money, Dad. I could help some." She rubbed her temple, the headache pooling there again. Returning to Baird was not an option. "Okay, so how much were you able to come up with?"

"Thirty thousand. That's it."

"And would our relations have an invested interest in the properties?" she asked.

"No, just payment of the loan and interest as soon as we're able."

She let out her breath. "All right. I'll see what I can do. You should have told me."

"Are you sure that you don't want to mate with Guthrie sooner and—"

"Nay! I'll do something. I'll call you back when I've got some idea of how much money I can get together on short notice. Love you and Mum."

They quickly said their good-byes, and she was getting ready to call her bank and broker when a knock sounded on the door and she nearly jumped out of her skin. She waited for a second, hoping whoever it was hadn't been standing there for some time and heard her talking about the money over the phone. Or anything else, like how she wasn't going back to Baird.

She didn't want to get the MacNeills involved. She didn't want them paying her parents' debts to Baird. They might not even agree to such a thing, as much animosity as they had for Baird's pack. And they might not have the funds to loan her parents the money, either. Or if they did have the money, it was probably all invested—as carefully as Guthrie took care of their finances—just like most of hers was.

She opened the door and found Guthrie standing there, frowning. She felt her whole body warm uncomfortably, worried that he knew what this was all about.

"Baird?" Guthrie asked.

She didn't want Guthrie and his family to know the financial bind her family was in. Some things were just private. If she'd *already* been mated to Guthrie, that would have been different.

"I…was just talking to my parents. Checking on them to see how they were doing on their trip."

"What's wrong, Calla?" He placed his hand on her cheek. "You're ice cold."

"I took the call outside until I realized how cold it was out there without a coat."

He took in a deep breath of her, smelling her anxiousness as a wolf would. He took her hand and led her to the two chairs and table in a corner of the room. Instead of guiding her to one of the chairs, he sat down and pulled her onto his lap. He wrapped his arms around her, warming her.

She didn't need this right now. Wanted it, aye, but she needed to learn if she could find out anything about the money. She felt stiff in his arms, unable to relax.

"Okay, tell me what's going on."

"They asked me to run to the bank and take care of some business for them."

Guthrie looked like he didn't believe that was all there was to it. Not the way she was reacting. She wanted to ask him how long he'd been standing at the door.

"Do you need money?" he asked, coming straight to the point.

"Personal finances aren't something one discusses with just anyone," she said, frowning at him. He *had* listened at the door! Or overheard some of the conversation when he approached. That was the problem with enhanced wolf hearing.

He began stroking her back, trying to get her to relax. "I overheard something about financial difficulty, though I hadn't meant to. Let me help."

"Nay, Guthrie. This isn't any of your business."

"All right. Then do you have enough money to cover the expense?"

"Guthrie, some things are…well, just not discussed."

"But if you need money, I can get it for you—"

"Nay." She got off his lap. "I really need to go into town and see what I can do about this."

"It's that urgent?" he asked, standing.

"Aye, it is."

"It's too late to do anything about it tonight. You'll have to wait until morning."

She was so flustered that she hadn't even realized it was way too late for anything to be open.

He hesitated, then pulled her into his arms and held her tight. She didn't embrace him back, wanting to get this over with as soon as possible and unable to think of anything else. But he didn't seem to care, or maybe he understood she was feeling ultra-distressed. He rubbed her back again, and she looked up at him, fighting damnable tears. How could he be so caring and tender when she was trying her damnedest to keep her mind on business and maintain her family's secret? Should it get out, her family's business and their home would be lost.

"You can always talk to me about anything," he said, then kissed her lips gently, a no-pressure kind of kiss.

That made her swallow hard as she nodded and pulled away.

"I could sell my carriage house and move into my parents' manor house…"

"It seems a shame to split up your parents' estate. What if you leased it out? Or used it as a bed-and-breakfast?"

"My parents were looking into having one. Their estate is near the lake, and the mountains are close by for hiking and climbing. A river for boating. Aye, it could work. And the income from that could help to pay off their debt." She hadn't realized her mistake until she'd said it. She hadn't meant to tell Guthrie this had all to do with her parents.

"It could. We need to settle this little bit of business between us first, though."

"I don't want you to feel pressured into making any decisions about us right now. You and your family have done so much for me already, and—"

"Calla, this is not about saving your parents from a bad debt. Your family has been friends with ours forever. We would help out as much as we can anyway—especially considering what must be at stake. Protecting you from Baird was something we would never have given another thought." He took a deep breath and took her hand and kissed it, his gaze focused on hers. "I would have you for my mate, Calla Stewart, if you will have me. If you're not ready for marriage, then we'll wait. Though it could possibly kill me."

"What about your family? How will they view this?"

"Lass, if we didn't mate, my brothers, and possibly my mother, *would* kill me. I'm sure my Aunt Agnes would. And there are my brothers' mates and my cousin Heather. I can't tell you how long that list goes. Getting Ian to capitulate to have the festivities at the castle was enough to make everyone love you. Me, most of all."

She smiled a little.

"What about *your* parents?" he asked.

She felt her face flush with heat. Guthrie smiled. She didn't want to tell him that her parents wished her to marry him—afraid he would believe it was all about wanting the MacNeill clan to help pay their debts. And her parents weren't like that. Not normally. They'd want the best for her, and they knew the MacNeill pack was a good family-oriented pack to belong to. But Calla had to tell him the truth.

She toyed with the buttons on Guthrie's shirt. Then let out her breath. "They already suggested I marry you."

His eyes sparkled with delight. "Why didn't you say so?"

"Because...because it sounded too much like they wanted me to marry you just so they would have your clan's financial backing."

"Lass, the only thing that is truly important is how *we* feel about each other." He stroked her hair.

She loved it when he did that. "I think you know how I feel about us," she said softly against Guthrie's ear. "I just wanted to make sure neither of us was getting too involved too soon, but...I do love you."

"And I you," he said, but the way he was smiling at her made her believe he'd known how she felt all along.

"My parents won't be home for a while longer so we can't have a wedding—a very *simple* wedding—until then, but in the meantime..."

He smiled a little, waiting, expectant, eager.

"I...see no reason to wait—for a mating. If this is what you truly want."

"Hell, yeah, Calla. Haven't I been hinting at that for some time now?"

Chapter 17

CALLA'S WARM BREATH AGAINST GUTHRIE'S EAR MADE his whole body heat with interest. And the way her silky hair felt threaded through his fingers, and the way she was so lovingly pressed against his body.

He smiled at her, suspecting his expression was wolfishly hungry looking, the way he felt. Weddings weren't exactly necessary for *lupus garous*. Once they had consummated sex, they were mated for life, just like their wolf cousins. But because of titles or transfers of properties down family lines for wolves that didn't have a pack, some were having human weddings. Once they mated, they were happily committed forever.

"Would it be clichéd to say that you've made me the happiest wolf in the world?" he asked.

"I love you," she said with sincerity and a smile.

He suspected Baird would want to kill him if he knew how quickly Guthrie and Calla had found compatibility and the need and want to mate. No holding back for a yearlong wait. They were perfect for each other. Oh, aye, they would have issues as all couples did, but he knew they were right for one another.

She kissed Guthrie on the mouth and he was so ready for this. She was just too appealing. His hand slipped under her hair, and he leaned down and kissed her deeply, passionately, no holding back.

She broke free from the kiss, her heart beating a

million miles a minute, her breath ragged. "We'll wait to tell anyone we're mated, aye?"

He doubted they could put on a charade for very long in front of his people without them suspecting as much. Hell, if he couldn't hide how he'd felt when his last girl-friend left him, he certainly couldn't hide how he felt about mating Calla.

"For how long, Calla?"

"Until we resolve the financial situation? I...I don't want the pack to think this is all about money and our mating isn't really about what we wanted," she said, looking worried again.

"As close as we've been to each other? No one would think that."

"Aye, but..."

"Calla..." As much as Guthrie wanted to tell every-one that they were finally mated, he didn't want Calla to have any reservations about it. "It's fine with me if we wait to let everyone know until we've cleared up the financial dilemma. Though I have to warn you that when I go skipping into the great hall for breakfast tomorrow, the clan will know something is up."

She laughed and began kissing him all over again—with passion, craving, and lustful need. That fed into his just as quickly. He hadn't realized how much this would change him. The concern over her financial position melted away, when normally he would have been chomping at the bit to get the problem resolved as quickly as possible.

But Calla—she made all the difference in the world to him. He knew then without a doubt that the she-wolf was the right one for him. Someone who could make him step away from his fascination with the world of numbers and enjoy something a million times more pleasurable. Someone he could love and cherish, protect and play with. Next time they got into a snowball fight? He was taking her down. Forget snowballs. He was tackling her in front of everyone.

He wanted the closeness, the way her belly was pressed against his groin, making him crave her all the more. Their touching heated his blood, sizzling, luring. Her heart raced with rabid expectation. And the beat of his heart kept pace with hers. His breathing was just as uncontrolled as he licked her soft mouth and sank his tongue between her parted lips, deepening the kiss.

Then he realized she was frantically trying to reach the buttons on his shirt and unfasten them. That had him pulling away and removing her boots and then his. He slipped her sweater over her head and tossed it aside. He grappled for the button and zipper on her pants, managed to unfasten them, and finally slid them down her legs, but only while he kissed down her thigh and up the other.

"Why did we wait this long?" she said, her voice hushed as she combed her fingers through his hair. He jerked off his shirt and they melded back together, his hands caressing her back until he reached the fastener on her bra and began to unhook it. "Why couldn't we have done this a year ago?" she groaned, rubbing her sexy body against his.

He was having a terrible time unhooking her bra with the way her hot little body was stoking his fire.

"Because we needed to make the other mistakes to learn that what we have here is truly special." The bra came undone. He pulled the straps from her shoulders and tossed it aside. He marveled at her breasts that he had so enjoyed already.

He kissed them each reverently and then, with purpose, devoured the rosy bud on one, caressing the other with his hand. She was so hot, and she was his. She dazzled him. Made him feel like a warrior who had found a maiden to cherish, to love. He growled with a wolf's primal need, then cupped her buttocks and pulled her tighter, her nails raking down his back like a wolf in ecstasy.

He lifted her until her legs were around his hips and then carried her to the bed. She wouldn't let go, and that was fine with him. They ended up on the bed, her legs still wrapped around his hips. His mouth on hers, he kissed, licked, and tasted the wine on her lips, the only thing she had managed to drink.

She hadn't eaten enough at dinner, he remembered. He had every intention of taking her downstairs to raid the kitchen later after everyone had gone to bed.

"You still have your pants on," she complained, tugging at him to take them off.

He was aroused to the nth degree, wanting to be inside her, to slake her need and his as well. He hurried to stand and remove his pants. He swore it had never taken him this long, even when he was in a rush to strip and shift in a moment of danger. She had so thoroughly turned him inside out. As soon as he removed his pants and briefs, he was ready.

She smiled at him.

"And you, lass," he said, his voice unsteady as he ran his hands down her waist, snagged her panties, and pulled them off.

The red curls covering her sex were wet with arousal, telling him that she was just as ready for him as he was for her. He joined her on the bed and began to coax her into climax, his fingers stroking her nub, his tongue stroking hers. Hot satisfaction raced through his blood as she arched and moaned at his rousing touch. He was torn between wanting to bring her to fruition at her own pace and wanting to drive his cock deeply into her—because then the mating would be complete and they would be together, a mated pair always.

Calla was going to die—and she had never thought it would happen like this. Never had any man made her feel this special and loved. As much as she'd been fighting this attraction between them, worried it was too soon, she knew now he was perfect for her. She was so close to the edge, her pulse and his racing as if they were wolves running across a glen. She was so wrapped up in the way he was making her blood sizzle, his strokes undoing her. She tried to continue to knead his muscles, feel the delectable way they moved beneath her touch, and smell the delightful muskiness—hot wolf, man—making her all the more turned on.

And then she felt as though she was racing to the top of the highest peak in the Highlands when she cried out. Guthrie belatedly covered her mouth with his, but it was *way* too late. She was certain everyone in the castle had heard them.

She was still on her sex-filled high when Guthrie eased into her and began to thrust.

This was it. The mating Guthrie kept thinking he'd have, but that had never come to pass. He was so glad it hadn't and that he and Calla were finally together. Being with her like this felt better than right. Her body arched against his as his mouth sought hers, and he penetrated her with his tongue. She moaned and he continued to surge deeply into her, stroking her tongue with his to build the sweet, painful anticipation. He could feel her tensing, her inner muscles clenching, and nearly smiled when she cried out again, his own release following. A feral growl of contentment, satisfaction, and fulfillment slipped from his throat.

She smiled up at him, then nipped at his shoulder. "Everyone in the whole castle heard me."

"Well, not *everyone*. Most likely," Guthrie said.

She frowned up at him.

"Probably most," he said smiling, "but not all. I'm sure *somebody* was fast asleep."

She groaned. He snuggled against her, kissing her cheek and wanting to do this again and again.

"You know you'll have to leave and return to your own bed, or everyone will think we are mated wolves for certain."

"Hmm, all right," he said, sliding the covers over them and then pulling her against him.

"This isn't returning to your bed."

"Aye, I will."

But he didn't. And he had no intention of doing so. And *she* didn't insist.

～〜～

When it was nearly midnight, Calla woke, her stomach grumbling, and that woke Guthrie too. He smiled at her.

"I'm hungry. But…you don't have to go with me."

He sighed. "I told you I would also be hungry after all that loving."

She was glad. Despite knowing how to get there on her own, she really loved his company. He got out of bed and threw on a pair of boxers. She slipped into a tank top and shorts, and pulled on a robe. Hand in hand, they made their way to the kitchen.

They had made chicken sandwiches when they heard light footsteps approach. Calla wanted to slip out a back way, but Guthrie got her a glass of milk and then kissed her cheek and led her to the kitchen table.

Julia walked into the kitchen and smiled. "I'm glad to see you're eating, Calla." Then she proceeded to fix some hot cocoa for herself. "Everything all right?"

"Just…hungry," Guthrie said, and Calla wanted to poke him in the ribs.

She couldn't help feeling so anxious. None of this— the mating or the financial difficulties—had been discussed yet with Ian and Julia, and she was afraid she'd blown the secret about their mating when she'd cried out while they were making love. Not to mention, here it was midnight, and Guthrie was in his boxers and she was in a robe. What was she thinking?

Thankfully, Julia didn't say anything more. She just got her cocoa, smiled broadly, and said cheerfully on her way out, "Good night."

When they had heard her footsteps fade toward the stairway to the bedchambers, Calla let out her breath. "She knows, doesn't she?"

"I didn't even have to skip into the great hall for breakfast."

Calla groaned.

—◌◌◌—

Julia rejoined Ian in bed and he quickly pulled her into his heated embrace. "You are so cold, lass."

"Aye, and you can warm me up."

"So what did you learn?" He kissed her cheek.

She looked up at him, smiling. "I just got some cocoa."

"Aye, after you heard two pairs of footsteps leave Calla's guest chamber."

Julia snuggled against Ian's chest. He was too much of a wary wolf. "I don't know what was bothering Calla at the evening meal, but I suspect it was nothing too terribly bad, or Guthrie would have said something about it to you already. They were eating sandwiches. Which made me think that Calla was okay."

"And?"

"And?" she parroted, teasing Ian, knowing just what he truly wanted to know, just like she had wanted to learn.

"Ah, lass, you can't hide your other reason for checking up on them."

"I went to get a cup of cocoa."

He chuckled and stroked her hair. "*After* you heard them leave Calla's room."

Julia let her breath out. "All right. Yes, they're mated."

"Good."

"You're glad, then?"

"Aye, no more of Guthrie being upset over losing the wrong she-wolf, and this means you'll stop leaving me in the middle of the night to get cocoa. Right?"

"You love warming me up," she reminded him and started kissing him, and he said something about how much he was going to love doing so.

Chapter 18

THE NEXT MORNING, CALLA WAS SLEEPING SOUNDLY—too soundly, after making love half the night with one hot, sexy wolf—when she realized the time. Guthrie's leg was resting across hers, his arm lying on top of her breasts, and there was no moving him.

"We…I've got to go to the bank. I need to shower and get ready." Already, she was feeling blue again about the whole money situation. She wished she could take care of this on her own and not involve the MacNeills.

"Aye, lass." He kissed her lips. "I'll return to my room, shower, and get dressed, then meet you here."

"Maybe we should go down separately."

He chuckled, shook his head, and kissed her forehead. "See you in a minute." His expression told her in no uncertain terms that he was escorting her down to the meal like her mate would. The only difference was that they still had separate bedchambers. But she suspected that would change soon.

She took a deep breath as she went into the bathroom. She just hoped Ian and the rest of Guthrie's kin wouldn't be too upset with Guthrie for taking her as a mate and the financial mess they would be involved in if they attempted to help her and her parents out.

She'd tried so hard to bury the worry last night, wrapping herself up in loving Guthrie and attempting to block out anything else.

She *loved* him. Twice, she'd woken and began to concern herself about the money, and both times, Guthrie had sensed she was awake and fretting. He assured her everything would be fine, that they'd take care of it when the banks were open, and then took her mind off it by making love to her again. And she truly loved him for it.

Now that it was time to have breakfast and afterward meet with her broker, she again wasn't hungry. Seeing Ian, Julia, and the rest of their kin just made her feel guilty, though she swore everyone was smiling even more at them—if that was possible.

And it wasn't *just* the women who were interested. *Everyone* was. She should have known, since Guthrie was so well liked. Then again, it was a pack mentality, and she wasn't used to that. She'd love it, if only she didn't have this financial burden hanging over her head.

"Calla," Guthrie whispered to her, "eat if you can. We'll be fine."

She'd managed two bites of a scone, and then when Ian and Julia left the high table, having finished their meal, Guthrie quickly rose with Calla.

"I've got to get my coat." She hated how choked up she sounded.

She thought he would leave her alone and go talk to Ian about her distress, but he pulled out his cell phone and said, "Ian, Calla needs to make a run to the bank. Can you see who would be up to going with us?"

They headed upstairs to her room, and he waited for her while she retrieved her coat from the closet.

"We have to go to a couple of other places too," she said.

He raised a brow.

"My parents and I are on some of the same accounts." God, if Baird wiped out her parents' funds, he could sue for hers too, since her parents' names were also on her accounts. She could be just as broke as them in a heartbeat. Ruined. When she'd always been so careful with her own savings.

Ethan and Jasper were busy with the cows, so Duncan and Cearnach met Guthrie and Calla downstairs in the foyer. He could tell from his brothers' expressions that they knew something was up, which was why Ian had sent them and not some of their more distant kin.

Guthrie felt sick knowing Calla was dealing with something beyond her control. He guessed she was about ready to collapse in tears, yet she was fighting them, eager to attempt to settle this in her own way. He loved how tough she was, but he still wanted to make Baird pay for everything he'd done to her.

He intended to speak with Ian privately as soon as he could. He needed to know how Ian wished to handle this. Once she was speaking with a broker in private, he would call Ian. Guthrie would have done so while she was getting her coat and purse, but because of the distressed state she was in, he didn't want to leave her alone for even a minute. He wanted to show her that he was her mate and would stand behind her, no matter what.

Money. Blackmail. Whatever Baird was threatening her with, Guthrie would protect her. More than anything, Guthrie had wanted to mate with her and resolve that issue before all else. Together, they could handle anything.

Later that morning, when they arrived at the building where Calla's broker was, they waited for a bit in the lobby. Duncan and Cearnach stood near the door, watching out for trouble, while Guthrie and Calla remained in the waiting area outside the broker's office. She was so anxious that she couldn't sit. He suspected she would have been wringing her hands if he hadn't been holding one of them and telling her she wasn't alone in this.

As soon as the broker asked her into his office, Guthrie pulled out his phone, his brothers joining him.

"What's up?" Cearnach asked.

As second in charge of the pack, Cearnach had every right to know. But Guthrie wasn't leaving Duncan out of this, either. He suspected they were going to have a wolf fight with the McKinley pack over this.

"Calla's in some kind of financial trouble. I suspect it has to do with Baird," Guthrie said.

"Bloody hell," Cearnach said. "I told her not to trust the slimy bastard."

"Aye." Guthrie called Ian and told him what he had overheard, and his brothers stood close, listening and watching the building for any signs of trouble. "She said she talked with her parents and had to take care of some banking business for them. I can't call them at the moment. Can you? See if they can shed some light on this?"

"Aye, will do, Guthrie. Just don't let her out of your sight. We don't want her martyring herself over this. If she needs money, we'll take care of it."

Guthrie loved his brother. The MacNeill wolves couldn't have had a better pack leader. "Aye, I told her I would do so, but she wasn't willing to accept my offer at first."

Ian didn't say anything for a moment.

"Ian, are you still there?"

"So…you're mated?"

Guthrie hesitated. He didn't want to betray Calla's trust, but he didn't want to lie to Ian, either.

"Julia told me she had the impression that you were," Ian offered comfortingly, sensing where Guthrie was coming from and trying to let him off the hook a little.

Guthrie took a deep breath and let it out. "Calla didn't want anyone to know yet. She was afraid the pack would think she mated me so we would bail her parents out of whatever financial woes they're having."

"Congratulations," Ian said, sounding proud of him, and Guthrie was glad he wasn't upset over not having been told before this.

He glanced at his brothers, having forgotten they were listening in on the conversation. They were both grinning from ear to ear and giving him a thumbs-up.

"Well, I'm glad for the two of you. I couldn't be more pleased. But you know how our mother is. So you'd better let her in on the secret sooner than later. How much money is involved in this deal with Calla and her parents?" Ian asked.

"A half million." Guthrie hated to say it.

Ian digested that. Then swore.

Guthrie saw Duncan and Cearnach snap their gaping jaws shut.

"All right. Let me…let me call her parents and see what they know about this. I'll get back to you. Just don't let her out of your sight," Ian said.

"Got it." As if Guthrie had any notion of leaving her alone for a second. He ended the call with his brother and slipped the phone into the pouch on his belt. "Ian's calling her parents."

"Hell, Brother, we all were fairly certain you and Calla would be mating soon, but…did you ask her properly?" Cearnach asked.

Guthrie shook his head. He watched the doorway to the broker's office, wanting to pace but forcing himself to stand in place and keep an eye out for her.

"We'll take care of it," Cearnach said. "You know Ian will want to do everything for her that we can."

Being more pragmatic, Duncan said, "I want to congratulate you and your lovely mate, but I'm in agreement with Cearnach. Couldn't you have told me at breakfast?" Before Guthrie could respond, Duncan asked, "Well, you're our financial manager, Guthrie. Can we do it?"

"It'll take a hell of a lot of finagling. We'll have to sell some of our stock. We'll have to see what her parents say and what Calla has in her piggy bank. Maybe among all of us we can come up with the funds."

Guthrie's phone jingled and he saw it was Ian. "Aye, what did you learn?"

Ian explained all about the loan.

"Bastard," Guthrie said.

"Aye. Guthrie, her mother and father both want you to marry her. They told me they believe you'll be good for her, and they know the MacNeill pack is the kind of wolf family she needs. So looks like you're not in any hot water there."

Despite the severity of the situation, Guthrie smiled. They'd marry when her parents returned. Nothing lavish, just the pack and her parents, most likely. The pack would be poorer again. But the pack members always had each other and pulled together when needed. They would manage somehow.

"You're our financial wizard. They have gathered thirty thousand. See what Calla has, and then let me know if we can put up the rest."

"I will, Ian." Guthrie glanced at the doorway to the broker's office as he heard the doorknob turn.

Calla exited, saw him and his brothers, and headed for them. She looked beaten, not pleased with the news.

"Calla, you can't believe that we'd let you do this on your own, lass," Guthrie said, taking her into his arms. "Ian and Julia run the pack, and they've okayed me using pack funds to help you out. As second-in-command, Cearnach is in total agreement."

Cearnach nodded.

Duncan said, "Me too, if anyone cares."

Guthrie smiled at him. "As financial manager, I'm signing off on it. The rest of the pack will agree that there is no way they're turning you over to the McKinleys, and we'll do what we have to for one of our own."

She looked up at him, a question in her beautiful green eyes as they filled with tears.

She sniffled and swallowed hard and then broke down, tears dribbling down her cheeks as she wrapped her arms around him. "You can't," she said in such a wee pitiful voice that his heart broke for her.

"We can, and we will."

"Do you know how much? You couldn't have enough."

"Somehow, we'll have enough."

"Half a million?" she whispered to him.

He held her close and took in her worried scent, her sweetness and softness, and loved her. "Aye, lass. Somehow we'll manage."

"But, Guthrie, you can't. You could be as destitute as me. You can't do that to your pack for me or my family."

"We would do it for our pack members, lass, whatever it takes. Your father and mother gave me their blessing to wed you. We'll talk about it more later, but we might have to plan something simple."

She gaped at him. Well, he hadn't meant to say so in front of his brothers. He was doing this all wrong. His brothers smiled at him and shook their heads.

"Ian said Julia told him about…you know…that we mated. And my brothers were listening," Guthrie said somewhat hesitantly.

"And we couldn't be happier," Cearnach told her reassuringly.

"About time, by our reckoning," Duncan said, trying to cheer her.

"So there's nothing to worry about," Guthrie said. "We'll take care of it."

Cearnach said, "Guthrie, can you at least get on bended knee for the lass?"

Guthrie frowned at his brother. "In an office building?"

"Don't you dare," she warned Guthrie. Turning on Cearnach, she added, "You, mind your own business."

Calla explained that she had close to two hundred and seventy thousand in stocks that she had her broker sell off to help pay the debt. Calla looked despondent, but Guthrie was impressed. He felt terrible for her that she would have to use her savings and investments to pay off her parents' debt, but her business smarts and quick thinking would help mitigate the loss. She was everything he had always wanted in a mate and more.

Guthrie arranged to sell off the necessary stocks that the MacNeill clan had as well and prepared to pay off her parents' loan. The interest the Stewarts would pay back to the MacNeills was much less than what Baird was charging them, and as long as they could get their hotels back into full operation, her parents should be able to pay off the funds over time.

Calla seemed numb over the whole situation as her parents signed the loan agreement over the Internet. Guthrie squeezed Calla's hand as they returned to the car.

They got into the backseat of the vehicle while Cearnach drove and Duncan sat up front.

"As soon as the money has cleared the bank to pay off Baird's loan, he'll have no more claim to your parents' properties. Once your parents are financially able, they can begin to pay back the monies they borrowed from us."

"And my earnings. I will help—"

"When we get home, I want to discuss our financial situation with you."

Her eyes filled with tears.

"Ahh, lass, only in a good way."

She nodded and he kissed her. "I don't know how I can thank you," Calla said again. "You and your pack."

"Our pack," he said.

Duncan said, "We have you to thank for convincing Ian to open up the castle to bring in so much money. I don't think I've ever seen him so cheerful. Seeing how much our pack enjoyed the activities, he was well pleased."

"I only wish I'd learned you had returned to the area,"

Cearnach said, "and I would have brought you to Argent Castle so you could have done all this a year ago."

When they arrived at the castle, Guthrie took Calla up to his office, wanting to show her the finances, since she would be bringing in income beyond what the others brought in.

"What a lovely office," she said, admiring his large oak desk, the Turkish carpet, and the seating area where he discussed finances with pack members—four brown velour chairs and a couch to match, with a curve-legged oak coffee table in the center.

Some of the ladies had made him gold-embroidered pillows to set on the chairs and couch to give more of a homey appearance. And a couple of throw blankets were neatly folded over the arm of the couch, where he'd taken a wolf nap or two and then continued working late on the finances.

"We have a communal pot to pitch our incomes into. We each have our own savings, but the community money is for the whole of the pack—for the upkeep of our ancestral home, for food, celebrations, and special needs. I want to show you just how we can figure things and bring more money into the accounts."

"Well, my earnings and the rental income from the carriage house should help to pay the loan back," she said, watching as he turned on his computer. "I need to move some of my things out of my home, some I can store at my parents' place. The rest of the furnishings will stay so that it's sufficiently furnished for bed-and-breakfast guests. As to the rest…"

"We'll move your other stuff here. We can do that this afternoon after the meal if you'd like."

"Okay."

He watched to see her response. She was frowning, but he didn't sense distress, only that this was going to be a lot of work. He was eager to get her moved over completely, though he'd forgotten about that part of it. Once they had mated, he'd felt that was all that needed to be done. She was here. That was all that was important.

"Everything's going to be fine." Guthrie pulled up some of his spreadsheets.

"Impressive," Calla said next to his ear, her warm, sweet breath tickling it as she leaned close to observe the charts.

In that instant, he was thinking a lot more about Calla's assets, rather than the finances. He couldn't believe anything would distract him from showing off their books.

"You're so meticulous with your accounts," she said, her breast touching his shoulder.

"Aren't you?" He was thinking about pulling her onto his lap and snuggling with her while they looked over the finances.

"Wait. I'll get my laptop and be right back."

He sighed. He should have just taken her straight back to bed when they returned to Argent Castle. What had he been thinking? "All right. I'll print these out, and we can have a seat over there and look them over."

In a few minutes, Calla was back with her laptop and sitting on the couch. He joined her with his handful of papers. She turned on her laptop and pulled up her financial records.

He smiled. "You're just as meticulous about your records."

He'd suspected she might be since she was able to talk to him about her financial data without having to look up her records.

She started analyzing his stocks and earnings. "Wow, this is great."

"Just as yours are," he said, admiring her—and not just for her financial figures.

"Our combined assets will grow over time and..." She paused when he began brushing her hair with his fingers.

"Aye, our joining of assets will be in both our best interests."

He shoved his papers aside, took her laptop, and set it on the coffee table, then pulled her into his arms. He began kissing her, then remembered the office door. But when he broke off the kiss, he saw that Calla had already shut it. Had she had the same notion as he had?

With the door closed, no one would intrude. When he napped, he always shut the door. Otherwise it was always open to pack members who wanted to discuss their finances with him or kids who needed math tutoring.

She smiled and began to unbutton his shirt. "No worries. I locked it when I returned with my laptop."

"I love when you are thinking the way *I'm* thinking. I love *you*," he said, pulling off her sweater, then yanking off his own. He'd never imagined making love on the sofa where he'd take a quick wolf nap in between figuring out the pack's finances—and with the loveliest she-wolf, who was now his mate.

"I just wanted to say that we are together in anything we do, you know. Even when we are apart. If you ever feel the need to talk to me about anything, if you're ever upset with me, just say so. I don't want anything to ever come between the two of us."

He'd understood her need to protect her parents' reputation and solve the financial crisis on her own, but he never wanted her to feel that she had to do anything like that again. They were a team now.

She smiled up at him with the most devilish look as she reached for his belt. "I'll remind you of this conversation later if you change your mind. It goes both ways, you know."

He grinned at her as he helped her to unbuckle his belt.

"I still don't know for sure—do you or don't you go regimental when you wear your kilt?"

"Ahhh, lass, what do you think?"

She ran her hand over his crotch, his cock straining for release, and he hurried to pull down his pants.

"Regimental. And you, lass, under that long Stewart plaid skirt?"

She smiled wickedly at him.

He smiled back. "Then next time we're wearing our plaids, we'll have to do something about it." He could just envision the two of them like that and wished that after the previous festivities when they had worn them, they would have had the chance to see for themselves. But they hadn't quite come this far at the time, and they had a lifetime together now to experiment all they wanted. The very next kilted occasion…well, he couldn't wait.

He stripped off the rest of her clothes and the rest of his, the room toasty warm. She was bared to him, her strawberry blond hair draped across his sofa, her smooth, soft skin light against the chocolate velvet and gold-embroidered throw, the red thatch of curly hair between her legs begging him for further exploration, her green eyes smiling as she waited for his touch.

She smiled at him and he sighed. "You're beautiful. How could I have ever gotten so lucky?"

"I keep asking myself the same question—about my getting lucky with you, of course."

He chuckled, loving her sense of humor. Then he pulled her legs apart so he could nestle between them and rub his cock against her mound. He smelled the way her pheromones were already stirring, her scent changing from sweetly seductive to hot and enticing. Everything about her was tantalizing—her soft skin, her round breasts, her erect nipples, her tongue-moistened lips open to him. He kissed her, tasting her lips, and licking and nibbling at their sweetness.

She moaned as he rubbed against her feminine folds.

Her legs wrapping around him, she rested her heels against the back of his thighs, her body receptive as she moved against him.

She groaned as he plunged his tongue into her mouth and began stroking her as his cock rubbed between her legs. Feeling her arching against him, as eager to find release as he was, he wanted this to last. She had the most amazing mouth, her tongue just as intriguing as she chased after his, stroking and making him smile. And she smiled right back.

He loved making love to her. He was so glad they hadn't waited any longer than this because the painful obsession he'd had to get close to her like this, to share of himself as she opened herself up to him, had been strangling him. Now, they were one, and he couldn't have been more pleased.

His skin was overheated, all because of one little she-wolf, her hot body making his blood sizzle. He kissed her again, loving her lips beneath his, the power of her kisses nearly making him come. Or maybe it was the way her body rubbed against his cock or her heels pressed against the back of his legs or her fingers combed through his hair.

He thought he would get the chance to stroke her clit, but before he had the opportunity to make her come using his fingers, him rubbing his cock against her made her cry out, and he quickly covered her mouth to kiss her long and hard. A little too late.

He slid inside her and felt her muscles contracting, pushing in all the way and slowly pulling out, then plunging deeper, harder. She felt so good wrapped tightly around him, and he leaned down and suckled a nipple. She groaned and lightly scored his back with her fingernails.

"You are so good," she whispered against his ear as he leaned down to lick her neck.

"Lass," was all he could get out as he plunged into her, over and over. She rocked against him, gripping his hips with her hands now as if afraid he would leave her before she could come again.

He rubbed and thrust until he felt her spasm around his cock. He couldn't hold on and released, letting go of the control, pumping into her, emptying his progeny into her womb, adoring her.

"Damn, woman, how we can go from analyzing finances to hot sex…"

She pulled him down for another kiss. "We just love each other's assets way too much."

Chapter 19

AFTER LUNCH, GUTHRIE HAD TO TALK TO IAN AND Julie about the finances as Calla explained how much she earned and about renting out her place. Other issues came up that afternoon that Guthrie had to deal with and Calla agreed that they would get a fresh start in the morning to move her things. She truly was anxious to get settled permanently at Argent, but Guthrie had the best way of getting rid of her worries, though she hoped no one had noticed that she and he had slipped off to bed so early.

Getting a really late start the next morning, Calla was ready to begin preparing her place to open as a bed-and-breakfast. She was grateful that the MacNeills had helped to pay her parents' loan off, but she wanted to start earning an income from renting her home as quickly as possible so she could repay the loan to the MacNeills and they could reinvest it. She hated owing money, even if technically her parents owed it. They were a family unit, and that was all that mattered.

She was afraid that Guthrie wouldn't want to bother with moving-in details this soon. Baird had not been interested in the details of domestic life—which was why they hadn't discussed her moving in with him. She guessed he'd just assumed she'd take care of it all in due time. But Guthrie?

He was ready to get this done. He actually talked

all about it with her—including what she could change in his bedchamber so she'd be comfortable there. She loved that about him and reminded herself *not* to compare him to Baird again.

"You're not in any hurry, are you?" she asked, smiling as he rushed her down the stairs.

"The sooner we get you moved over here permanently, the sooner you're all mine." He smiled wolfishly at her.

She chuckled. "That sounds *awfully* possessive."

"I just don't want you to feel like you're having to live in between Argent Castle and your carriage house."

She truly loved him; he was being so considerate of her.

"As for my office, we can fix it up so that you have plenty of room for your own desk and files or whatever you need."

"Thanks, I'd love that. On both accounts. You don't mind if I move my frilly pink curtains into the office, do you?"

Smiling, he looked at her with a raised brow.

She chuckled. "Just teasing. By doing this today, we'll be home in plenty of time to rest up before the Christmas party tomorrow." She couldn't wait. She and Julia had sneaked off to plan the whole affair in secret, clueing in some of the ladies, who would help set up the games, and Cook and her assistants, who would prepare the special treats and meal. Calla had gotten the biggest kick out of hearing Ian cajoling Julia to tell him what all they had in store for the party, but she wouldn't say.

Guthrie slipped his arm around her waist and kissed

her forehead. "I can't believe you've left me out of the loop on the Christmas party."

She smiled up at him. "Remember, no swordplay."

He sighed. "I don't plan on us returning from your house after moving your stuff just so we can rest up a whole lot, either. You haven't scheduled the celebration too early, have you?"

"Thankfully, Julia wanted it to be a late-afternoon affair."

"I'm glad for that."

Guthrie asked Ian whom he could spare to help them move her things to her parents' home, while she okayed it with her father over the phone. "Aye, aye, Dad. We're…" She smiled up at Guthrie as he observed her. "Mated."

Her father whooped and hollered, and she envisioned him seizing her mother, embracing her, and twirling her around as she screeched in the background.

"And the wedding?" her father finally asked, his excitement cheering her.

"Nothing elaborate. Just a gathering of families and that's it," she said.

"You still have the wedding gown."

"Of course. The store doesn't take back used wedding gowns."

"Your mum said she'll call Guthrie's mum and talk to her."

"No big wedding, Dad. We can't afford it. Just something simple."

"All right."

"I'm moving in with Guthrie."

"Aye!"

She laughed. "You sound like you're eager to get rid of me."

"Nay, lass. We're so glad you're mated to Guthrie and have a pack to live with."

"Good. I want to move some of my things to your place."

"Anything."

"And I want to rent out my place as a bed-and-breakfast. I was thinking…"

"Way ahead of you there. We'll manage it, and we'll rent out the five extra bedrooms in the manor house. Your mother has wanted to do this forever. She loves to cook—you know how she is. This was just the incentive we needed."

"Good. We're headed over there now, and when you return home, we can see what the MacNeills' schedule looks like and plan a quick wedding."

"Your mum wants to talk to you."

Calla took a deep breath, bracing for the inevitable.

"Calla, oh, Calla, we're so very proud of you," her mother said. "As soon as we end the call, I'm talking to Lady Mae."

"Keep it simple. Nothing extravagant. I mean it." Calla didn't want to hurt her mother's feelings. By *lupus garou* tradition, her parents had never officially been married in a church, though they had legal documents to prove Calla was their only daughter and heir. Still, she knew how much this meant to her mother, that Calla would marry Guthrie in a church.

"Of course, dear. We wouldn't think of anything too costly. Flowers—"

"No flowers. They're too expensive." If it had been summer, Calla would have cut some roses from her garden.

"Oh, all right." Her mother began crying.

"Mum?" Tears sprang into Calla's eyes. She couldn't bear it when her mother cried. "What's wrong?" She didn't believe having no flowers would upset her mother so much.

"I'm just so happy for you," her mother sobbed.

Calla smiled and sniffled. "Me too. I have to go. I'm moving most of what I can today. An ice storm is coming in, so we've got to hurry."

"All right. You take care of that handsome Highlander. I always told you that you should have paid more attention to Cearnach's younger brother."

"Aye, you're right. A mistake I'm rectifying. Love you, Mum. See you soon." Calla ended the call and put her phone in her purse. She'd forgotten how her mother had said she should have gotten together with Guthrie some time or another. Just to see if they would suit because both of them were actually like-minded about finances and, well, a whole lot more. But Calla hadn't had a chance once she returned to the area and Baird had so quickly swept her off her feet.

"Are you okay?" Guthrie asked, helping Calla into her coat.

"Yeah. They're both ecstatic." She wiped her nose with a tissue.

"You had me worried there for a moment."

She smiled up at Guthrie and tugged on his belt. "My mother was overwhelmed with joy and began sobbing."

"Ah, mothers. Got to love them."

She laughed. "Aye."

Duncan, Cearnach, Jasper, Ethan, and Oran all volunteered to help with the move. Ian figured they didn't need any more men than that, and that was probably too many. But they all insisted on going. Heather went along to help Calla pack. The other ladies were mysteriously absent.

The weather was supposed to worsen later in the day, so they left right after breakfast. A heavy mist already cloaked the area with a ghostly white blanket.

When they reached Calla's carriage house, she felt overwhelmed with the idea of packing up everything that she didn't want to leave behind. It seemed like a lot more work once she realized how much paraphernalia she had stuffed in closets, under beds, in drawers, and in cabinets.

Guthrie rubbed her back. "We don't have to do this all in one day, lass. We can take as much time as you need."

"Aye." But she wanted to do this. To get it over and done with as quickly as possible. At least she had only lived here for a year and hadn't accumulated many years' worth of things. Plus, the last time she'd moved, she'd gotten rid of a lot of stuff she didn't need.

She started in the kitchen and began giving orders, thankful everyone was here to help and thinking maybe it wouldn't take too long after all. "All the food needs to go. You can leave it in my parents' fridge and cupboards. The dishes will stay here. I'll go through the rest of this and see if there's anything I want to take. Guthrie, you can box up my clothes. I'll take all of them with us."

"Got it." He took a couple of boxes down to her bedroom. Ethan and Jasper unloaded her fridge and all the food from the cupboards.

She directed Duncan and Cearnach to help pack up all of her financial files and office supplies. She and

Heather went through the rest of the house, collecting keepsakes that Calla would leave at her parents' home for now and taking anything else that renters didn't need for a comfortable stay.

Packing everything up that would go to her parents' house first would take a lot longer than she'd thought. The men figured they'd get it done quicker if all six of them started hauling everything over to her parents' place while Calla and Heather stayed at the carriage house and continued to pack.

The men would leave all the boxes in Calla's old bedroom, knowing that her parents would not rent her room out, and she'd come back and sort out everything later. Some of the boxes were going into a storage unit on the property, and the men would need a little time to put away all the food.

Heather smiled at Calla. "I'm so glad you mated Guthrie. We'll have to have a grand wedding."

"Nay," Calla said. "After what your pack had to do to help my parents and me out, I want something really simple. We can dress up. And that's it. Someone in the pack can take pictures, and our honeymoon will be enjoying family here."

She realized then that she would be spending Christmas with her new family. "Can…can my parents come to the Christmas celebration?"

Heather hugged her. "Aye, of course. They are family now too."

Calla let out her breath. "This is all so new to me."

"You'll get used to it right away. If Guthrie ever gets to be a problem, you just tell me. I'll let his mum know. End of trouble."

Calla laughed.

They both sat down to wrap her fragile decorations—family pictures and other mementos—in paper, then tucked them into a box. It seemed so strange to be packing up her stuff like this and not needing her home any longer. Living in the castle was bound to be more fun, though—seeing everyone and having more people to bounce ideas off—and she really looked forward to another open house with crafts and games and a holiday bazaar like they'd had this year.

Heather smiled at her. "You've made everyone so happy. We all worried about Guthrie after his last breakup. I didn't really care for the woman. But the two of you are just perfect for each other. I've never seen Guthrie so sure of this being the right move to make."

"With the other woman, he thought she was the right one too, didn't he?"

"As far as his ego went, aye. She fell all over him and, well, he thought if the woman adored him that much, they had to be right for each other."

"Then she left him for her old boyfriend."

"Aye, but before that, she started belittling him in front of others. We all like Guthrie. He's a good man. She had no business putting him down like she did. She just made up stuff to complain about."

"I didn't know that," Calla said, shocked. She shook her head.

"Then there you were. He was fighting with himself, trying so hard not to share the same space with you."

"Because of the last girlfriend."

"Aye. But then he couldn't help himself where you were concerned. The two of you have a common interest in finances. Not everyone has a good head for numbers. And…well, any of us who were decorating the tree… When it was suddenly knocked over and Guthrie rescued you and you kissed him for such a gallant deed—we knew where it was headed."

Calla chuckled. She hadn't thought of it in either of those ways. Before she got to know Guthrie, she had assumed he was going to be the Scrooge of the family. She would never have guessed that she would end up planning an event like the holiday bazaar with him. And the kiss? Only an impulsive, exciting, and reckless bit of fun. Or so she'd thought at the time. She'd treasure that special moment with Guthrie forever. She could just imagine some of the MacNeill kin saying to the kids she and Guthrie would have someday, "Did you know that your mum and dad were caught kissing underneath the Christmas tree way before you were born?"

She smiled at the thought and wrapped another picture.

The back door suddenly creaked open. Both Calla and Heather looked in that direction, but they couldn't see who was there, if anyone.

Calla couldn't imagine why anyone was using the back door. The men had all left through the front door, and Guthrie had locked it on the way out. She had some patio furniture out back, but she had no plans to take any of it with her. She was going to leave it there for the prospective guests. Beyond that, trees lined another cobblestone drive that led to the back side of the property.

Concerned, Calla rose to her feet. Just as Baird came into view.

With a soft gasp, Heather jumped up and backed toward the front door.

"Don't move," Baird warned Heather with a threateningly deep voice.

"Go," Calla said to Heather, her voice firm and angry as she continued to stare Baird down. He looked angry, tense, and determined. "This is between Baird and me. Heather has nothing to do with it." Besides, she knew Heather would go for help.

As soon as Heather raced for the door, Baird went after her. Calla jumped him, knocking him against the wall. She held on to him in a tight body hug. He cursed her as he tried to peel her arms and legs off him.

In her panic, Heather struggled to get the door unlocked while Calla fought to keep Baird from going after her. She prayed Heather would manage to get out of the house before Baird could shove Calla aside and reach her. He finally managed to jerk Calla away from him, nearly making her fall. She regained her balance and tackled his whole body again before he managed another couple of steps toward the entryway.

Heather threw open the door and it banged against the wall. She sprinted outside.

Calla felt a tiny bit of relief, but she held on to Baird, afraid he might still be able to catch Heather before she got very far on the driveway. He finally shook loose of Calla, cursing up a storm. She jumped on his back as he headed for the door.

"What do you want? You got your money!" Calla yelled at Baird.

"I wanted *you*, damn it, Calla. Giving your parents that loan was to tie you to me *in the first place*. Your parents were indebted to me. You were always the good little daughter. When you wouldn't agree to come back to me, I had to play that card. To save your family from financial ruin, you were supposed to return, beg me to take you in, and—" he said, struggling to get her off his back, but she held on as if her life depended on it. Which she was afraid it might.

"And then I was supposed to give you my savings? Sell my carriage house and hand you the profits? Turn over my income to you? My savings would have paid for the money you borrowed from your pack. When my parents paid off their debt to you, any repayment of the loan would have been your money and not your pack's. Except for the commission your brothers and cousin would get from the deal. Isn't that right?"

"The money would have been *ours*," he corrected her, still attempting to reach the doorway and stop Heather.

Heather was screaming, yelling, trying to get the men's attention as she ran for the manor house, her boots pounding on the cobblestone driveway.

"Nay. You would have controlled every aspect of it," Calla said, still struggling. "Cearnach was right. Once a pirate, always a pirate. Your loan has been paid back, one hundred percent legally. You have no control over me or my parents."

He finally reached the door and saw how far Heather had gone. Instead of going after her, he slammed the door and locked it. Calla jumped away from him, now that he was unable to go after Heather in time. He had murder in his eyes. "You mated that bastard, didn't you?" His mouth twisted with hate. "You put me off for a whole year and you've already mated him? You've been dating

him for what, two weeks?" He glanced around at the
packing boxes. "That's what this is all about, isn't it? I
thought you had sold your house to help pay your parents' debt, but you wouldn't have had time."

The fury in his voice scared her.

She raced for the back door, but he quickly caught
up with her, grabbed her, and held her pinned against
his body this time. She struggled to free herself, but he
was too strong.

"Let. Go. Of. Me," she growled, trying to infuse her
voice with as much steel as possible to hide her fear.

How long would it take before Guthrie and the others
came to rescue her? She had to delay Baird, though she
was afraid he'd just attempt to kill her rather than allow
Guthrie to have her for his mate.

Baird tried hauling her toward the back door.

"Nay, let go of me, Baird! Your pack has its money
back. You don't need me any longer."

"They have the money back, aye. But the only way
they'll forgive me for taking it in the first place without the pack members' mutual consent is if I mate with
you and bring your income and properties to add to the
pack's holdings."

"I'm already mated to Guthrie. For life. You just said
it yourself. You know I can't mate you."

"I don't care. I still need you."

"Or what?" she asked, still fighting to free herself as
he made headway to get her to the back door.

"Or I'm out. The same with my brothers and my
cousin who conspired with me. We're all out. Without a
pack. Without money. Power. Nothing. So you're coming back with me."

"You think the MacNeills will allow it?" she said, trying to reason with him.

"I don't have any choice. Can't you understand that?" he said, angered.

"You'll be alive, Baird."

"I'll be *nothing*."

There was no reasoning with him. She couldn't free herself from him, no matter how hard she tried. He must be parked out back. No matter what, she couldn't allow him to take her with him.

All she could think of doing was shifting. She'd never tried it before when she was fully clothed. She'd never heard of a *lupus garou* managing to shift while wearing clothes.

But she was desperate. If she had her wolf's teeth, she could bite him. Even with her just making the shift, she knew he would have a hard time holding on to her.

She called on the urge to turn, her body stiffening slightly, and he quickly said, "Oh, no you don't."

She saw his fist right before he struck her, and she tried again to pull away. He hit her hard. Pain radiated through her skull, preventing her from concentrating enough to complete the shift. A flash of recall of when he'd done it to her before followed. She wished to God she had her wolf's teeth bared. Then her world instantly dissolved into inky blackness.

Chapter 20

GUTHRIE AND THE OTHERS DROPPED EVERYTHING THEY were doing when they heard Heather screaming and shouting that Baird had come back for Calla. Heather was crying and running as fast as she could toward the manor house, which was about a thousand feet from the carriage house.

They rushed outside, and Guthrie bolted for Calla's place, Duncan and Oran keeping pace as Ethan and Jasper raced behind them.

"Stay in the manor house," Cearnach said to Heather. "Call Ian."

And then he hurried off to catch up with the rest of them. When Guthrie reached the carriage house and twisted the doorknob, he found it locked. "Calla!"

Duncan yanked out his standard *lupus garou* lockpicks and worked on the lock, while Guthrie and Cearnach sprinted around the other side of the house, in case the back door was open. His heart thundering, Guthrie saw Baird's red car peel off down the long cobblestone drive to the main road. But no sign of Calla in the car. Not that he could see anyway.

Guthrie and Cearnach hurried inside the back entryway, where the door hung wide open. Guthrie hollered at Duncan and the others, who were searching in the back rooms, "Any sign of Calla in the house?" He worried then that Baird might have killed her and run.

"They're gone," Duncan said, stalking down the hall-way. "She's not here."

"All right. They headed off the property the back way," Guthrie said, hurrying for his car just as lightning blazed across the darkening sky and thunder cracked. The rains started right after that.

Duncan and Cearnach climbed into Guthrie's car and Guthrie drove off. Oran and Ethan took off in the other, following them, while Jasper stayed behind to watch over Heather—just in case they had unexpected trouble from more of Baird's kin.

Cearnach called Ian on the speakerphone. "Baird's taken Calla hostage. He's headed onto the main road. We're in pursuit."

"Out here, the rain is changing to sleet. Be careful," Ian warned. "Keep me posted."

By the time they got to the main road, they couldn't tell which way Baird had gone.

Duncan quickly got out of the car, sniffed the wet air, then got back in the car. "His recent car fumes indicate he headed left."

They were off again, the car roaring down the road and Guthrie going way faster than was probably safe. But no one told him to slow down. If any of their mates had been abducted, they would have felt the same way.

He just hoped they weren't too late.

The roads wound back and forth in the hilly country, some of it edging steep cliffs that dropped away to the cold sea.

Guthrie's heart rate hadn't slowed down from the moment he had heard Heather's frantic cries.

Usually his brothers would reassure each other when

something was wrong—saying they would take care of it. In this case, everyone was silent, anxious, watching for any sign of Baird's car and trying to see if it hadn't driven off on another road along the way. No cars were traveling on this road at all, though, most likely because of the bad weather.

The road surface hadn't completely frozen yet, but the rain hitting the windows was definitely mixed with sleet as it slid down the windshield and began to accumulate like chunks of glass.

A couple of times they slid on the road. Cursing, Guthrie cut back on his speed when he saw in his rearview mirror that Oran's car had hit an icy patch and dovetailed into a ditch.

"Oran's in the ditch," he quickly told his brothers.

Duncan got on the speakerphone to Ethan in Oran's car. "Hey, are you two going to be okay?"

"Yeah, go after the lass," Ethan said. "Don't lose her. We're going to try and get ourselves back on the road and catch up as soon as we can. We'll keep in touch."

Cearnach was on the phone to Ian again. "Oran and Ethan slid on a patch of ice. They ran off the road, but they're both fine." He gave their location. "We're continuing on this route. No sign of Baird's car yet."

"Okay. We'll send someone to pick up Oran and Ethan if they aren't able to make it back to the road on their own. What about Jasper and Heather?"

"Back at the manor house."

"They may have to stay there overnight. We've got a new problem. The ice storm has brought down"—Ian paused—"electric lines. The electricity just fluttered." Silence. "It just went out. Some roads are impassable, according to the weather reports. Lines are down all over the area around here."

"Wait, what about the other ladies?" Duncan asked, sounding worried.

"They, ah, went shopping, when you went to pack Calla's things," Ian said.

"They went Christmas shopping? In this weather? Are they crazy? Are they back yet?"

"Nay. They were supposed to be back already, but they called and said the car slipped on ice and managed to hit a telephone pole. No one's injured. But they're shaken up a bit. I'm on my way with a couple of other men to get them."

Cearnach shook his head. Duncan growled.

"They…didn't want anyone to know about it," Ian said as Guthrie and the others heard car doors slam and the engine roar to life over the phone. "But, they didn't go out for Christmas shopping."

"What then?" Duncan asked, his tone of voice furious.

"They went shopping for wedding gifts for Calla and Guthrie."

Calla's head was pounding—again. Thankfully, Baird hadn't struck her in the same place that he had hit her before. So she'd have a new bruise and a new lump on her temple, other side. She wanted to kill him. Her heart was beating a million miles a minute. He was driving beside the cliffs near Elaine's castle ruins. She recognized this stretch of highway, the place that Cearnach's vehicle had been pushed off the cliffs by Baird's own kin. Which is what had led to her calling it quits with mating Baird.

She felt the car slipping and sliding on ice. The sleet slithered down the windshield and the side windows, and the ice piled up at the bottom of the glass. Every time the tires slid, she sucked in her breath. Baird glanced up at the rearview mirror. Cold, dark eyes stared at her. She almost didn't recognize him.

She wanted to tell him to watch the road, as bad as the conditions were, or even better, to stop the car and let her out, but even making a sudden stop could send them over the cliff. She wanted to plead with him, but she didn't feel she could say anything further that would change his mind. Not now. He was hell-bent on his own destruction and hers. The only hope she had was that when he took her back to his pack and she told them she was mated to Guthrie, they'd let her go—to avoid riling the whole MacNeill pack—and deal with Baird in their own way.

Then the car slid on ice again, and the words slipped out anyway. "Baird, slow down!"

He just growled and ignored her.

She knew it was crazy, considering the more worrisome concern of how Baird could very well end up killing them both, but still, she thought about the Christmas party she and Julia had planned for tomorrow and how she might never be there to help set it up. Most of all, she thought of Guthrie and the short time they'd had together as a couple, and wished with all her heart that they'd gotten together sooner.

Baird shook his head. "You're the reason I'm in such a mess."

As if. She didn't want to antagonize him further, though she did have a question she wanted answered, no matter how much he might not like her bringing it up.

"Why didn't you try this hard to get back together with Ivy? Why all this trouble for me?" Calla was still irritated with him that he'd set up the meeting with her and that it hadn't been chance or love at first sight. She wanted him to know that she knew all about Ivy and how he'd met her the same way.

"I knew she wasn't the right one for me. I didn't pursue her because *I* called it quits. Did she tell you differently? She wanted to get married. Pleaded with me to come back. She called a dozen times after I left. Even came to my house after I had ended the relationship. Bothered my brothers by asking them to let me know she needed to talk with me."

Calla couldn't believe it! Then Baird had to know how *she* felt about being stalked. But was he telling the truth? Had Ivy lied?

"After you split up, did you go to the same places you had taken her before?" Calla asked.

"Nay. She frequented them. I wasn't about to put up with her fitful scenes any longer. She was spoiled, used to getting her own way."

"But…" Calla wanted to tell him that he was behaving just like Ivy. But she realized then why Ivy hadn't had him thrown out of her ball. Ivy had wanted him there. Maybe she had hoped that Calla and Baird would get into a fight, so she could move in and entice Baird to be interested in her again.

"Why did you come to the masquerade ball, then?"

"Ivy called and said you'd arrived. I didn't come to see her. She knew that but was hoping she and I could get back together. It would never have happened."

The car slid again, and he didn't slow down even a

wee bit. Calla's heart nearly gave out as she buckled her seat belt and grabbed the door handle. If the car went over the cliff, would she be better off as a wolf or a human? Seat belted as a human seemed like the best bet, though neither option was exactly ideal.

As soon as she had that thought, the car hit ice and spun around, her heart and stomach spinning with it. They were going too fast, tires vibrating so violently that she felt as though they would shake loose from the rims.

Then suddenly they were going straight down the side of the cliff. Her heart was in her throat. Instead of the road in their path, she saw trees and rocks. Jagged rocks scraped the underbelly of the car raw, the metal screeching and grinding, tree limbs snapping.

For some inane reason, she hated that he was destroying the trees. Forget about what would happen when the car crashed at the bottom of the cliff and resulted in the destruction to their bodies.

Branches tore at the doors, scarring the paint job. The rocks shredded the tires, and they boomed as the air whooshed out of them. Both the windshield and the back window wore spiderweb cracks all across their width, the wipers still sweeping across the windshield, clearing the sleet away only to be covered in the slippery stuff again. The car slammed to a stop, and a jarring jolt crashed through every bone in her body.

It wasn't over. They were hanging precariously midway down the cliff, hung up on rocks and trees, the only things that kept them from falling any farther. Baird wasn't moving, his head slumped over the steering wheel.

"Baird," Calla cried out, torn between wanting to leave the car without him and wanting to ensure he wasn't going to try anything further to injure her. Her clothes were damp from the run in the sleeting rain, and her head was still pounding furiously.

She leaned forward a little to try to reach him, but the car shuddered, and she realized then how precarious their situation still was.

"Baird," she said again. She wanted to open the door and jump out and take her chances, but she was afraid *any* move she made would shake the car loose and send it plummeting to the bottom of the cliff. She saw then that a tree trunk was jammed against her door.

Baird slowly raised his head and groaned. He glanced up at the mirror as if he suddenly remembered her in the backseat, then glanced at the door. She realized before he even swung open his door what he intended to do.

"Nay, Baird, don't! We can't move. The car isn't stable enough, and any slight movement could send us down to the rocks below," she said.

"Says you," he said.

Her heart was hammering so hard that she was sure it would break through her ribs any second.

She'd have to climb across the seat to the other passenger door or attempt to maneuver over the driver's seat to exit through Baird's door, if he managed to get out. Baird pushed his door open partway, and the car shuddered and slipped and caught, a rock keeping the door from swinging very far and the narrow gap making it difficult for him to squeeze out. He wasn't wearing a seat belt, but the car was at an odd angle and he was having a time climbing out. She remembered what Cearnach's car had looked like after Baird's kin had sent it flying over the cliff. It had turned into a squashed metal can. If she lay on the floor, would she fare better?

The car moved again.

"Bloody hell," Baird swore as he struggled some more, then managed to fling himself out of the car.

The vehicle slid another five feet or so, and her heart went with it. It ground to another precarious stop.

From the rear window, she could see Baird clinging to a tree, not out of danger yet himself. Then he pulled out his cell phone, moving around to lean his back against the tree to brace himself. "I'm where Cearnach's car went off the cliff. I need to get picked up on the road south of here. I'm okay, but the car is probably not going to make it." He glanced back in Calla's direction.

"I can't get her out of the car. I don't know what we're going to do. I guess we'll tell the pack I had an accident. Which I did. Tell them that Calla was coming with me and didn't make it. There's not much else I can do." He smiled at Calla, the look pure evil. "Nay. I can't get her out without risking my own neck." He listened for a second and said, "Pick me up, Vardon. We're still in this together." He slammed his cell in his pocket and began stripping off his clothes.

She got the impression Vardon didn't like the circumstances any more than she did.

Baird hadn't even tried to get her out! Did he think the pack would buy his story? And let him get by with it? She hoped that if she didn't make it, they would deal with him the way she wanted to right this instant.

Ignoring him and concentrating on what she had to do to save herself, she wondered—could she climb the cliff face better as a wolf? Could he? He must have thought so or he wouldn't be getting ready to shift.

She was afraid to unfasten her seat belt in case the car started moving again. Then she'd be in more danger, thrown through a car window or stuck in the car as it plummeted down the cliff, or no telling what. She heard the sound of tires screeching up above and her heart nearly died. If it was Guthrie and his family coming to rescue her, or really anyone, they could end up sliding off the cliff like Baird, slam their car into Baird's, and send her crashing to the bottom. Their vehicle would land right on top of Baird's car…and her.

Then she saw that Baird had shifted and was trying to make his way down the cliff as a wolf. She realized he had to, or face the wrath of Guthrie's family, if that's who was up above on the road. Baird was getting away.

She listened for the sound of anything up above.

Silence.

Then the slamming of doors from farther down the road. Running boots pounded on pavement, nearing the location where Baird's car had sailed over the edge. Three men, it sounded like. Good thing she hadn't shifted, in the event that whoever was coming wasn't Guthrie and his kin. Someone else might try to rescue her if she was a woman, but not as a wolf.

Rocks rolled down from above. Gooseflesh erupted all over her skin as the rocks bumped the flattened tires.

"Calla!"

"Guthrie." She barely whispered his name. "I'm okay!" she shouted. She wasn't *really* okay, but she wasn't exactly injured—except for the new bruise on her temple—and she had to let him know that. But then she was scared for him. What if he slid to his death on the cliffs?

"Don't move!" he shouted back.

"The car keeps moving," she said, hating that she couldn't get out of this by herself like Baird had done. But she would have to do a lot more moving around in the car than he did just to reach a viable exit. Her door was no longer wedged against the tree trunk, but a branch still prevented her from opening the door.

More branches snapped behind her. More rocks skittered down, striking other rocks. She was afraid any one of them would shake the car loose and spell disaster.

"We're coming!" Cearnach shouted. "Just...just don't move." He was to the right of her, with Duncan behind him.

"We're almost there," Guthrie said, sounding really close now on the left side of the vehicle.

"All right." She hated sounding so meek, but she felt even talking would send the car sliding.

Guthrie managed to reach the car and came into Calla's view, holding on to a branch, the same one that was stopping her from opening her door.

"Guthrie, be careful," Calla said.

He smiled at her as if he wasn't worried about his safety, only hers, and the notion amused him, despite the circumstances.

"What do you want us to do?" Cearnach asked, peering in through the opposite window.

"You and Duncan hold on to the door handles if you can. Calla, I want you to unfasten your seat belt. I'm going to break this branch and open the car door. I'll pull you out and then we'll take it from there."

Undoing her seat belt was harder than she'd ever imagined since her hands were shaking so much. She feared the car would take off and she'd need her seat belt in place, but Duncan and Cearnach grasped the door handles and nodded. Guthrie braced his feet against rocks. As soon as she nodded, he pulled the branch aside and broke it with a jerk. The car stayed put.

He reached for her door handle. "Okay, I'm going to open the door, and you get out and I'll grab for you at the same time."

Again she nodded, unable to say anything because she was so scared. What if she was half out of the car when it broke loose and continued its journey? What if it ran over her foot or dragged her down? Anything could go wrong.

He pulled on the door, but like the driver's door, this one was stuck on rocks and only opened partway.

"Can you make it out this way?" he asked, his voice urgent.

"Aye, I think so."

She inched her way out, the icy rain making the mossy rocks all the more slippery. She had one foot on the ground and was taking another step when she felt the car shudder. Guthrie grabbed her hand and pulled her a little as she tried to slip out through the narrow opening.

The car moved a few inches. Which meant she was closer to being free, but she wasn't out yet.

"Hurry, Calla," Cearnach grunted as he still held on to the car with a titan grip.

And then Guthrie drew her the rest of the way out. When the car didn't move for a moment she thought she'd panicked for no reason. Until the car creaked.

Guthrie quickly hauled Calla farther away from the vehicle, and Cearnach and Duncan let go of the door handles and jumped back completely out of the car's path. They found solid footing, but the car slipped on the slick rocks, began to pick up speed, and raced down the rest of the way, crashing with a horrendous bang at the bottom. Calla jumped a little in Guthrie's arms.

Guthrie held her tight in the sleeting rain, both of them smelling like wet wool. She was chilled to the bone, but she was so grateful to be in Guthrie's arms.

"Where did Baird go?" Guthrie asked.

"He stripped and shifted. As a wolf, he made his way down to the beach. He heard your car stopping up above. Well, he heard *a* car. He might not have known it was you. He managed to call his brother, Vardon, and told him to pick him up south of here on the road." She didn't bother to mention the part about Baird looking right at her, still trapped in the vehicle, and telling his brother he was unable to rescue her. Guthrie would be angry enough as it was.

"Cearnach, can you help Calla back up the cliff?" Guthrie said, holding her tight and pressing against a tree to help them keep their footing, both of them getting wetter and colder.

None of them had coats on. All of them had removed them to pack and to drop off the boxes and unload the food at her parents' home, and they must have rushed straight from there. Everyone was just wearing wool sweaters, trousers, and boots—and getting soaked.

"Nay," Calla said.

"I'm going after him," Guthrie said. "Cearnach?"

Calla began to pull off her sweater.

"What are you doing?" Guthrie asked.

"Going with you. If you're chasing after him in your wolf coat, you're not going alone."

"I'm going with him," Duncan said.

Guthrie hugged her tight. "It's going to get ugly. Hell, if you try to shift, the way you've got to be feeling, you could pass out. And then you and I could be more at risk on this steep incline."

The adrenaline was still pumping wildly through her blood. She frowned at him, not wanting to remain behind but realizing he could be right—as much as she hated to admit it.

"I don't want to stay at the car," she said, knowing why Guthrie didn't want her to be with them. Sure, he didn't need her help, but it was more that he didn't want her to see the wolf fight that was likely to occur, she thought. Guthrie was her mate now, and she wanted to be there for him.

"Will you stay, please?" he said, stroking her cheek, his eyes worried.

Her head hurt so bad that she realized everything Guthrie had said was true. As much as she hated this, she nodded, kissed him, and then allowed Cearnach to lead her back up the hill, slipping the whole time.

Guthrie waited a heartbeat to watch Cearnach help a struggling Calla climb the hill. She would never have been able to shift and make it down the cliffs, not as dizzy as she was and with the sleet making everything so slick.

He and Duncan stripped as quickly as they could, considering how steep the cliffs were and how they had to brace themselves on trees while they undressed. They shifted, then made their way down the slope where it was more like a mountain goat's path, but fine for the wolves. When they reached the bottom, they saw that the car was upside down, looking similar to Cearnach's when it had landed at the bottom. The occupants would have been crushed.

Guthrie was glad Calla had stayed behind. Taking her by force when she was already mated to another meant Baird would never respect their boundaries. And Guthrie was afraid that even if he killed Baird, Vardon would need to be dealt with next.

Guthrie chased after Baird's scent along the beach, Duncan keeping up with him. He hoped Calla had reached the car by now and was inside where she'd at least be out of the sleet.

Rocks jutted out into the water, and they had to swim to reach the other side. Wolf prints indicated the wolf was running.

Guthrie had to stop him this time.

Chapter 21

THE SLEET WAS STILL COMING DOWN, BUT IN THEIR wolf coats, they had the outer guard hairs to keep the water from soaking them. Guthrie's feet dug into the sand as he made his way to the next group of rock outcroppings in the same direction Baird had gone. Guthrie had wanted to keep Calla from seeing the wolf fight, though he understood her need to be there to show her support for her mate. He still hadn't wanted her to have to witness this.

They had to hurry. What if Vardon and some of his kin came to rescue Baird? What if they outnumbered Guthrie and his kin and attempted to grab Calla again? Guthrie had to prevent it from happening.

He swam around the rocks to reach the next beach and saw Baird trying to make it up the cliff. Here, the cliffs were even steeper and there was no way for a wolf to manage any farther than a third of the way up. No way Baird could make it in human form either, not without clothing to keep warm in the wintry sleet, or boots and gloves to protect his hands and feet on the rocks. Baird turned and was beginning to make his way back down to the beach when he saw Guthrie and stood stock-still.

When Baird made a move to head the rest of the way to the beach, Guthrie thought Baird would fight him. Until Baird ran for the next outcropping of rocks— heading straight for the water. Guthrie ran full out as if

he were chasing prey in an attempt to catch up to Baird
before he dove in and swam away.

Within reach, Guthrie leaped at Baird, landing on
his back. Baird yipped in surprise, then growled and
twisted around. The two reared up, both too alpha to
submit. Snarling and growling, Guthrie bit at Baird's
face as he bit back.

Guthrie tasted Baird's blood and they both rose up
on their hind legs again, forelegs trying to get purchase,
their teeth clicking against each other's. Baird tried to
stay on top but lost his balance and went down on all
four paws. He ducked his head suddenly and bit low,
aiming to bite into one of Guthrie's legs. Guthrie jumped
back, avoiding Baird's wickedly snapping jaws. Baird
tried for the water again, and Guthrie jumped against his
right flank and bit him in the back.

Snarling, Baird turned to retaliate. Their teeth connected again and then, unable to bite anything vital
above, Baird again went for Guthrie's foreleg.

This time, as soon as he bent his head low for a
lunging bite, Guthrie went high and grabbed him by the
neck. Baird snarled and tried to shake Guthrie loose.
But Guthrie was too angry and too determined to let
him go.

Knowing this was his last chance, Baird continued to
thrash about, trying to get free, and Guthrie continued to
try to get a better grip.

Then they heard a car braking up on the cliffs.
Sliding. Stopping. If it was Vardon, he wouldn't know
that Baird had come this far, but Calla and Cearnach
could be in danger. Then the car began rolling toward
Guthrie's vehicle. Hell. Guthrie could just imagine them

discovering that the car was his, shoving it off the cliffs, and stranding him and his brothers and Calla.

Calla!

With the distraction, Guthrie lost his grip on Baird. The wolf dove into the sea and out of sight, and Guthrie growled at his lost chance, but Guthrie and Duncan had to reach Calla and Cearnach pronto.

Guthrie and Duncan raced across the beach, dove into the water, and swam around the cliffs. As soon as they hit the other beach, they dashed across it and to the cliffs where Baird's car had fallen. The road was not visible from the beach and they had quickly begun the climb up when they heard a car stop south of where Guthrie's car was. Vardon and his kin would know it was Guthrie's car. Even if they didn't recognize the vehicle itself, they could smell that he was here with two of his brothers. They'd know that some of the MacNeills had gone after Baird.

Cearnach wouldn't be enough of a threat if he had to face too many wolves. Guthrie heard Baird's kin talking and tried to climb carefully, not wanting to send any rocks tumbling down the hill to alert them that he and Duncan were coming.

"Let's grab the girl and give Guthrie's car a proper send-off," Vardon said.

Guthrie had to stop them at all costs.

"What about Baird?" Robert asked.

"What about him?" Vardon said.

"I don't like this at all," Robert said. "If they already killed your brother, maybe the pack will let us off with just a warning. But if we take Calla, you know the MacNeills will want all our blood."

"You control the finances," Vardon said. "You okayed the transfer of funds. So no, I don't believe they'll let us off that easily. Either way, we need her as a bargaining chip. Let's grab her."

Guthrie hadn't reached the road before he heard Robert shout, "Cearnach's coming as a wolf!"

Robert didn't get another word out as Guthrie reached the road and saw Cearnach chasing Vardon and the others. Calla was lying beside Guthrie's car as a wolf, giving Guthrie a terrible shock.

He raced to her, while Vardon and Robert ran for their car, slipping and sliding on the icy pavement. Vardon's younger brother, Oliver, was already diving into the backseat of the car. Robert and Vardon scrambled into the car, and then they sped off. The tires slid on the ice and the car careened across the road, spun back around in a circle, and headed straight for the cliff. And dove over it.

Branches in the path of the car snapped, rocks tumbled, and then there was silence until a loud crash sounded below where the car met the rocks. Another bang, and then silence.

Duncan joined Cearnach at the edge of the cliff and watched for any sign that the men were alive.

Guthrie realized with relief that Calla was still breathing, and he licked her face until she stirred and blinked groggily.

He quickly shifted. "Are you all right, Calla? Can you shift?"

She let out her breath, then shifted. As soon as Guthrie saw the bruise on Calla's other temple, he was angry with Baird all over again. He quickly pulled her sodden sweater over her head and then helped her into the rest of her clothes.

He eased her gently into the car. "Stay here. I'll be back in a couple of minutes."

She nodded, leaned back against the seat, and closed her eyes, shivering violently. "I'll be right back," he repeated. Then he shut the door, shifted, and raced along the road as a wolf to join his brothers.

Guthrie peered over the cliff, the same one that Baird hadn't been able to climb because it was so steep. The car had taken a swan dive into the rocks below and had landed on its side. No one was moving inside the vehicle that they could see. The younger brother had been thrown from the vehicle and lay motionless against a tree. No sign of Robert or Vardon, who were probably trapped inside the smashed-up car, Guthrie assumed grimly.

But Baird had gotten away. Guthrie and his brothers went to retrieve their clothes where they had stripped out of them, shifted, and hurried to dress.

"No way to check the car out unless we go back down, take a swim again, and poke around at the wreckage," Guthrie said to his brothers. "Next best thing is to call their next of kin and let them sort it out."

"Aye," both Cearnach and Duncan agreed. Being second in charge of the pack, Cearnach normally would have taken care of the matter, but because Baird had stolen Guthrie's mate, Guthrie would inform Baird's pack of the business. As soon as he got into the car, his brothers quickly following, Guthrie wrapped his arm around Calla and hugged her shivering body tightly against his. "What happened," he asked, "when Vardon and the others arrived?"

"When we heard the car coming, Cearnach went into the woods to shift. When I saw Vardon's car, I shifted so I could protect myself, but I guess I fainted. I'm glad you're okay," Calla said.

"That was the best thing you could have done, Calla, as it turns out. They could have broken into the car and grabbed you if we hadn't been able to stop them in time."

Duncan started the car and turned the heat on high, though the Arctic blast from the vents nearly transformed them into frozen statues before the car warmed up. And then, very slowly, Duncan drove back to Calla's parents' estate.

Guthrie got his phone out to call Baird's other older brother, Skinny. He was the biggest wolf in the pack, but normally more even-tempered than Vardon. He was apparently more interested in his artwork than running the pack, but Guthrie wasn't sure how he was going to take the news. It could go either way.

He had to tell Skinny that Baird and the others had brought this all on themselves, if they were dead—and before any rumors started to circulate that the MacNeills had intentionally taken them out. "This is Guthrie MacNeill. I'm calling to tell you that Baird stole my mate and his car went off the cliffs." He gave the location. He could hear Skinny's heavy breathing, but the oldest McKinley wasn't saying anything.

"After the crash, Baird called Vardon, and he and Robert and your younger brother Oliver came to help him out."

Calla cleared her throat. Guthrie glanced at her. "Tell

Skinny that Baird didn't bother to try to rescue me from the car."

Guthrie stared at her for a moment, furious with Baird. "Did you get that?" he asked Skinny.

"Aye," Skinny said. "The others?"

"Their car went over the cliff as well. Roads are really icy up here."

"Yeah, but they slid on the ice because they were hightailing it out of here after trying to abduct me *yet again* and push your car off a cliff *yet again*," Calla said, folding her arms and looking cross. Guthrie smiled a little at her. His brothers were grinning.

"Survivors?" Skinny asked.

"Not sure. Baird made it out alive, but he ran off." Guthrie wanted to say "like the coward he is," but he was trying his damnedest to be diplomatic since they didn't need a big fight with Baird's clan.

"Here, let me have the phone and *I'll* tell him," Calla said, clearly not interested in diplomacy at the moment. "Tell him that we're mated, but Baird knocked me out and kidnapped me anyway."

"I heard," Skinny said. "What of my brothers and my cousin?"

"For all we know, Vardon and Robert could very well be alive. We can't see them. The car is on its side, and all we can see is the underside. Oliver was thrown free of the vehicle, but he could have only been knocked unconscious. We can't tell from way up here. Whoever retrieves them will have to swim to reach them, or maybe get some climbing gear and go after them that way. In this sleet, no matter what, it will be a risky business," Guthrie said.

Skinny grunted.

"We don't want any more trouble between our clans. Calla is not returning to your pack, and the loan to her parents has been repaid," Guthrie said.

The phone clicked dead in his ear.

Cearnach let out his breath. "He hung up on you."

"Aye."

Guthrie called Ethan next. "How are the two of you doing? We're on our way there. But it's so icy that it's going to be slow going."

"We're fine. Glad you're all right. I take it you've got the lass? And she's okay?"

"Aye. She's with us and just fine. I can't say the same for Baird's brother, Vardon, his cousin, or younger brother." Guthrie explained what had happened. "As long as we don't have any accidents, we'll be to your location in a wee bit."

"Did you want us to run back as wolves?"

"No. We'll pick you up."

"Good. See you soon, but you drive careful, you hear?"

"Aye." All they needed was to all be stranded out here in the freezing weather.

Cearnach called Ian to update him on everything, putting the conversation on speakerphone. He ended with, "Skinny hung up on Guthrie, so we have no idea how the McKinley pack is going to respond to this."

"If Vardon's alive, he might try to stir everybody up like he always does. Or Baird might, if his pack doesn't actually kill or exile him and his brothers. Not sure about the others. Robert's kind of a 'tuck tail and run' kind of wolf. Oliver is a total yes-man. If someone says fight, he'll be there, but if he's on his own, he'll be out of there. Not sure about the others in the pack. Those who are angry about Baird and his close kin stealing the money may figure it is justice."

"That's what I was thinking. We'll be ready for them if they decide to take this further. What about the ladies?"

"They're home safe, anxious to get word from you. We still have no electricity. Can you hold out if Skinny and any others intercept you on the road in an attempt to pay you back for this latest calamity?"

"Aye. I'm certain they'll have the same problem reaching us as we have in returning to Argent Castle," Cearnach said.

Calla snuggled closer to Guthrie. As soon as they picked up Ethan and Oran, it would be a really tight squeeze in the small hatchback. It seated four comfortably, five was a snug fit, and six was impossible unless Calla stretched out on the men's legs or someone rode in the trunk. Or maybe if she sat on Guthrie's lap.

"All right. I'd send men as reinforcements, but I don't want anyone else stranded. Just keep me informed. Let me know when you reach the Stewarts' manor house."

"Aye. Don't worry about Ethan and Oran. We'll pick them up on the way." Cearnach ended the call and then punched in another number. "Jasper, we're returning to the Stewart manor as soon as we pick up our stranded men. Keep a lookout. We might have company—and it won't be the good kind." He explained all that had happened as Guthrie stroked Calla's wet hair.

"Ask if they still have electricity," Guthrie said to Cearnach.

Cearnach asked, then shook his head at Guthrie.

"Does the manor have a gas water heater?" Guthrie asked Calla.

"Aye. Two of them."

"Great. I'm sure we could all use a hot shower," Guthrie said.

"All of you can borrow some of Dad's clothes, I'm sure," Calla said.

After picking up Oran and Ethan, they weren't sure they could all fit in the car. All of the men were around six feet tall. Calla was about five and a half, but Guthrie didn't want her sitting in the trunk.

"I'll sit in that," Oran said, winking at Calla.

She opened her mouth to say something, but Guthrie quickly said, "Good idea." He wasn't letting her sit back there, being chilled to the bone already, not when he wanted to keep her tucked against his body. Even at that, it was a tight squeeze, but that helped to warm them up a bit.

They were steaming up the windows, though, and Duncan had to turn the defroster on high, along with the heat, as wet as they all were.

When they finally reached the manor house, Cearnach hurried to open the hatchback to let Oran out. He'd practically been curled up in a ball, sleeping on the floor of the trunk. Cearnach laughed. "Now I know why you wanted to sit in the trunk."

Jasper and Heather rushed outside to greet them, wearing their jackets and gloves and looking much warmer.

"So I take it we're staying here for the night?" Jasper asked. "Even though we have no electricity."

"Aye. It's the same at Argent Castle," Guthrie said.

"It would be safer starting out tomorrow after the ice has melted off."

"We have lanterns and candles," Calla said, the day already turning dark. Though as wolves they could see well at dawn and dusk. "We can still cook something. We have a gas stove."

"We've got the fire going in the den too," Jasper said.

Guthrie was more concerned about sleeping arrangements and speaking to Calla in private. He really wanted to stay with her in the carriage house alone. But his brothers were already looking at him like they knew what he was thinking. They were ready to disagree with him on splitting up their forces, though they'd give him the chance to make that decision on his own.

"We all stay in the manor house," Guthrie conceded, knowing that it was the safest thing to do.

Everyone eagerly concurred.

Inside the house, Heather said, "I'll take everyone's wet clothes and hang them to dry by the fire."

Jasper asked, "Is there anything that we could cook that I can start making?"

"You can cook?" Calla asked, sounding surprised.

"Aye. Not sure about your fancy Scottish dishes, but I make mean Texas chili with the right ingredients."

"You're welcome to anything in the fridge or the cupboards." She turned to Guthrie. "Can you cook?"

The brothers laughed.

"Well, it *was* a much-guarded secret that my brothers and I could cook, but I think the truth is out," Guthrie said, taking her hand and leading her to the stairs. "Let's get out of these wet clothes."

She let out her breath in frustration. "You only

moved things that needed to come here. So my clothes are still at the carriage house, packed in boxes to take to Argent Castle."

He frowned.

"We can get the boxes," Cearnach said.

"Wait, I packed them. So I know which ones she'll need." Guthrie hugged her and kissed her lips. "I'll be right back."

"Okay, I'll take a shower while you're gone," Calla said.

"I'm going with you," Duncan said to Guthrie. "You realize we're not going to be able to return home tomorrow without another vehicle."

"Aye, we barely made it here with the number we had already. And we also have Jasper and Heather to take home. We wouldn't be able to carry any of Calla's things with us, either."

Guthrie and Duncan ran to the car in the sleeting rain, slipping a little on the cobblestone drive. They climbed inside the vehicle, then drove back to Calla's place. As soon as they parked, they raced to the covered porch. Guthrie tried the doorknob, figuring they hadn't locked it in their rush to rescue Calla. Sure enough, it twisted open.

He felt wary all at once. It was completely dark out and the same inside. He smelled Baird's angry scent and Calla's angered and fearful scent, and that made Guthrie's temper rise. Even though he knew the man couldn't be here, Guthrie couldn't help but feel that Baird was in the house again.

"Come on," Duncan said, nudging Guthrie to go with him to Calla's bedroom.

They both were taking deep breaths—scenting the air

to make sure no one else had been in the house while they were gone or was here now—as they stalked down the hallway to her room. Guthrie found the right box, then lifted it and carried it back down the hall.

"Is Calla all right?" Duncan asked. "Shelley had some trials of her own, but every lassie deals with them differently."

"Aye, she'll be fine." As soon as they ate, Guthrie was taking her to bed, snuggling with her, and talking.

"We're all here for you," Duncan said as they drove back to the house.

Suspicious, Guthrie said, "Why are you bringing all this up?"

"Just, if she's upset about you trying to kill Baird, all of us will help you and Calla deal with it."

"I'll talk to her privately later about all of it."

"Aye."

Sometimes Duncan surprised Guthrie. His younger brother tried to pretend he was all warrior all the time. But at times like this, Guthrie saw Duncan for who he really was—concerned about others' feelings and ready to step in and help out.

Still, Duncan's unease worried him a little. "You can talk to me about anything, you know," Guthrie said to his brother as he parked the car.

Duncan took a deep breath and let it out.

Hell. "What?" Guthrie asked.

"I was just concerned when she wanted to go with us so badly. That maybe she had it in mind to protect Baird. I didn't want to mention it, Brother."

"Aye, well, I'll talk with her later."

"Aye." Duncan looked guilty for saying anything.

Guthrie attempted a smile and slapped him on the shoulder. "Hey, she got the best man out of the deal. And that's all that matters."

Duncan smiled a little. "Aye, you're right there."

Guthrie grabbed the box from the backseat and they headed for the house. He loved his mate unconditionally, no matter why she had wanted to go with him so badly when he took off after Baird. Guthrie couldn't fault her if she'd been concerned about either of them. She had promised to mate with Baird first, and Guthrie had to take that into account.

Chapter 22

"WE'LL POST GUARDS THROUGH THE NIGHT," Cearnach said as Guthrie carried the box of Calla's clothes into the house.

Duncan locked the door. Oran had been watching them through the window, making sure they got back all right without further incident.

"But we want you to stay with Calla through the night. Jasper's going to watch out for Heather," Cearnach continued.

"Sounds good to me." Guthrie smelled chili cooking. He should have known Jasper would make something like that. He'd already cooked it at the castle, shooing away Cook who was fussing about his preparing meals in her kitchen and making a mess of everything. Though Guthrie was surprised that the Stewarts already had all the ingredients for it. The MacNeills hadn't been stocked with just the right things until Jasper wanted to make it.

"Chili, eh?" Guthrie said to Cearnach.

"Aye, Jasper is in seventh heaven, talking about the Texas chili cook-offs and the famous chili he entered. *Again*."

Guthrie snorted and shook his head.

"We all took turns taking showers and grabbed some of Calla's dad's clothes. She's upstairs waiting for you," Cearnach said.

"Chili will be served in another forty minutes," Jasper called from the kitchen.

"Where's Ethan?" Guthrie asked Cearnach.

"Helping him. The three brothers always did the cook-offs together. Ethan and Jasper are arguing about how much chili powder to put in the chili. We told them to go light on it."

"Hey," Jasper said, "I'm going to enter my…well, Ethan and Teague's and my chili in the second chili cook-off in Scotland next year."

"See you in a minute," Guthrie said and carried the box upstairs. Duncan had already disappeared, but then Guthrie heard a shower running so he figured Duncan was taking one now.

When Guthrie reached Calla's bedroom, he found her buried under the covers.

"Are you all right?" he asked, setting the box on the floor and closing the door.

"Oh, aye, I'm just cold, waiting for my clothes. Can't dry my hair. And it's freezing up here."

"I'll start a fire."

"Nay, go ahead and get a shower and dress, and we'll go downstairs and join the others."

"All right." He had to get out of these wet clothes. He planned to talk to her as soon as he washed up and dressed. In the middle of the shower, the water turned cold. And he jumped out of it. Bloody hell. He was already freezing.

He grabbed a towel, figuring that Duncan had used up the last of the hot water. Calla had placed some clothes for him to wear on the bed and had left.

He hoped the hot chili and the fire would warm him

up, but he knew just what else would as soon as he and
Calla went back to bed.

The chili was hot, and the fire nice and warm as Calla
snuggled next to Guthrie on the love seat and the others
sat on various couches and chairs around the fire. The
guys were talking about how to get back to Argent Castle
with only one vehicle, while Guthrie sat quietly with
Calla, not saying a thing. Watching her, looking concerned. She was afraid she'd ruined Julia's Christmas
Eve party by having come here to get her things. Why
hadn't she waited until the weather was better? Why not
after the party?

She stared into the fire. Why had she ever gone out
with Baird? What a mess that had all turned out to be.
She hated to see it end this way, but she knew after he
struck her the second time and took her hostage that he
was never going to stop coming after her. She would
have feared for her safety and Guthrie's, always looking
over her shoulder.

She thought for sure Guthrie had killed Baird, but
then to learn he was still alive? And still a potential menace? What of the others? Had Vardon and his brother
and cousin perished? Would the others in the pack come
after them? She couldn't quit worrying about how this
whole situation could escalate.

Cearnach got on the phone and called Ian to ask
him how he wanted to handle the car situation to get
them home.

Heather began grabbing empty bowls to wash.

"Might as well just leave them to soak," Calla said,

joining her. "We won't be able to wash them really well until the electricity comes back on."

"No hot water," Heather said, her hand under the cold water running out of the spout.

"I used up what was left of it," Guthrie said, joining them. "I'm on guard duty upstairs. Ready for bed, Calla?"

After all they'd been through, aye, Calla was ready.

"Not fair that you two are automatic electric blankets for each other," Heather teased.

Guthrie smiled a little, then took Calla's hand. She loved the strength and gentleness of his touch. "'Night," she said to Heather, giving her a brief hug with her free arm. "See you in the morning."

"Aye. Try to get your sleep, you two."

Guthrie hurried Calla through the house to the stairs. "Seems we were doing the same thing only this morning, except coming down the stairs at Argent Castle," Calla said.

"Aye, lass. Are you truly feeling all right? You seemed so quiet while we were eating."

"You too," she said.

"I was worried about you." He took her into her bedroom and shut the door.

They quickly dispensed of their clothes and climbed into bed, then snuggled together. "I was just anxious about the Christmas party Julia and I had planned for the pack."

"Ah, lass. We can have it any day and everyone will be happy to do so. It matters not which day it is. All that's important is that no one was injured." He kissed her temple right below where she was sporting a new bruise. "Except for that."

"It just looks awful, but it doesn't feel bad now."

He rubbed her arm and said, "You weren't too upset with me for wanting you to stay behind when I went after Baird, were you?"

She sighed. "You can't know how angry I was that he'd first take me hostage and then leave me to suffer the crash he got me into. I didn't want to see him killed, but I wanted to show you that I was there—for you. No one else."

"Because of your injury, I was certain you'd be better off staying safely in the car. I never thought Vardon and that bunch would be so close by," Guthrie said, kissing her cheek.

"I thought you had the better idea when I was having so much trouble getting to the road and my head was pounding so much."

"While I went after Baird, all I was contemplating was that I could lose you and we hadn't even had a chance to really be together."

"I was thinking the same thing. That I had wasted a year with Baird, caused all this trouble for your clan, my parents, and myself, and here I could have been like this with you instead." She inserted her leg between his and snuggled closer, her head against his chest. His hands swept down her back and cupped her buttocks.

"Hell, yeah, lass. I was pondering the same thing. I probably shaved a few years off my brothers' lives as I took a few of those icy curves a little too fast."

"Oh, God, nay. I couldn't have lost you too."

He kissed her slowly, not wildly, impatiently, but more to give her tender loving care after her ordeal. She loved him for it. She never thought of herself as a wilting

flower, but after the horrible experience with the car accident, worry that she would never see Guthrie again,
the fight, and the fear that Baird's kin would cause them
more trouble, she so appreciated Guthrie's gentleness.

And yet as they kissed slowly, their tongues dancing,
the friction between their bodies making her hot and
hungry for his penetration, she began to slide fiercer and
faster against his throbbing erection, stroking her fingers
through his hair, wanting more, quicker, deeper, harder.

He was of a like mind. *Thank the heavens.* She loved
how he would do anything to please her. He groaned
with need and separated her legs so she was straddling
him, her breasts brushing against his lightly haired chest,
her nipples so sensitive. She was soon wet for him, her
own woman's core throbbing with the need to have him
inside her, thrusting, claiming her as she claimed him.

He moved his arm between them and began to stroke
her fast and hard. She was ready to scream out with
pleasure, getting on her knees, barely able to breathe
because she was so hot, her legs spread to him.

So much for slow as he plunged two fingers into her
and she came down on them, all her composure splin-
tering into a million fragments of bliss. Before she could
collapse on top of him, he was holding her hips, center-
ing her, and plunging his cock deep inside her.

Riding him was just as pleasurable as his hands
cupped her breasts and he massaged them while her
inner muscles tightened her hold on him. Like her, he
couldn't last, as if all the pent-up anxiety they'd felt earlier in the day was released. After several hard thrusts,
he filled her womb with his heat.

Then she was able to collapse. But they didn't separate

and she loved the way they were joined, feeling his heat and love surround her as he pulled the covers over them. This wouldn't be the last time they'd make love tonight, proving to the world and themselves that they were mated wolves and no one could tear them apart.

Guthrie's arms were wrapped around Calla after another bout of lovemaking. She'd fallen asleep again, her head nestled against his chest, her leg in between his. She felt right there, like she had always belonged.

Then he heard a noise that brought him to instant alertness. He listened, trying to discern the sound he'd heard. He didn't know who was serving on guard duty at this time of night, and though he hadn't mentioned it, he really didn't like being here at the manor house with Calla until the issue with Baird's pack had been resolved. The Stewart's manor house just wasn't half as secure as the castle with its fortified walls.

Seven hours had passed since the incident on the cliffs. Time enough for Skinny to get some of the McKinley pack together and come to mete out justice if they could make it on the icy roads. Unless they arrived as wolves, their nonslip paw pads having a better chance at maneuvering over the ice.

Guthrie slipped out from under Calla and pulled the covers back over her. He threw on a pair of boxers, intending to strip them off and shift if there was trouble. He padded down the hallway, listening for the sound he'd heard. He wasn't sure what it was, having been half asleep at the time. He made his way quietly down the stairs, until one of the steps squeaked.

Downstairs, Duncan was sleeping on the sofa in the living room by the fire in his wolf coat. Cearnach heard the stairs creak underneath Guthrie's footsteps and came out of the kitchen to investigate.

Cearnach didn't speak to him, but motioned to the front of the house. He'd heard something too. Guthrie touched Duncan's shoulder, and his eyes shot open as he shifted, threw on a pair of boxers, and grabbed a sword. It wasn't his, so Guthrie assumed it was one of Calla's dad's.

Guthrie held his finger to his lips, and Duncan nodded and rose from the couch.

The stairs creaked and they all turned to look as Calla headed down in her wolf form.

Guthrie motioned for Calla to stay with Cearnach and Duncan. He had to wake everyone else so they'd be ready, false alarm or not.

As soon as he climbed the steps, Guthrie knew Calla was following him. He wondered if she thought to guard him.

He was about to open the guest room where Heather was sleeping, when Calla ran for the room at the end of the hall, her parents' bedroom, and growled softly.

Bloody hell. Guthrie jerked open the door to Heather's guest room, saw Ethan sleeping in the chair across the room, and whispered, "Ethan, trouble."

Ethan shot out of his chair and began to toss off his clothes. Guthrie hurried down the hall, smelling where Jasper had gone, but the door was already open, and Jasper was in his wolf form.

Jasper and Ethan joined Calla at the door, though Ethan, being the fatherly sort, nudged at her to leave.

Guthrie wished he could be in his wolf form also, if wolves were in the room, but someone had to open the damn door.

He twisted the knob quickly, knowing that doing so slowly wouldn't make any difference. All of them could hear the doorknob turning. He threw the door aside, and the growling that came from within warned him that there were three wolves in the room.

And Guthrie wasn't suited up for battle.

Calla was having fits. She recognized the men in the room at once. That damned Vardon had survived the crash and no doubt was the instigator in coming here to fight Guthrie and the others. The younger brother, Oliver, was also here. And so was Robert Kilpatrick. She half expected Baird to be running the show, but he wasn't there.

Immediately, Vardon went after Ethan, and Calla stood her ground, despite Ethan trying to force her away. She wasn't buying his protectiveness. Until Guthrie had time to shift, she was helping the other men.

Jasper was fighting Robert, and Oliver couldn't get beyond them because they were battling it out in the doorway, the MacNeills on this side in the hallway and the McKinleys still in the bedroom.

Then Guthrie raced past her, barking at her to get back, which she did, only to give them room. She wasn't hiding in a room somewhere. Guthrie took on Vardon, the biggest of the three McKinley wolves. Cearnach ran into the fray—taking on Robert. Jasper and Ethan fought Oliver. They were older wolves—more experienced in fighting. Still, Oliver had youth on his side and was able to get away from their snapping jaws more quickly.

Calla worried then about Duncan being alone downstairs, but she assumed he was guarding down there in case this was a ruse so others could come in a different way and flank them. Sure enough, she heard a window breaking on the back door. She didn't know how many wolves would come in, so she scooted down the stairs to help Duncan.

"Lass, nay," Duncan shouted, but this was her fight too.

If she hadn't gotten involved with Baird in the first place, none of this would be happening now.

She raced across the stone tile floor in the kitchen and saw Baird in his wolf form. From the way Baird moved, he appeared to be in a lot of pain, but he didn't hesitate to come after her.

She growled her fiercest growl and leaped at him. She figured Duncan would take over any minute, as soon as he could strip out of his clothes and shift into the wolf. But she had to take the initiative before Baird hurt her—again. Only fatally this time.

She lunged at Baird's neck, and he yipped and fell away. He wanted to kill her. She could see it in his narrowed eyes, his lips drawn back in an angry snarl, and the low way he snarled at her right before he lunged at her.

But he couldn't rise up on his hind legs to force her down. Most likely due to his injuries. The enamel of their wicked canines clashed and she tasted her blood, damn it, right before another wolf sailed past her.

Guthrie. Where the hell was Duncan?

Calla stepped back, ready to spring if Guthrie needed her, but as viciously as he tore into her tormentor, she knew Guthrie wouldn't make the same mistake twice.

Over the sound of their growling and snarling, she listened for any sign of trouble anywhere else in the house. The fight upstairs sounded like it was over, and then Cearnach was beside her, checking her over.

Then Baird collapsed on her parents' kitchen floor, and they all waited for him to shift back to his human form. Duncan had shifted and dressed and gone outside. She was about to go with him to protect him, but Cearnach barked at her to stay back. She barked right back at him. Damn it. She could help Duncan if he needed her.

She saw Heather coming down the stairs as a wolf, and Calla wondered where she'd been all this time.

Ethan hurried outside. Fine. Guthrie was still checking out Baird to make sure he really was dead this time, so she ran up the stairs to ensure that the other wolves were no longer any trouble.

She found Vardon, Robert, and Oliver's bodies, now in human form. Then she heard a car door slam and padded over to peer out the window. Skinny. He talked to Duncan for a moment. Another man was sitting in the front seat of the vehicle, but he didn't make any move to get out. Then Duncan raised his voice and motioned to the house. Skinny shook his head, got back into the car, then drove off.

She frowned. *What?* The McKinley pack couldn't have left the bodies for the MacNeills to deal with. She hated that it had come to this, that Baird and his kin couldn't have left well enough alone. She felt bad about it, but she knew they had made the choices that sealed their fates.

"What happened to you?" Calla asked Heather once they had shifted and were dressed.

"I would have helped, but there wasn't any room to maneuver in the hallway where they were all fighting."

Calla was glad Heather hadn't been involved in the battle between wolves.

And in the middle of the pitch-black night, the MacNeill men were all out digging graves for the four dead men, their own pack having washed their hands of them.

~~~

Exhausted, they finally managed to return to Argent Castle the next day in a cavalcade of cars, just in case the MacNeill wolves had any more trouble. When they arrived home, everyone there kissed and hugged the returning pack members.

Julia took Calla aside. "We can delay the Christmas Eve party and make it a Hogmanay celebration if you're too worn out."

Calla was tired, but not that exhausted. "Nay, I've waited so long for this that I can't wait any longer. Are we ready?" She wanted to celebrate the holidays, anything to get her mind off what had happened.

"Everyone was concerned about your return, but yes, we're ready."

Calla had noted that Oran and Ethan did not return with the rest of them. Before she could ask about them, Julia was hurrying to show her the various activities they had going on. Games were in progress for the little ones—puzzles and board games and treats—while the adults had returned to playing charades and other games once they learned everyone was safe.

Later, they feasted on bread and butter and smoked

salmon and Scotch pie. The Texas triplet brothers and Shelley had slaved over making tamales, a Texas Christmas tradition.

When Calla heard Oran's voice, she looked in the direction of the entrance to the great hall and could hardly believe her eyes. Her mother and father smiled at her as Ethan took their coats and handed them to another pack member. Calla rushed to greet them, tears in her eyes.

"You came home," she said, hugging her mother and thrilled to see them.

"Aye, we couldn't miss the first Christmas Eve party you've ever set up, and we've been invited for Christmas. How could we resist?" her mother said, hugging her back. "Your father and I are so proud of you."

Then her parents joined them for the meal.

In Scotland, Christmas wasn't celebrated as much as New Year's, but with all the Americans now living with the pack, things were changing, and the pack was happy to enjoy all the fun.

In a Scottish tradition, kids gathered around the fire and tossed their lists to Santa into the flames. Smoke curled up from the burning paper and carried their messages to Lapland where Santa lived.

A Yule log cut in the summer from a rowan tree had been dried and saved and was now brought into the kitchen, where pack members toasted to it while circling it three times. Then it was taken to the main fireplace in the great hall to burn.

Fires in all the fireplaces would remain lit all night long, as it was the tradition to scare away evil spirits to keep them from coming into the house—or in this case, the castle—on Christmas Eve.

Later that night, while Julia showed Calla's parents to their guest chamber—actually, Calla's but she'd promptly moved into Guthrie's—Calla and Guthrie went out to the garden room, where she was expecting the party to continue for another hour or so.

Instead, they found chestnuts roasting on the fire and mulled wine waiting for them, Christmas music softly playing in the background and cinnamon candles lit, the only other illumination besides the fire in the fire pit. It was a lovely, intimate time for them to share after the big party.

She noticed then that her Christmas stocking and his were hanging off the coat stand and she smiled. "Who planned this?"

"Didn't you?" Guthrie asked, taking her into his arms.

She smiled. "Must have been Julia or the ladies. Want to open our stocking presents first?"

"Ahh, lass, all I need is you." But Guthrie grabbed their stockings and cuddled with her on the couch where they opened the gifts to each other. For her, a super-duper online scheduler and three books on creating memorable parties.

She loved them.

And for him, a financial planner, a fancy pair of argyle socks, and a package of bonbons. He laughed. "You'd been eyeing these at one of the stores."

"Aye, for you," she said, smiling.

"Do you want one?"

She grinned. He laughed.

They danced then to the music, but when they finally headed for the keep and his bedchamber, the place was all quiet except for Julia, on her way back from getting her required cup of hot chocolate.

"The party was the best," Julia said. "And now that you're family…"

Calla laughed. "I get to plan it for free, aye, next year?"

Julia gave her a hug. "It was all in the plans from the start."

They watched her head to the stairs to the bedchambers.

"I think Julia had this in mind all along," Calla said, loving his family as much as she did him.

Guthrie wrapped his arm around Calla and headed for the stairs. "So do I."

––––– ⁓⁓⁓ –––––

Bright and early the next morning, candles were lit in all the windows to guide strangers to warmth and safety. Everyone gathered around to see the ashes in the great hall fireplace. A foot-shaped pile of ash pointed toward the inside of the house, foretelling a new arrival that would come in the New Year.

Everyone sat around the huge Christmas tree and unwrapped presents. What Calla hadn't expected was for Guthrie to get her a MacNeill plaid skirt, with the ladies' help in picking the right size. She gave him a hug, her eyes misting with tears. She was now truly one of the pack.

She had bought him a lovely soft wool sweater that she could snuggle up against, so it was as much hers as it was his.

But the most special gift was Julia's Christmas present to Ian. A baby-sized kilt. Everyone was thrilled.

And several commented on the prediction of the Yule log's ashes.

Ian smiled broadly, lifted Julia from the chair and hugged her, then swung her around in his arms, and everyone looked on and cheered. Guthrie squeezed Calla's hand, assuring her she would be there one of these days.

All the ladies hurried to give Julia hugs after that.

They sat down at noon to a Christmas feast of turkey with all the trimmings, bannock cakes made of oatmeal, and a chocolate cake from Sweden. Mulled wine, champagne, and whisky were served too.

At each place was a Christmas cracker—a cardboard tube covered in colorful gift wrap twisted at both ends. Each was handmade and personalized for the recipient by another member of the pack. Everyone took their cracker in their right hand and crossed arms with their neighbor to grasp his cracker with their left hand. With a tug, the crackers made small pops or bangs all around the great hall. Inside the crackers were colorful paper crowns that everyone, from the youngest to the eldest of the wolves, proudly placed on their heads.

Each cracker also contained a joke, love poem, or limerick, as well as a small gift.

Calla smiled at the sparkly coin purse that Guthrie had given her. "That's all I have money for now," she joked.

He opened his and found a sterling silver money clip personalized with his initials—and laughed.

"Before long, we'll fill the coffers all over again. Don't you worry, lass. And thank you. I love my gift." He leaned over and kissed her. Though he was starving for the meal, he craved returning to bed with Calla even more.

She kissed him back and opened her note. "To my dearest, Calla, the love of my heart. Ahh, Guthrie," she said and pulled him into a tighter hug and another kiss.

"I'm afraid I'm not much of a poet and that was the best I could do." He opened her note to him and smiled. "To the hottest wolf in a kilt, fighting or not, with the sexiest legs a lassie ever set eyes on." He chuckled and ran his hand over her lap, covered in her new plaid skirt.

A bonfire was lit outside after the meal, and everyone went out to dance and sing while the bagpiper played. Calla hadn't realized all the fun she'd missed out on when she was living alone. She loved the big pack's traditions and danced the afternoon away with Guthrie, glad he loved to dance too. An English Christmas tea followed that with cheeses, crackers, pigs-in-blankets, Christmas pies, and snowman buns.

She didn't think she'd ever had this much fun—until she retired to be with Guthrie that night. Who knew that she could live on so little sleep?

The day after Christmas, they planted the Christmas tree in the ground—a new tradition for the pack—so no one was saddened about the tree decorations coming down. Besides, next up was Hogmanay, the Scottish New Year, and the anticipation of those celebrations was just beginning.

And then there'd be a wedding that the whole clan was taking part in, using Calla's book on planning parties on a budget.

Best of all, although Calla and Guthrie were starting the New Year a little broke, they had all the love they could share—and *that* they would never find lacking.

Read on for a sneak peek at the next book in Terry Spear's jaguar shape-shifters series

Jaguar Pride

AT DUSK IN THE CORCOVADO NATIONAL PARK IN Costa Rica, Melissa Overton barely heard the constant sound of crickets chirping all around them. Prowling through the dense, tropical rainforest as a jaguar, she listened for the human voices that would tell her that her prey was nearby.

Waves crashed onto the sandy beaches in the distance as she made her way quietly, like a phantom predator through the tangle of vines and broad, leafy foliage, searching for any sign of the poachers. Humans wouldn't have a clue as to what she really was if they saw her—to them, she'd just be an ordinary jaguar. And she and her fellow jaguar shifters planned to keep it that way.

Her partner on this mission, JAG agent Huntley Anderson, was nearby, just as wary and observant. Martin Sullivan, director of the JAG Special Forces Branch—also known as the Golden Claws and only open to jaguar shifters as a force that protected both their shifter kind and their jaguar cousins—had ordered them to capture a group of poachers. After that, Melissa and Huntley were to let the Costa Rican authorities take it from there, which didn't sit well with Melissa. She understood Martin's reasoning, but she'd rather end the poaching in a more…*permanent* way.

An ocelot caught her eye, but as soon as he saw her, he quickly vanished. It was May and the rainy season had just begun—a time when many tourists avoided the area, as flooding made hiking more dangerous. She and Huntley made their way through the tiny section of over 103,000 acres of tropical rainforest, searching for Timothy Jackson, the leader of the poachers, and his men. Intelligence at JAG headquarters stated this was their favorite area to poach exotic cats from. Jackson was an enigma. He'd fought bravely in the desert on two combat tours and left the service with an honorable discharge, but when his wife took their baby daughter and ran off with another man, the shame and anger seemed to have consumed Jackson. He'd finally quit his job as a Veterans Administration clerk and had turned into something dark and twisted.

Stepping through snarled roots and wet and muddy leaf litter, Melissa's paws didn't make any sound. She moved through the towering tropical trees with her ears perked, listening for human voices.

Wearing his black jaguar coat, Huntley was sniffing the air nearby, pausing to listen. Darkness had claimed the area, the trees and rapidly approaching rain clouds blocking any hint of light at dusk. Though Melissa's golden coat, covered in black rosettes, was difficult to see at night if anyone should shine a flashlight on her, Huntley was even harder to see, making him hauntingly ghostlike. In broad daylight, his rosettes could be seen, but in a darkly elegant way. She'd never tell him though. As hot as he looked, he probably knew it well, and she didn't want him to think she was interested or anything. Not when they were both currently seeing someone else.

She loved working with him, though.

Black jaguars, a melanistic form, averaged about six percent of the regular jaguar population. The jaguar shifters weren't sure about the ratio with their own kind. Huntley's mother was a beautiful black jaguar, and his dad, golden. Both his brother, Everett, and sister, Tammy, were golden also. For whatever reason, Huntley's coat appealed to Melissa, especially on missions like this. He seemed like a Ninja warrior in jaguar form, sleek, agile, and deadly. And she liked that he was wild, like she was, able to live in their native environments without a hitch.

She realized more and more, she should have hooked up with a cat like him to date—and not a city cat like Oliver Strickland, who didn't ever shift or want to experience his wild side. How boring was that? She had believed if she showed Oliver how much fun it could be, he might change his mind. She should have known that altering someone's personality wasn't going to happen unless the person wanted it to. Oliver was strictly a human who kept his jaguar persona hidden from everyone. Including her.

Switching her attention from thinking about her tame boyfriend and her hot JAG partner, she listened again for any human sounds. Nocturnal animals were out hunting, which included all the wild cats that lived there—the pumas (also known as cougars, mountain lions, and a variety of other names), margays, ocelots, oncillas (a small wild cat, also known as the little spotted cat), and the jaguar. All wild cats being territorial—the jaguar was king.

Melissa and Huntley were searching for the poachers at night because that's when the men were most likely to be hunting. This was the second day of trying to locate the poachers, and she wanted to find them *now*.

Mosquitoes buzzed around her, and she was glad for her jaguar fur coat. The sound of insects roared in the thick, humid air. An owl hooted. A vampire bat flew overhead, and she was kind of surprised to see it, as they often stayed near herds of cattle. She glanced up at the cloudy sky. Vampire bats didn't like hunting during the full moon when visible. Only the stout of heart would come to the rainforest during the rainy season. That meant more of a chance for her and Huntley to catch those who weren't there just to sightsee.

Martin had said that the poachers had been seen hunting their prey in this very area—suspected to be hunting here at night, sometimes when the jaguars went to the beach to eat sea turtles. It was the perfect hunting ground for the poachers, who would use the beach to escape with their bounty. She loved it there in the South Pacific region. This was a favorite vacation spot for her, so she hated to think that poachers would be there hunting any of the beautiful cats. Or any of the animals, for that matter.

Startling her, she saw two spotted cubs sniffing around the ground, and immediately Melissa stood still. A mother would be nearby. And dangerous. Melissa couldn't tell from this distance and without being able to smell the cubs' scents whether they were jaguar cubs or pumas. They were so similar before they were six months of age that they were hard to tell apart. In the tropics, jaguars and pumas were known to overlap territories to a degree, unlike in other locations, though if the puma came across a jaguar, he'd give way to the bigger cat.

Her heart pounding, Melissa caught sight of the mother—a tan-colored puma. She nudged one of the cubs, who looked to be about four months old. And then the mother and her cubs disappeared into the rainforest.

Men's voices deeper in the rainforest caught Melissa's attention. She couldn't make out what they were actually saying. Huntley was beside her in an instant. Were the men camping in the rainforest? She'd heard at least three different voices. She could smell whiffs of smoke from their campfire. She and Huntley headed in that direction, growing closer until they could hear the three men talking—about rugby, girlfriends, and sex. *Australians*. Most likely they were not who she and Huntley were looking for.

"Hey, mate, look at this. Hold the light closer."

One of the men was holding a flashlight as they looked at a tiny, neon orange poison dart frog sitting on a broad green leaf.

They thought that was exciting?

To give the men an experience of a lifetime, and before Huntley could dissuade her—if he thought to, or before he did it first—she ran near the camp and past it. She caught one of the men's attention before she disappeared into the rainforest.

"Holy shit!" the man said, scrambling to his feet.

"Was that a—?" another man said.

She heard Huntley chasing after her.

"Two of them?"

"A black jaguar?"

"Did anyone get a shot of them?"

The men were so excited that they continued to talk about their experience, wishing someone had gotten a picture of them.

Both Melissa and Huntley were well out of sight, having disappeared into the foliage seconds after their appearance in camp.

Huntley was close enough that he brushed his shoulder against her hip in a playful way—amused at what she'd pulled, and playing along. She grinned back at him, showing a mouthful of wicked teeth.

He grinned in response.

He *could* have gone on a path parallel to hers, staying hidden, but *no*, he had to follow her, probably giving the tourists a near heart attack when they saw not one but two jaguars.

She smiled, never knowing what to expect from her partner. He would likely say the same about her. Sure, he would have an inkling of what she was about to do from the way she would shift her footing, tense her body, preparing to lunge or run. But he wouldn't have enough time to react.

Wouldn't the tourists just love to tell the park rangers that they had spied two jaguars running together? Jaguars rarely made an appearance for them. A black jaguar was even rarer. But a female and male running together? In the jaguar world—as opposed to the jaguar shifter world—the big cats only did that when they were courting.

She smelled the salty ocean and headed that way, intending to see if maybe someone had ditched a boat at one of the isolated coves. She and Huntley finally made it to one of the beaches, where the warm ocean

waters lapping at the sandy shore teemed with marine
life, brightly colored coral, and rock formations. She
sniffed the ground and the air, trying to smell any sign
of insect repellent or suntan lotion. *Neither.* She glanced
at Huntley. He shook his head, indicating he hadn't
smelled anything, either.

Then they spied a jaguar at one end of the beach
searching for sea turtles. She'd read where the park
used to have over a hundred jaguars and now it was
down to between thirty and forty. This jaguar was one
of the lucky ones.

She and Huntley avoided it and took off in the opposite direction. She ran along the sandy beach, her
paws leaving imprints in the sand, then she and Huntley
reached the mouth of the river—and saw fins. Bull
sharks—only one of a few kinds of sharks that could
survive in fresh and salt water. She was surprised to see
so many, as by all accounts, illegal poaching of shark
fins was decimating the numbers.

Melissa and Huntley needed to cross the river to get
to the other beach and continue their search for a boat
tied off on the shore. She was certain this wasn't an ideal
spot to traverse.

But Melissa found it awfully tempting. She attributed
having such a reckless nature to her father, who had always encouraged her and her twin sister, Bonnie, to take
risks, when their mother would have had a stroke had
she known.

Melissa studied the water again, wanting to take the
quickest path to the beach on the other side. The bull
sharks were definitely feeding, their fins showing, then
disappearing and reappearing. She thought she counted

about eight. The problem was that the farther away from the mouth of the river she and Huntley got, the more trouble they could have with crocodiles and caïman added to the mix.

Huntley nudged her to get her to move through the rainforest further. She grunted at him. What did he think? She was a daredevil? Well, she was, to an extent.

Lightning briefly lit up the gray clouds and then thunder clapped overhead, making her jump a little. Then the rain started pouring down. As deep as the river was, they would have to swim, not walk across it like they could in the dry season. Jaguars *were* powerful swimmers, so at one point where the river narrowed a little, they finally made the decision to go for it, side by side, protecting each other's flanks.

Her heart thundering, she crossed the warm river. A small croc was resting on the shore, eyeing them, another slipped into the water, and a bull shark passed by. When she and Huntley finally reached the other side, they bolted out of the water and away from the riverbank. They headed again through the rainforest until they reached the beach along the coast.

For a moment, they just stood there, the rain pelting them as they listened for the sound of a boat engine or men talking. She smelled gasoline down the beach. Her heart began to beat faster. The gasoline smell had to have come from a boat. She and Huntley loped toward the cove hidden by trees.

When they reached the edge of the beach and looked right, they saw a boat sitting in the protected cove. She felt a hint of relief and a thrill of the chase. If it was the poachers' transportation, they could escape with their "catch" without having to leave via any of the park entrances. She had to remind herself that others used boats to reach the shores for tours, so this might not be a poacher's boat.

She and Huntley drew closer under the cover of the rainforest, though it was pouring and dark.

Then they heard something moving through the brush. She and Huntley stopped.

"Hurry up," a man said, heading in the direction of the beach.

A light wavered through the dense foliage. The men had to be human, not shifters, or they wouldn't have needed the man-made light.

Suddenly, someone came out of the rainforest in a different direction. A man yanked up the zipper of his trousers while he watched for his comrades. Dressed in a white shirt and pants, he stood out in the black rain that soaked him and everything around him.

"Any trouble?" he asked the three men as they broke through the vegetation and reached the beach.

"Carlton got careless, and the cat scratched him bad," one of the men said, two of them carrying a burlap sack between them with what was likely their live bounty inside.

Cats. Which kind?

A third man was carrying another burlap sack, while the last man was holding on to his shoulder as if his injuries were severe, his shirt and fingers bloodied. He groaned in pain.

All of them had rifles slung over their shoulders and sheathed machetes hanging from their belts.

"Whatcha get?" the lookout asked.

"Puma and two cubs."

Melissa ground her teeth, thinking at once of the puma and her cubs that she and Huntley had spied earlier.

"Hot damn."

"Help Carlton into the boat, will ya? Where's Jackson?"

Jackson. The man—and his cohorts—that they'd come for. And he wasn't here? *Great.*

"Taking a dump. Something didn't agree with him, and he's about an eighth of a mile back there."

"And you left him alone?"

"Hell, he told us to get going. If you want to watch him doing his thing, *you* go back and do so."

Melissa had no intention of letting these men remove the pumas from the park. But both she and Huntley hesitated to make a move. If they attacked now, Jackson could all of a sudden show up and shoot them both.

Then, figuring they had to chance it before the men got the cats in the boat, Huntley growled low, Melissa's cue to attack.

They had one attempt to get this right while the men still had their hands full with carrying the sacks and the lookout was trying to help the injured man to the boat. They had so many rifles and machetes between them, it was a dangerous move on the jaguars' part.

Huntley went after the two men holding the bigger cat. Melissa lunged after the lone man holding on to the sack with the cubs. The JAG agents wouldn't kill the poachers if they didn't have to. But the agents had to use an economy of movements and quick action to do this right.

Huntley struck the first man that he could reach in the head with a swipe of his paw, his claws extended, knocking him out cold. Melissa used a similar tactic with the other man. Thankfully, a jaguar's sweep of a paw could stun its prey, knock it out, or kill it. They were trying hard not to kill the men, as much as she regretted her orders.

She immediately went after the lookout, who was panicking, struggling to get his rifle off his shoulder. The injured man looked dazed and didn't react. She coldcocked the lookout, then went after the injured man. Even if he couldn't fight well, she didn't want to chance it. Once she slugged him hard, and he'd joined the lookout lying unconscious on the beach, she turned to take care of anyone else.

Huntley was checking on all of the men to ensure they were really out and not playing dead.

She tore open the first of the burlap sacks with her teeth. Two sleeping spotted cubs. One of them she recognized as the same cub she had seen earlier. Melissa tore the other sack open and found the mother, tranquilized like her babies. She felt badly for them for having experienced this, but glad they would have a good outcome—*this time*.

Huntley had shifted into his attractive human form—that she was trying hard not to look at too much—as he examined each of the men's IDs, verifying the poachers' names before he called the park ranger. They had to move quickly before Jackson arrived on the scene.

"Wish we'd gotten Jackson, but we might still be able to. At least we got the rest of his men, for now," Huntley said, pulling a cell phone out of one of the men's pockets. Huntley's dark blond hair was dripping wet, his blue-green eyes studying her as he called the authorities.

She grunted her approval, then dragged the momma cat in her burlap sack into the rainforest to hide her. By the time she had returned to seize the sack containing the cubs, Huntley was speaking on a cell phone in Spanish, relaying to the ranger station that some very bad *hombres* had been caught attempting to poach a puma and her two cubs. He read the men's names off their IDs, then tucked their IDs back into their pockets. "The puma and her cubs are sleeping in burlap sacks in the vegetation nearby to keep them safe, but you can find the men and their boat at the following coordinates." He proceeded to tell the ranger the location of the cove. "One other man, the leader in charge of the poachers, is named Timothy Jackson, and according to his men, he's still in the rainforest."

Huntley ended the call and disabled the boat by pulling the control box apart, removing a few things, and tossed them into the ocean, just in case.

She was supposed to watch Huntley's back, and that meant any other delectable part he showed off. All his parts were remarkable, as toned as his muscles were, and though she didn't want to admit looking, he was very well endowed. She felt a little bit guilty, especially since he had a girlfriend and she had a boyfriend. Still, she was only human—well, and jaguar—so she blamed the interest on both. Besides, looking but not touching was acceptable, right?

She swore he was fighting a smile, probably flattered just a little that she *was* interested.

"I'd prefer to sink the boat with them on it," Huntley said gruffly as he joined her.

She roared in agreement. A sunken boat would make a great coral reef structure for fish in the future.

"It will take hours before anyone can arrive, unless they send a boat, and even that will take some time," Huntley said. "Maybe we can still get Jackson."

Huntley shifted back into his jaguar form—though some would call him a black panther, that wasn't correct and he preferred being referred to as a black jaguar—and quickly joined her. She led him to the mother and cubs and stayed there, watching over them, protecting them. The mother and the cubs would probably sleep through the night, long enough for the park rangers and police to reach this location. Melissa and Huntley climbed high into a tree, not wanting to face a very hostile mother puma that would be dangerous while she protected her young once she woke.

They listened for any sign of Jackson approaching. They couldn't see the boat or his men from there, which was why it was a safe place to leave the drugged cats. Either Huntley or Melissa could have gone searching in the rainforest for the bastard, but their training had taught them to stick together as much as possible while they conducted a mission in the wild.

They would stay hidden unless they heard Jackson reach his men—then they'd pay him a visit and knock him out, too. Otherwise, they'd wait until the rangers and police arrived and ensure the mother and her cubs remained safe, just in case any other poachers happened onto them. Not likely, but she and Huntley couldn't leave their safety to chance.

A short while later, they heard some kind of movement near the cove. Melissa hated leaving the mother and the cubs alone. Huntley indicated with his head that she should stay with the pumas, but she couldn't let him risk his life in case Jackson saw Huntley and fired a shot to kill.

She and Huntley leaped down from the tree, then stealthily made their way to the cove. A couple of tapirs were rooting around. No sign of Jackson. Disappointed, she and Huntley returned to the pumas and jumped back in the tree to wait.

The problem with the rainforest and all the creatures that lived within was that everything made a noise, and because of the cats' enhanced hearing, they heard *everything*. So they investigated the cove five more times before they figured that Jackson had to have discovered what had happened to his men, found he couldn't start the boat, and took off on foot. According to the mission briefing, he had lived in jungles for much of his life, so she could see him being nearly as stealthy as them.

Three hours later, they heard men speaking in Spanish— police, two rangers—all surveying the area for any sign of the cats. When they searched the rainforest and found the sleeping cats, they took pictures and checked them over, never looking up to see the jaguars in the tree above them. In the dark, they wouldn't see them anyway unless they flashed their lights in that direction, but who would ever believe a couple of jaguars would be watching them?

Ensuring the three pumas were well, the men returned to the beach.

In the boat, they'd found the cages, weapons, and tranquilizers—enough evidence to put the five men in jail. "The caller said there were six men," one of the police officers said. He read the names of the poachers that she and Huntley had taken down. "But the ringleader? Jackson? He's not here."

Letting her breath out in annoyance, Melissa hated that they hadn't caught Jackson too. She glanced at Huntley, his eyes narrowed and he looked just as pissed as she felt.